BLUEWATER KILLER

A SERIAL MURDER MYSTERY SET IN FLORIDA
AND THE CARIBBEAN

BLUEWATER THRILLERS
BOOK 1

C.L.R. DOUGHERTY

Copyright © 2011 by Charles L.R. Dougherty

All rights reserved.

No part of this book may be reproduced in any form or by any electronic or mechanical means, including information storage and retrieval systems, without written permission from the author, except for the use of brief quotations in a book review.

rev. 2024

BLUEWATER KILLER

Bluewater Thrillers Series

Book 1

A Serial Murder Mystery set in Florida and the Caribbean

Leeward and Windward Islands

- Anguilla
- St. Martin
- St. Barths
- Saba
- Statia
- Barbuda
- St. Kitts & Nevis
- Antigua
- Montserrat
- Guadeloupe
- Dominica
- Martinique
- St. Lucia
- Barbados
- St. Vincent
- Bequia
- Canouan
- Mustique
- Carriacou
- Union Island
- Grenada
- Venezuela
- Trinidad

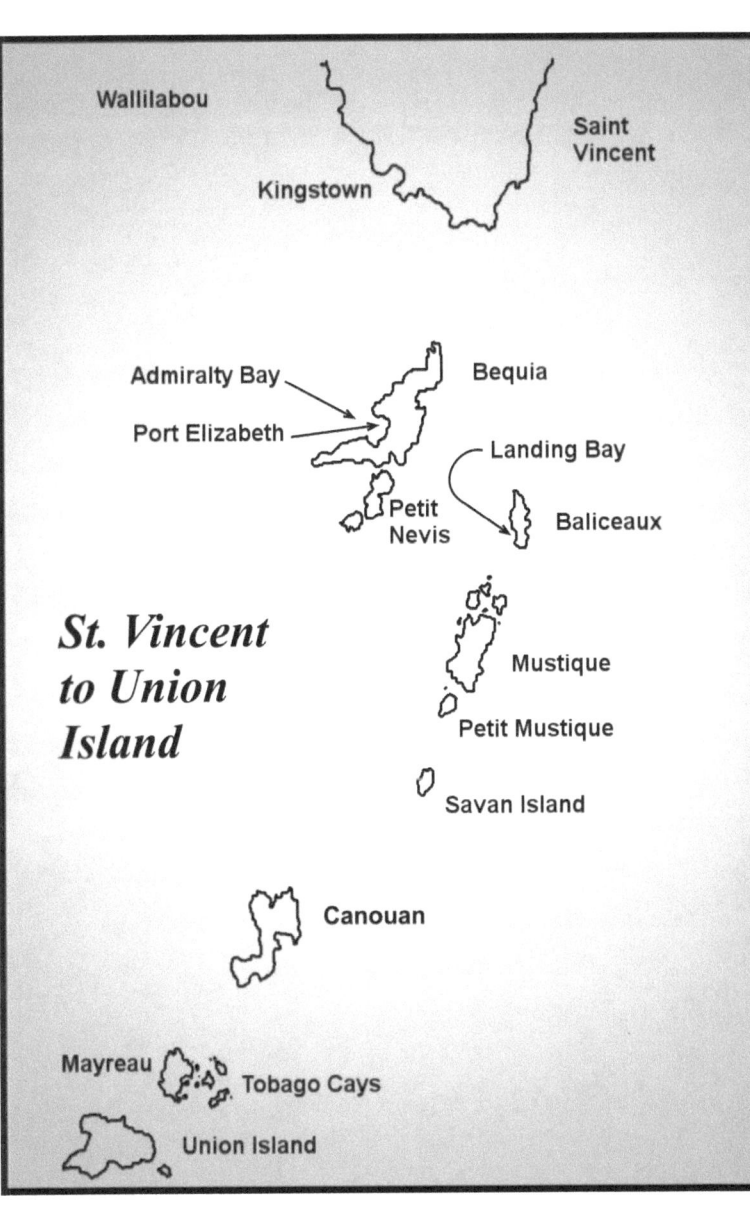

PROLOGUE

THE SUN HAD JUST DIPPED BELOW THE HORIZON, AND THE SEA surface was lit by that lingering glow that fades to darkness so quickly in the tropics. The man on watch in the freighter's wheelhouse caught a glimpse of safety yellow among the waves a few hundred yards off the bow, and then darkness fell.

A strobe light caught his eye as the scrap of yellow faded from view. He called to one of the off-watch crewmen to go up to the bow as a lookout while he altered course slightly, wondering what they would find.

The helmsman throttled the big diesel down and disengaged the transmission, allowing the ship to coast as they approached the strobe. A few yards from the flashing light, he went to full power astern for a moment to stop them.

The man on the bow turned on a powerful handheld spotlight. The helmsman climbed down from the wheelhouse and joined him.

In the light's harsh beam, they could make out a young woman in a bright yellow life vest. She gave no sign that she was aware of the ship looming a few yards away. They called out, but she didn't respond, rolling with the waves, her head and arms moving loosely.

The waves blocked their view every few seconds. The sea was rough, and the man who had been steering didn't think he could maneuver the ship well enough to retrieve the woman.

He went back to the wheelhouse, to the little cabin where the captain was asleep, and woke him. The captain took the controls and put the ship close alongside the person.

When the ship's pilot ladder drew abreast of their target, a deck crewman hanging on the last rungs of the ladder snagged the life vest with a boat hook. The helmsman joined him on the ladder and they brought the woman aboard, hoping they would be able to revive her.

1

HE DRIFTED INTO CONSCIOUSNESS, FIGHTING IT THE WHOLE WAY. The harsh light of the sun burned through his eyelids. He clamped them closed, in hopes that he would drift off again.

"Where am I?" he asked.

No one answered, but his instincts told him that it wasn't a good place. As he raised a hand to his throbbing head, he smelled the corrosive vapors of jackiron rum wafting from his shirt.

Have I been drinking? Not much of a drinker, but I feel hung over.

Moving his hand to the floor, he felt the surface beneath him — hard, lumpy, and damp. *Cobblestones?*

He forced his eyes open again, a little bit at a time. His surroundings rolled past in surreal swirls. His instincts were right. He was nowhere good, and nowhere familiar, either.

Sunlight beamed from a hole, high up in one of the walls. He turned his head, trying to look the other way, but instantly regretted the effects of the motion.

Retching, he rolled onto his side to avoid choking. As the waves of nausea receded, he took in the uneven stone floor stretching from his cheek to the iron bars comprising the wall opposite the one with the hole in it. *Bars? I'm in a cell.*

"Where am I?" he asked again, in a loud voice.

Still, no one answered.

Ignoring his body's protests, he forced himself to a sitting position. He paused, waiting for his surroundings to stop their circular motion.

Alone. Dead quiet, but...

In the distance, he could hear voices, raised in gospel song. There was a subtle but noticeable calypso undertone to the familiar music. As he registered the rhythm, the notion that he was in the islands formed in his mind.

I'm hung over and in jail, somewhere in the Caribbean. Church service. Thirsty. Hungry. His stomach growled.

He crawled over to the bars and pulled himself to a semi-erect position. His vision swirled again; he clung to the bars to keep from falling.

Careful about moving my head so fast. He looked out into a dim, rough-walled corridor, broken pieces of oyster shell visible in the construction. *Definitely in the islands.*

"Hello," he called. "Anybody there?"

He listened as the sound of his voice died in soft echoes. Still grasping the vertical bars of his cell door, he shook it to make a noise and get someone's attention. To his surprise, the door swung out into the corridor with a loud screech of rusty iron hinges.

He stumbled, shuffling to stay on his feet, as he followed the arc of the swinging door. He paused, hanging on the door to regain his equilibrium. After a few seconds, he released his grip on the door and moved a little way into the corridor, taking in the empty cells to either side of his.

"Hey!" he yelled, rewarded by an increase in the throbbing pressure behind his forehead.

No one answered. Leaning on the wall, he worked his way down the corridor toward what appeared to be an exit. Reaching the end of the corridor, he peered through a narrow archway into a sort of waiting room.

It was dirty but neat, in that way unique to official spaces in small Caribbean countries. There was a bench along one wall. Along the opposite wall, there was a counter, with a window of scarred, yellowed Plexiglas, like the ticket booth at a defunct theater.

There was nobody behind the window. He stumbled out into the empty waiting room. Looking around for a moment, he blinked in confusion. A single door stood open, leading outside.

Still unsure of his footing, he shuffled out into the morning sunlight, expecting to encounter a policeman at any moment. He was a little worried about how he would explain his accidental freedom if anybody challenged him.

As he staggered out of the door, he looked up and back, over his shoulder. A signboard hanging above the portal bore the legend, "Police."

He recognized his surroundings, now. *Bequia.*

Bequia is a delightful little island just south of the main island of St. Vincent. The streets were deserted, and music poured forth from every house of worship.

Sunday, for sure.

His grasp of his situation increasing, he recalled that he was here on his sailboat. He made his way to the town dock, remembering as he walked with uncertain steps that he should find his dinghy tied up there. *Better get back to the boat and get myself out of town. No telling what I've gotten myself into.*

There were several rigid inflatable dinghies, one of them his, tied at the end of the dock. He had painted the name of the mother ship, *Sea Serpent*, in 3-inch-high letters on both sides when he bought it. The dinghy was locked to the dock with a heavy cable and a padlock.

He fumbled in his pockets. *Empty. No keys, no money, either. Police probably have it unless somebody beat them to it.*

Normally, he would only have been carrying a little local currency and his keys. He would have left everything else locked away aboard *Sea Serpent*.

He scrounged around the foot of the town dock, looking for something that he could use to liberate the dinghy. Picking up two almost-intact bricks, he carried them out to the end of the dock. He put one brick down on the dock and pulled on the cable holding the dinghy.

Gaining some slack, he twisted a kink into the cable, positioning the kink on top of the brick. After smashing the kinked cable repeatedly with the other brick for a few minutes, he succeeded in breaking the cable.

He dropped the bricks in the dinghy, climbed in, and fired up the outboard. His head was clearing now, thanks to the adrenalin and the activity, and he was aching with his need for water and food.

Looking out to the west, he spotted *Sea Serpent*, swinging to her anchor out near the harbor entrance. He brought the dinghy alongside her and shut off the outboard. He set the bricks up on the side deck.

The companionway was locked, as he had expected it to be, but a few quick blows with one of the bricks solved that problem. He dropped the bricks over the side.

At least nobody bothered the boat while I was ashore.

He went down the companionway ladder and rummaged in the refrigerator, finding a bottle of cold water. He swigged it down, feeling it soak into the dry tissues of his mouth and throat. He got a pot of coffee and a pan of scrambled eggs going on the galley stove.

His physical condition improving, he checked in the chart table to find that his wallet, passport, and ship's papers were where he always left them. He scanned the papers, discovering that he left St. George's, Grenada, on Wednesday, October 19, and had not yet cleared in with customs and immigration in St.

Vincent and the Grenadines. A glance at the digital wristwatch hanging by its strap above the chart table confirmed that it was indeed Sunday morning, October 23.

According to the clearance documents from Grenada, he had been bound for Rodney Bay, St. Lucia. He probably spent Wednesday night at an out-of-the-way anchorage and got into Bequia the next night, most likely after Customs and Immigration had closed for the day. That would have been Thursday night, but now it was Sunday. He frowned.

Puzzling over the missing time made his headache worse, but he forced himself to think through his probable itinerary. He couldn't account for Thursday, Friday, or Saturday.

The papers from the chart table provided no record of his having cleared into Bequia, which he would normally have done the morning after an evening arrival.

Maybe I got here late last night. He shook his head, dismayed at the gap in his memory.

His eyes fell upon the ship's log, sitting on the tabletop in front of him. He opened it to the last entry; he had anchored in Petite Martinique late in the afternoon on October 19. There were no more recent entries in the log. He found that strange, as he was meticulous about records.

There was no official record of his arrival, unless he had lost his copy of the clearance paperwork. He checked his passport for an entry stamp, but there was none. He always asked the immigration officer in Bequia to stamp his passport, even though they didn't routinely do so. He liked clean records. His whole life, he had carried this legacy of parental control. *All rules must be obeyed.*

Since he wasn't carrying any identification, the police wouldn't have known who he was. *They didn't even lock my cell; I couldn't have been in much trouble.*

He wanted to know how he had come to spend the night in jail, but he had no idea how to find out without risking being reincarcerated. *Screw it. It doesn't matter. But I'd better get moving, just in case. St. Lucia here I come.*

As he leaned down into the cockpit to start the diesel, he noticed splattered blood all around the drains. *Did I catch a tuna?*

He couldn't remember. Tuna often bled a lot. He shook his head. *I always clean it up right away, so it doesn't stain the teak.* Cleanliness and order were deeply ingrained in his psyche.

Puzzled, he grabbed the windlass control from the cockpit locker and went forward to raise the anchor. He noticed more bloodstains, all over the teak decking forward of the coach roof.

What happened? Looks like somebody butchered a hog. I don't land fish up here.

He shrugged off his confusion and raised the anchor, lashing it securely in its chocks, ready for sea. As *Sea Serpent* drifted toward the mouth of the harbor, he uncovered the mainsail and laid the jib out on the foredeck, ready to hoist.

Out of the lee of the land, the breeze began to fill in, and he raised both sails. While he clambered back to the cockpit, the breeze blew the bow off to port and the sails began to flog on the starboard tack. He sheeted them in for a close reach, heading for the west side of St. Vincent, and shut down the diesel.

As *Sea Serpent* worked her way out into the open water beyond the shelter of Bequia Head, the wind built to a steady 20 knots from the east. He trimmed the sails and set the wind-vane steering.

Gonna go below; get a quick shower. Late morning, no traffic to worry about. Everybody else left hours ago. He turned on the radar, set a two-mile guard band to warn him of other vessels coming too close, and went below deck.

2

STRIPPING OFF HIS FILTHY CLOTHES AS HE ENTERED THE HEAD, HE was taken aback to find feminine undergarments hung out to dry on the towel bar.

On the counter, he saw a woman's shower bag with a few typical toiletries in addition to a comb, a brush, a safety razor, and a toothbrush. *Where did those come from?*

Nobody else was aboard — at 40 feet overall, *Sea Serpent* didn't have anywhere for a stowaway to hide. The undergarments were dry, so he put them on the berth just forward of the head along with the shower bag and cleaned himself up.

Shaved, showered, and teeth brushed, he put on fresh shorts and a clean T-shirt. *Feel human again.*

About the time he finished, he sensed from the change in *Sea Serpent's* motion that she was in the open water of Bequia Channel. Back up in the cockpit, he did a quick 360-degree scan of the horizon.

No other vessels were in sight, and it was a beautiful, clear day. *Sea Serpent* rolled along at her seven-knot hull speed under perfect sailing conditions.

He climbed back down the companionway into the main

cabin and took a quick look around, trying to figure out where the woman's clothes came from. In one of the lockers above the starboard settee, he found an unfamiliar duffel bag.

He normally kept that storage space clear for use by the occasional guest, but he couldn't remember having any company. He put the duffel bag down on the settee to open it and noticed an Air France baggage tag on one of the handles.

The flight was from Charles de Gaulle to Antigua several months ago. *Doesn't tell me much.*

He unzipped the bag to find a typical sailor's stash: well-worn foul weather gear, a good, sharp rigging knife on a lanyard, a couple of pairs of clean cut-off jeans, one pair of clean but well-worn full-length jeans, half-a-dozen cheap, souvenir T-shirts, two string bikinis, and a pair of beat-up sea-boots stuffed with several pairs of rolled-up woolen socks. *This woman was a seasoned sailor, not a tourist.*

Feeling around the sides of the bag, he found a zippered pouch, which held a wallet, a French passport, and a dog-eared spiral notebook. He opened the passport and discovered that it belonged to Danielle Marie Berger.

Even in a typical passport mug shot, she was a looker, a little French pixie with short, curly blond hair and an impish smile. *You're cute. Where'd you go, anyhow?*

The wallet contained a crisp 100 euro note and a few hundred Eastern Caribbean dollars in used small-denomination bills. There were no credit cards, although there was an ATM card for a French bank.

He noticed a week-old ATM receipt from the RBTT bank in Bequia. *That's how she got the cash down here. Did I leave her in Bequia?*

A French driver's license in the clear plastic window of the wallet matched the passport. There were no photos of family or friends, and none of the other miscellaneous items that he carried in his own wallet. *Danielle travels light.*

Opening the spiral notebook revealed that it was about one-third filled with notes in a neat script. *I can't read much French, so it's not too helpful, Danielle.*

On the last page, he noticed the date, 20 October, underlined. Following that, he read, "*Sea Serpent*, Mike Reilly, Mayreau, SVG." He frowned. *That's my boat, and my name.*

Mayreau is a small island about five miles north of Petite Martinique. Mike often stopped there for a night or two between Grenada and Bequia.

Working backwards through the notebook, he found that Danielle had been crew on the British yacht, *Rambling Gal*, for almost a year. Several of the stamps in her passport also listed *Rambling Gal*.

Head hurts. The sails began to flutter, making a racket. Mike zipped up the sea bag, stowed it back in the locker, and scrambled topside to mind his ship.

3

THE NEW GIRL ARRIVED IN BALICEAUX ABOARD THE *ERZULIE FREDA*, a small Haitian-flagged freighter that was delivering a shipment of drugs from Venezuela. Santiago Rodriguez, known to his minions as Big Jim, went aboard the decrepit little rust bucket to check out the merchandise before allowing it to be off-loaded.

She was unconscious, sprawled on the pilot berth in the wheelhouse, a blanket thrown over her wet, clammy body. There was an inflatable life vest on the cabin sole by the berth. The vest had lost pressure through a large gash down one side. Big Jim saw that there was a water-activated strobe light attached to the vest, still flashing.

The girl was strikingly beautiful, with short, curly blond hair and even features. Trim figure, but curved in all the right places, judging from the contours of the blanket. She would catch a man's eye, even in her bedraggled, comatose state.

"Who is she, Julio?" Big Jim asked the dirty, unshaven captain, who was unpacking a carton that had a picture of a microwave oven on the side. The packaging was hollow foam-plastic blocks, each containing 500 grams of pure cocaine.

Julio paused and looked up from his task, taking advantage of the interruption to swig rum from an unlabeled bottle on the table next to the carton. He gave an inarticulate shrug and went back to work. Big Jim wasn't sure if Julio was being rude, or if the shrug was his answer.

"I don't understand, Julio. Is she your lady?" Big Jim tried again.

Julio turned from the carton and picked up the bottle, wiping it on his filthy forearm before offering it to Big Jim, who shook his head. Julio stretched his back, putting both hands on his hips and rolling his torso, his joints popping. He turned his single, bloodshot eye on Big Jim, his jaw working as he sought the words to answer. He belched loudly and shrugged again, licking his lips.

"The lookout, he see. Sun set. Yella light flash, flash, flash. We pick she up. Busy, put she here. You want?" He took another swig of rum, waiting for Big Jim's answer.

"You know where she came from?" Big Jim asked.

"Prob'ly boat," Julio belched again. "Lifejacket bust when they drag she aboard."

Big Jim looked again at the flaccid lifejacket, prodding it with the toe of his shoe. It was of good quality and had a harness sewn into it. He recognized it by type as having most likely come from a sailing yacht, but there were no identifying markings other than the manufacturer's logo.

"How long ago did you pick her up?" he asked, turning his attention back to Julio.

"Hour. Mebbe two hour," Julio shrugged again. "You want, Big Jim?"

Maybe 15 or 20 miles from here, at the most, Big Jim calculated, before he responded. "Was she awake when you found her?"

"Nah. She mash up; out cold," Julio answered.

Big Jim flipped the blanket off the unconscious girl, noticing how the still-wet T-shirt molded to her well-formed breasts. His eyes traced the muscles in the long legs visible below her cutoff blue jeans. She had a good tan and looked well-groomed and well fed.

He put a hand to her shoulder and shook her gently. There was no response. He saw no obvious wounds, and probed gently in her hair with his fingers, stopping when he found a large lump on the left side of her head.

He spread the hair around the lump and found an open wound over an inch long. He could see the bone of her skull through the swollen tissue. The exposed flesh looked white, and it was puckered from immersion in seawater. The bleeding had stopped of its own accord, apparently, and her time in the sea had washed the blood away.

He felt a strong, steady pulse in her neck, and her breathing was smooth and easy. He reasoned that she must have fallen overboard from a yacht, maybe hit by a swinging boom during an unplanned jibe. The automatically inflated lifejacket had kept her afloat until Julio found her. It was odd that no one had come back to pick her up, unless she had been sailing alone, he reflected.

"Too bad for her she didn't use that harness in the lifejacket," Big Jim said. "At least then she would have stayed aboard her boat. What are you going to do with her, Julio?"

"Take to Haiti, if she come awake. I sell there. Is an Arab, he buy blond white women."

"She would be a lot of trouble for me," Big Jim said.

Julio grinned, showing an expanse of pink gum interrupted by the occasional blackened stump of a tooth. The bargaining process had begun.

"She very beautiful. Valuable to Arab. Healthy; young. She wake up soon."

"She might not wake up, Julio. Then she's worth nothing but trouble," Big Jim countered.

"No trouble. I put she back in the sea, she no wake up."

"Tell you what, Julio. You leave her here on Baliceaux, and

Rosa can take care of her. When we sell her, I'll take out Rosa's expenses, and we can split what we get for her with you. That way, you don't have to keep her alive and hidden all the way back to Haiti."

"Nah. No like Rosa expenses, and how I know how much you sell she for?"

"Okay, Julio. I'll send you an email and you can agree to the price before we sell her, and we'll split Rosa's expenses."

"You say the expenses in the email," Julio demanded.

"No problem. I can do that."

"If she die, no split any expense," Julio said, on a roll now.

"Okay." Big Jim nodded.

"If she die, you take scalp to show me she die," Julio said, rummaging in a drawer under the table.

Big Jim watched as Julio pulled out a camera and made two photographs of the unconscious girl. He shot a close-up of each side of her head and then brought the camera over to show Big Jim the pictures, her ears prominent among the damp curls.

Scrolling between the two pictures as Big Jim looked, Julio said, "Now, Big Jim, if she die, you and Rosa, you take she scalp, with she ear both, so I can know to believe."

"Okay, Julio. After we finish unloading, we'll take her to Rosa."

"Good. We got deal." Julio picked up the damaged life vest and moved to toss it over the side.

"Not here, Julio. Too close. Get rid of it somewhere else, okay?"

Julio dropped the vest on the deck and nodded. They returned their attention to removing bricks of cocaine from the plastic foam packing material on the table by the microwave cartons.

THE ISLAND of Baliceaux was in sight of the exclusive resort island of Mustique, both just a few miles southeast of Bequia. Baliceaux was a 300-acre island, politically part of St. Vincent and the Grenadines. Privately owned, the island was uninhabited except for a few smugglers who had recently set up shop, squatting quietly out of everyone's sight.

The smugglers were part of a loosely organized group of drug dealers calling themselves El Grupo. They had noticed that Baliceaux was at a crossroads of tourism and commerce but wasn't part of it all. Since no one lived on Baliceaux, it was simple to develop it as a transfer point for smuggling drugs, money, and other lucrative, illegal commodities. Regular payments to politicians in St. Vincent ensured that the smugglers' activities weren't disrupted by law enforcement.

Big Jim Rodriguez ran things in the Eastern Caribbean for El Grupo. He had used discreet Venezuelan contractors to build a well-concealed facility in the interior of Baliceaux. The compound had everything but a landing strip, which would have attracted attention. There were plenty of good landing strips on the adjacent islands, with ready access to Baliceaux by small boat, and Baliceaux had a small but well-protected natural harbor.

El Grupo's business focused on illicit drugs, but Big Jim dealt in other things as well. One of the commodities that passed through Baliceaux was flesh. The flesh was human, alive, and primarily, but not exclusively, female. Compliant, attractive women were of great value.

Big Jim handled the entire operation for El Grupo, including drugs and other contraband. Rosa Sanchez assisted him on Baliceaux. Rosa's job was to take care of the livestock, as they referred to their captives.

Many of the unfortunates who became temporary residents of the facility weren't in the best of health when they arrived. Some had been injured incident to their capture; others were addicted to various substances. Some, particularly specimens sold to Big Jim by their impoverished families, were simply starving, and they needed to be fattened up before they could be moved into retail distribution.

Rosa had been a medic in the Cuban military, back in the cold-war days when the Russians were still funding Castro's government. Her skills in dealing with trauma cases, honed in combat, surpassed those of many emergency room physicians in the islands, especially if the case had to be handled in a remote location.

Security was not much of an issue on Baliceaux, as there was no way on or off the island except for the boats supporting El Grupo's activities. There were guards looking after the stockpiles of goods in transit, but they were kept strictly away from the concealed compound that housed Rosa's charges. This eliminated any opportunities for her inmates to corrupt members of the security force.

When Big Jim and Julio carried the limp girl into the two-bed infirmary, Rosa set to work, stripping off the clammy, wet clothes and drying the girl off with the help of one of her assistants. Once they determined that she had no injuries other than the wound to her head, they put her into a hospital gown and covered her with a dry blanket. Rosa deftly cleaned and stitched the cut, and her aide attached an intravenous drip, so that they could keep the girl hydrated and nourished.

"What do you think, Rosa?" Big Jim asked.

"It is in the hands of God, Big Jim."

"When she wake up?" Julio asked.

"She could wake up any minute, or never," Rosa responded. "With no scan or MRI, we have no way to know what damage is inside the skull. She is a healthy, strong, young woman. If there is no damage to the brain, she will live a long time. With a head injury, nothing is certain. She may live a long time and not wake up. We can only care for her and wait, but I don't think the lump looks so big. She will come around, probably. She is very beautiful, no? Worth some waiting, I think."

LESS THAN 15 miles northwest of Baliceaux, the cape effect from the south end of St. Vincent caused the wind to clock. Mike disengaged the wind vane and steered by hand until *Sea Serpent* was in the lee of the island.

The sails started to slat back and forth as the boat rolled with the gentle swells when St. Vincent blocked the wind. He dropped the sails and fired up the diesel, engaging the autopilot to steer a northerly course. That would take him a couple of miles west of the island.

The gentle rocking of *Sea Serpent* and the drone of the diesel were making him drowsy. Mike checked the radar settings again, in case he should nod off, and went below to get his wristwatch from the nav station. Back in the cockpit, he set a 20-minute timer on the digital watch. If he fell asleep, the watch would wake him every two miles so that he could check for small boats. The radar would sound an alarm if a target came within the two-mile guard band. Mike closed his eyes and leaned back, wondering about Danielle. He passed three hours in a half-sleeping state, rousing to stop and restart the timer on the watch.

The sea state was more rambunctious as he approached the north end of St. Vincent, and the wind began to fill in. Soon, he could sail again. He went below to the galley and made a thermos of coffee and a few sandwiches. He would need sustenance before he reached St. Lucia. He took his supplies back to the cockpit.

Mike stowed the food before he shut down the diesel and raised the sails. He settled in to enjoy 30 miles of perfect trade wind sailing from the north end of St. Vincent to the Pitons at the south end of St. Lucia's west coast.

Once he was riding the smooth swell out in the St. Vincent Channel, Mike ate one of the sandwiches. His hunger sated, he poured some coffee and thought about the missing block of time and the mystery of Danielle and her sea bag.

Do I know Danielle? When was she on the boat? Where did she come from? Where is she now? Why's her stuff here? How did I end up in jail in Bequia? What about the blood on the foredeck?

One thing's for sure; I wasn't drinking. Couldn't have been an alcoholic blackout.

He was careful about his consumption of alcohol, along with all other aspects of his life. Losing control was anathema. He forbade himself to have more than one or two drinks in an evening.

But I reeked of jackiron rum when I came to. Shit, I can still smell it from my dirty clothes when I go below. I wasn't drinking, so how'd my clothes get soaked in rum? And I was wrong; that was no hangover. I got over it way too fast.

Maybe somebody knocked me out. But why? Who? Danielle?

He tried to reconstruct his last days in Grenada, but he couldn't conjure up any memories. This was his fourth trip northbound through the islands, so imagining how he might have spent his last few days in Grenada was not difficult. But he couldn't recall any specifics.

He passed five anxiety-ridden hours mulling over what might have happened, until he found himself off St. Lucia's Pitons around 7 o'clock in the evening. The two 3,500-foot peaks blocked the wind, and the sails began to flog.

Mike dropped them, lashing the jib along the port lifelines and the main along the boom. He was done with the sails for this leg of his journey north. Rodney Bay was 20 miles away.

Mike normally spent a few days there, resting up from the trip north from Grenada. This time, he wasn't sure how long it would take him to recover.

Mike was in the customs office in Rodney Bay Marina shortly after they opened. He helped himself to a clearance form and sat down at a table to fill it out while the agents dealt with the folks ahead of him.

"Good morning, sir," he greeted the customs agent as the other people moved away from the man's desk.

"Morning, skipper," the agent said, his eyes traveling over the form Mike handed him, as Mike took a seat in front of the desk. "Ah, *Sea Serpent*! Welcome back, captain. Nice to see you here again," the agent smiled. "Clearance from your last port of call?" He held out his hand.

Mike handed him the Grenada clearance document, watching as he circled the departure date and looked over at his desk calendar.

"Slow trip," the agent said, a question in his tone, looking at Mike over the top of his reading glasses.

"Yes, light air," Mike said, trying to sound disinterested.

"You stop anywhere?" the agent asked.

"Couple of nights at Petite Martinique, diving to clean the bottom," Mike said.

Petite Martinique, while part of Grenada, is sort of a no-man's land. It's an island several miles north of Grenada's northernmost customs port of entry and departure.

Boats headed north routinely clear out from St. Georges, Grenada, and spend a day or two at Petite Martinique in the clean, clear water. In the old days, it was a smuggler's haven. Some say it still is. In any case, it's a good excuse for a delay not documented by paperwork.

"*Sea Serpent* had a foul bottom after sitting in Grenada and not moving for the whole hurricane season," Mike said.

"Okay. We're glad to have you here. Enjoy your stay with us," the agent said, stamping the triplicate entry form with rapid-fire vigor.

Mike paid his fees and got his passport stamped by the immigration agent. He bought a loaf of fresh bread and a roti for lunch at the bakery downstairs from customs and took his dinghy back to *Sea Serpent*.

Now that he had cleared customs in St. Lucia, the question of those missing days had no legal implications. The issue of where he had been was now solely between himself and his guilty conscience. *Or so my ex-wife would say. I'm just not going to think about Danielle.*

4

"Look, Jim! Isn't that *Sea Serpent* over there?" Joann Morris asked her husband, as he threaded their dinghy through the anchored boats in Rodney Bay.

"Looks like her to me," Jim said, as he pulled alongside *Morris Dancer*. "We'll swing by and say hello to Mike and Dani after we get the groceries put away. Maybe they'd like to come over for sundowners this evening."

"Great idea," Joann said, tossing the dinghy painter over a cleat on *Morris Dancer's* port quarter as she scrambled up the boarding ladder. "They were a lot of fun the other night in the Tobago Cays. Wonder how long they've known one another? They didn't really say much about their personal history, did they?"

Jim passed the grocery bags over the lifelines to Joann and scrambled up after her. "No, they didn't, but they struck me as sort of an odd couple, you know."

"Odd how, Jim?"

"Well, they both had a lot of bluewater sailing experience, but she didn't really seem at home on that boat. She didn't know where stuff was stored. Remember, she kept asking him where things were in the galley, when she was setting out the snack food."

"So maybe he's the cook, you sexist pig. She probably changes the oil in the diesel for him," Joann said, teasing him, as they stored the groceries. "Let's eat some sandwiches and take a nap. Then you can zip over there to say hello and invite them for drinks."

MIKE HAD JUST FINISHED SCRUBBING *Sea Serpent's* deck with bleach and detergent. After a thorough rinse with the seawater wash-down hose, the bloodstains were almost gone.

A few days in the sun and a few more sails with the deck awash with salt water, and nobody will notice.

Mike rolled up the hose and hung it on the bow pulpit. He was stowing the bucket in a cockpit locker when a dinghy approached.

"Hello, *Sea Serpent*!" Jim called over the noise of his outboard. "You home, Mike?"

The dinghy coasted alongside *Sea Serpent* as Jim shut down his outboard. He reached up to grasp the toe rail as Mike closed the locker and stood up.

"Hello. What can I do for you?" Mike asked, a puzzled look on his face, as he tried to figure out who the man was.

"I'm Jim, from *Morris Dancer*," the man in the dinghy said. "Joann and I had cocktails with you and Dani aboard *Sea Serpent* down in the Tobago Cays the other day. I came by to invite you guys over for sundowners on *Morris Dancer* this evening. It'll just be the four of us, and we'll make an early night of it, 'cause we're out of here first thing in the morning. Heading up to St. Pierre. Gotta get to Antigua to meet the kids in a few days. That's us anchored straight across the bay — the little red ketch. Can't miss it. About 5:30 okay with you?"

Mike was looking down at his feet, his right hand massaging the back of his neck as he pondered the invitation. He looked up, ready to make an excuse.

Jim said, "No need for you to bring anything. We just stocked up. See you then," and started the outboard with a roar. He put it in forward and raced away before Mike could decline.

Mike went below and looked at the clock on the forward bulkhead of the saloon. It was 3 o'clock. He had two and a half hours to kill. He thought that maybe a nap was in order, so he stretched out on the settee opposite the dining table.

After tossing for 10 minutes, trying to get comfortable, he gave up. *Jim and Joann. Damned if I remember meeting them. At least he told me their names. And I guess it's "Dani," not Danielle. Wonder how long they were aboard? What the hell did we talk about?*

He made it sound like we were a couple, Dani and I. Shit! They think she's here. What am I gonna tell them?

Having given up on the nap, he made a cup of coffee and sat down at the nav station.

So Dani and I were in the Tobago Cays. Damned if I remember that. Her notebook said she met me in Mayreau on Thursday. We could have been in the Cays either Thursday night or Friday night.

Mayreau was only a few miles from the Cays, so it was not a stretch to think that he left Petite Martinique on Thursday morning and sailed to Mayreau. It would have only taken him a couple of hours. *I could have picked up Dani and sailed to the Tobago Cays that afternoon. Then sailed to Bequia on Friday or on Saturday.*

I might have spent one night in jail there, but no way it could have been two. It was Sunday when I left, so I must have gotten there Saturday evening. So I spent Friday evening in the Tobago Cays.

But what about Dani? How did she come to be aboard? How did we represent our relationship to Jim and Joann? Where is she, and why's all of her stuff still on Sea Serpent? And what the hell do I tell Jim and Joann?

Let's see. Dani spent a couple of days with me in the Cays to see how we got along. She's thinking about joining me for some long-term cruising. It was a trial run; that's all. She's wrapping up some loose ends, trying to decide.

I'll have to wing it. I don't feel good about this Dani thing, but maybe I'll learn something tonight. Anyhow, if I don't screw up too bad, it won't matter. I'll never see these people again. Maybe.

Why can't I remember her? Or where I was, even?

Dani had left behind what appeared to be everything she had with her. That and the unexplained bloodstains troubled Mike. Had he and Dani been victims of foul play? That kind of thing happened occasionally, but usually not in this part of the Caribbean.

With that thought in mind, he checked himself for unexplained cuts and bruises. Other than a tender swelling on the back of his head, there were no obvious signs of injury.

Where'd I get the knot? No wonder I felt hungover. Probably a concussion.

Shaking his head, Mike scrubbed his face and put on a fresh shirt in preparation for his visit with Jim and Joann.

"AHOY, MORRIS DANCER!" Mike said, as he brought his dinghy alongside the well-kept red ketch.

"Welcome, Mike," Jim Morris said, as he stepped out of the cockpit onto the side deck to take Mike's painter. "Come on aboard while I tie off your dinghy. Where's Dani?"

"Well, she was just with me for a trial run down in the Cays to see if we hit it off. If I'm lucky, she'll rejoin me in a week or two. She had some loose ends to tie up. Thanks for the invitation.

Pretty boat you've got here. What is she?" Mike asked, hoping to shift the topic of conversation.

"She's an old Halberg-Rassy 35, from the '70s. Joann and I bought her a few years ago. We spent three years of weekends getting her ready for cruising," Jim said, pride in his voice.

"I'm partial to older boats myself," Mike said, "from before they started building for the charter market."

"Yeah, you said that when we were on *Sea Serpent* last Thursday," Jim said.

One of Mike's questions had been answered without having been asked. Now he knew where he had been on Thursday.

"Good evening, Mike," Joann said, as she emerged from the companionway into the cockpit, a tray of snacks balanced in one hand. "It's good to see you again. I heard what you told Jim. Sorry Dani's not with you this time."

"Likewise," Mike responded, reaching for the tray to give her a hand.

Joann set up the folding table attached to the steering pedestal and took the tray back from Mike. She sat down and put the tray on the table.

"Have a seat, Mike. Make yourself comfortable. What would you like to drink? We've got some fresh rum punch."

Mike settled in across the table from her. "Sounds just right, Joann. Thanks."

Moments later, Jim reappeared from below, juggling three frosty glasses. Joann took them from him while he sat. She handed one to Mike and put Jim's down on the table.

"To new friends becoming old friends," Jim offered by way of a toast, once everyone had a drink.

"Friends," Mike and Joann said, simultaneously.

Seems like they bought my story. Might as well probe them a little bit.

"So, I told Jim that Dani's gone to tie up some loose ends and think about whether she wants to join me on *Sea Serpent* for a while. I'm fond of her, based on our short acquaintance, but I'm curious to know how she struck you two. You're a happy cruising couple; a single-hander who'd rather be half of a couple would welcome your advice."

"Well, Mike, it's hard to say, since we only just met both of you," Joann said. "We could tell Dani was new to *Sea Serpent*, but she's quite a sailor, I guess. That transatlantic passage she told us about was a hairy one, I thought. I can't imagine the guts it takes for a young gal to take off like she did. I would have never done something like that at her age."

"I sure hope not," Jim said. "I don't know what the kids and I would have done if you'd run away to sea and left us."

"Oh, hush! You know what I meant." Joann chuckled and smacked Jim on the shoulder. "I guess I'm not surprised that she jumped at the chance to join you on *Sea Serpent* when she met you in Mayreau."

"Why's that?" Mike asked.

"Those people she was crewing for. Can't imagine a worse match than a young, free-spirited French girl stuck on a boat with a stodgy British couple with three kids. They expected her to be a nanny as well as crew."

"Yeah," Jim said. "But she was kind of a spoiled brat herself, from her tales about her folks and their big old Perini Navi sloop."

"Well, they had it in charter most of the time, from what she said. Not like it was just the family yacht — it was a business, and she was paid crew," Joann said.

"Some business — a 120-footer that charters in the Med for a hundred grand a week," Jim said. "But you're right. She grew up working her holidays as deck crew on it, so I guess you can't say she was spoiled."

Mike sat, listening. He was gathering a wealth of information, and based on the way they were chattering, they weren't likely to ask too many questions.

"I did pick up some vibes that she didn't get along with her folks, though. Or at least with her mother. I kind of wondered if she had been a 'troubled teen,' and her Dad sent her to sea to straighten her out, maybe," Joann said, looking over at Mike.

"Hard to say," Mike said. "We didn't spend much time talking except when we were with you guys, so you know as much as I do about her, probably. I sure enjoyed her company, though. And she's a hell of a sailor. I hope she decides to give me and *Sea Serpent* a try."

"You two seemed like a good match to me," Joann said. "Hope it works for you, if your single-handing days are done."

"I'm kind of an accidental single-hander," Mike offered. "I started out with my wife aboard. We'd been a couple for 15 years when we took off. After a year of cruising, she kind of up and left. I was helping a friend deliver a boat from Nassau to Fort Lauderdale. When I got back to the marina we were in, she and all her things were gone. That was 10 years ago, and I haven't heard from her since. No clue how to get hold of her, either. She has no family, and she hasn't been in touch with anybody we knew from our shore-side life. End of story."

"Wow," Jim said. "Hope this turns out for you, then."

"To happier times!" Mike said, raising his nearly empty glass.

On that note, they all tossed back their drinks.

"Another for anyone?" Jim asked.

"No, thanks. I appreciate your hospitality, but I know you've got an early start tomorrow. I'd better let you two get some rest." Mike got up and reached for his dinghy painter.

"Okay, Mike. Thanks for coming over. Hope we see you up the way, and Dani, too," Joann said.

"G'night, folks, and thanks again," Mike called, as he motored slowly away toward *Sea Serpent*.

MIKE SCRAMBLED BACK aboard *Sea Serpent*, stepping carefully along the unlighted side deck to avoid tripping. Gaining the cockpit without stubbing his toes, he unlocked the companionway and went below, his mind still processing all the information he had gleaned.

Joann was a real talker. That was good. It helped him fill in some blanks, but he worried that she would be a willing gossip-monger if the opportunity arose.

Right now, nobody knew that Danielle Berger was missing, but that wouldn't last. From what Joann and Jim had said, Dani had parents who would expect to hear from her every so often.

Drinking a cup of coffee to counteract the effects of the rum punch he'd consumed, he considered what he should do. The right thing would be to report Dani's disappearance, but to whom, and what would he say?

His options were many, but he could see problems with reporting her as missing. Stickler for detail that he was, he still couldn't believe that he had picked her up in the Tobago Cays without having properly entered the country.

If he reported her missing, no matter to whom, the authorities would ask questions to which he had no answers. Envisioning the endless snarl of red tape, he gave up the notion of doing the right thing.

She'd entered St. Vincent and the Grenadines, which included the Tobago Cays, as paid crew on *Rambling Gal*. The fact that he had Dani's passport meant that *Rambling Gal* would be facing difficulties when her captain tried to secure outbound clearance from St. Vincent and the Grenadines.

Dani would have been listed as crew on their clearance documents. To clear for departure from the country, the captain would have to produce her passport. Official alarms would sound when *Rambling Gal* tried to leave. The sooner that happened, the more likely someone would connect Dani to *Sea Serpent*.

That was bad. On the positive side, the burden of explaining her disappearance would fall first upon the skipper of *Rambling Gal*. When he was unable to produce her passport, the officials in St. Vincent and the Grenadines would begin looking for her, even if her parents didn't start asking about her.

5

Jean-Pierre Berger's face was red as he listened to the shrill complaints of his ex-wife. He considered making static noises and disconnecting, one of the few advantages that cellular telephones offered, in his view. But that would only postpone the inevitable.

He would eventually have to deal with the Dragon Lady, as his current wife called Marie. He, more diplomatically, called her his starter wife, a term he had picked up from one of his American acquaintances.

"I know, Marie, she always calls on your birthday, and it is two days past," he restated her complaint, a trick he learned long ago from a marriage counselor. That at least kept her from screaming that he didn't listen to her.

"She may be at sea, or somewhere without telephones," he said.

That unleashed another tirade about their daughter's wandering life, for which, in Marie's opinion, he was wholly to blame. Pointing out that Dani was 25 years old and had chosen the vagabond life of crewing on yachts would gain him nothing.

Marie had expected Dani to work in her family's investment banking business. Dani had been successful there for a couple of years, but she found the call of the sea too strong. He was guilty of yachting. Who else was to blame for Dani's love of bluewater sailing?

"Yes, Marie, if I hear from her, I will certainly ask her to call you immediately," he said.

He heard the crash as she slammed her telephone into its cradle. That was yet another reason he didn't like cellphones. You couldn't terminate a call so dramatically, just by pushing a little button.

He thought Marie's worry was premature. Dani could take care of herself. She had inherited his innate toughness along with his love of the sea. Although she was slight of build, she was strong.

And her disposition was fierce. When she was in her teens, he had bailed her out of innumerable scrapes involving wrecked waterfront bars in some of the less reserved parts of the world.

NIGEL SMYTHE WAS DOING his best to stay cool. "As I explained to the customs officer at the next window over, I don't know where she is, and no, I don't have her passport."

This was his third time through, explaining a simple proposition to these post-colonial bureaucrats. *Give them autonomy and this is what you get*, he fumed to himself. *We were all better off before we gave them independence.*

"So, Captain Smythe, this Danielle Marie Berger is on your crew list, which you provided when you cleared into our country, right here in this office on 10 October.

"We have a record showing that you presented her passport, here in this ledger. My colleague, who was on duty at that time, he initialed the passport number for her on the crew list. That means that he examined her passport. You agree that she came into the country on your vessel, do you not?"

"Yes, I agree. I've told you that already. Why are we going over this repeatedly?" Smythe asked.

"Captain, you must understand that this is no small matter, this problem of your missing crew member. We must know where she is, and how she will support herself while she is here, and whether she can pay for her passage to leave our country when her time is up. You are responsible for her, when you bring her into our country as your crew. It is not the same as if she were a guest aboard your yacht."

"As I've already explained to your henchman over there, the last time I saw her was in Salt Whistle Bay, Mayreau. My wife and I left her on board with the children and went ashore to have lunch at the resort. We weren't gone over two hours. When we got back to the boat, she had cleared off. All her stuff was gone. The kids said she had taken the extra dinghy and gone ashore to look for some T-shirts at the market on the beach. She came back after a few minutes and fed them lunch. They settled down to watch a video while they ate, and she told them she was going for a swim. That's the last they saw of her, and all I know about her."

"Yes, captain, we have all that now. My colleague put it in his notes in the file, here, and he has faxed it to the office in Union Island. We are passing it along to the police down that way. They will be looking for her. Maybe she is in Mayreau, or Union Island, or Canouan. When they find her, perhaps we can clear this up, all right?"

"Yes, yes," Smythe said. "We've been over that. I need to clear out now. I have to take my boat to Antigua for storage, as I've already explained. My family and I have a flight back to England next week, so just stamp the paperwork and look for this irresponsible French woman later."

Smythe's diatribe was interrupted as another officer, this one in a customs uniform, stepped into the office with the immigration officer who held Smythe's paperwork and the passports.

The customs officer was holding a sheet of paper, which the

two discussed at length. The glass partition in front of Smythe kept him from hearing the soft conversation in patois that was taking place between the officials.

They were now turned away from him, avoiding eye contact. After several nods between them, the newcomer handed over the document to the immigration officer and left. The immigration officer, a somber look on his face, turned back to Smythe.

"Captain Smythe, my colleague has been talking with our superiors in Kingstown, and we are instructed to retain all your paperwork. This includes your ship's document of registry and your passports, as well as your copies of the clearance documents. I will give you a receipt for these items. You and your vessel are under arrest. Your wife and children are free to visit ashore here, but they may not leave the country, as they are witnesses in this matter. You, yourself, must not leave your vessel, and the vessel may not be moved until this matter is resolved."

"What?! That's absurd. I know my rights. I'll want an attorney. We'll just see about this. *Rambling Gal* is British flagged. You have no right to do this. I'll see you all out of your fancy uniforms and back chopping sugar cane before I'm through with you!" Smythe's face turned bright red.

"I am sorry that this has upset you, captain," the officer said, in his soft, well-modulated voice, 400 years of well-honed passive-aggressive behavior guiding him. "You may indeed wish to take some legal advice. In the meanwhile, here is the receipt that I discussed. We will be in touch. Good day to you, sir."

The officer slipped the document under the glass screen and turned away, walking into the back office and leaving Smythe standing alone at the counter.

AFTER A RESTLESS NIGHT spent reviewing the subject of Danielle, Mike decided that he should eliminate all traces of her presence aboard *Sea Serpent* before someone began looking for her. If a search led officials to *Sea Serpent*, he didn't want her personal effects found aboard. That would be much more difficult to explain than her presence aboard for a few hours in the Tobago Cays.

Disposal of her belongings would be a simple task, easily accomplished by weighting her sea bag with rocks and dropping it in a few thousand feet of water in the St. Lucia Channel on the way to Martinique. A simple task, but one that he sensed he should handle soon. The longer he held onto her things, the more likely he was to become embroiled in some endless red tape related to her disappearance.

He decided to go grocery shopping and pick up a few marine supplies at the chandlery in Rodney Bay before moving on. He would visit Customs and Immigration on his way back to the boat and clear out for Martinique. He could depart tomorrow morning and drop his parcel out in the channel. He'd make it into Cul-de-Sac Marin in time to clear in with French Customs and have a late lunch ashore tomorrow afternoon.

The Morrises had planned to stay in St. Pierre, at the north end of Martinique, for only one night, but their plans might change. Spending a few days at Marin would reduce the chance of Mike's encountering them again. Feeling better since he had a plan, he lowered the dinghy into the water and set off on his errands.

JEAN-PIERRE BERGER WOULD NOT LET Marie know it, but he had a cellphone number for Dani. After thinking about it for a while, he decided to give her a call.

He would tease her about upsetting her mother. She often did that, just to assert her independence. He understood well why she would do things like miss an expected birthday call, just as he understood why she had been unable to work with her mother in Marie's family's bank. Dani was a free spirit, and Marie's efforts at control infuriated her. That was another trait that she shared with her father, along with a love of the sea.

He took note of the four-hour time difference as he scrolled through the directory on his cellphone. It was early evening in Paris, so he might catch her before the cocktail hour in the islands. As the phone rang, he wondered if she were still crewing on that British schooner. He hoped she had moved on. He couldn't imagine how she put up with the fool who owned *Rambling Gal*.

She claimed that she enjoyed the three children, and she was enamored of the vessel itself. The last time he had spoken with her, though, she had hinted that the owner, Smythe, had begun to make untoward advances when his wife and the children weren't around.

Jean-Pierre could tell she was ready for a change, even if she hadn't recognized it herself. He wasn't surprised when the call went to voicemail. He left a message, chiding her for provoking her mother and giving her his love, asking her to call him when she could.

JEFFREY SAMUELSON WAS RESTING PEACEFULLY in his guard shack at the head of the trail from the beach in Salt Whistle Bay to the resort. It was the off-season, not that it made much difference. There wasn't much need for a security guard here, but it made the guests feel more comfortable, and it was a job, after all. He could sit here in his uniform, drowsing in the shade, and collect his paycheck every week.

Or he could join his friends, fishing around the reefs and hustling the tourists on the charter yachts. He had done that for several years. It had its moments. Some of those boats came equipped with good-looking women who could only afford half of a bathing suit. Usually they bought the bottom half, but, every so often, there was one who couldn't even pay for that.

The men with them spent all their money buying rum and fish and lobster from guys like him, he reasoned, so they couldn't pay for bathing suits for the women. He was glad for the business, back when he used to be hustling.

You could score some good money doing that, besides the views, but it was hard work, and the price of gasoline for a boat ate up a lot of the money. Yep. Guarding the fallen coconuts here on the beach was the better way to make it.

Every so often, he still got a look at some prime tourist ladies, too. There was the little French girl who brought her duffel bag by the shack last week and gave him $20 E.C. to watch it for her.

He had almost swallowed his tongue when she pulled her T-shirt over her head and slipped out of her cutoff jeans, all in one fluid, casual motion, while she was talking to him. She had on a skimpy bathing suit herself, and a good, all-over tan, he noticed.

She folded the clothes and zipped them into her bag before she took her dinghy back to the big green schooner with the British flag. She only stayed aboard for a few minutes before she jumped in the water and started swimming around the anchorage, visiting with the other nearby boats.

After a while, she was ferried ashore by a man in a dinghy. She put on her T-shirt and cut-offs and collected her bag, thanking Jeffrey. Jeffrey shook his head, smiling at the memory of the water droplets clinging to her lithe, tanned form. A gal like that could get a ride on any boat she wanted.

The ringing of a phone startled him out of his reverie. He looked under the counter, following the sound, and spotted the phone just as it quit ringing. He picked it up and examined it. It was one of those new ones that only the tourists had. It didn't have any buttons on it to make calls — just a smooth glass front. You couldn't get those in the islands, yet.

There was a picture of that little French girl on the screen. As Jeffrey tried to figure out how to work the phone, it let out a squawk and the picture changed to an image of a battery with a red band at the bottom. Then the phone died.

He stuck it in the drawer in front of him with the other things that had accumulated over the last few months. It must have fallen out of her bag. Maybe she would come back for it, and he could get a reward from her.

That was a fringe benefit of this job. He had made several hundred Eastern Caribbean dollars that way since he had been working here. It had been almost a week since she was here, but you never could tell about those yacht people.

"They come; they go. Nobody know why," his mother had always told him.

6

"Are we clear on your mission, Constable?" Sergeant Reynold Wiggers asked, worry in his voice.

Wiggers was near retirement, and he didn't have a great deal of faith in the younger generation of policemen and women. He was among the last survivors of the colonial era police force in St. Vincent and the Grenadines. The quality of the force had been in steady decline ever since independence, in his view.

Not that independence was a bad thing, he mused. No way he wanted to go back to taking orders from some pommy bastard. The Chief Super in Kingstown gave him enough heartburn. He didn't need these two kids screwing up a high-profile investigation. A missing woman from a foreign yacht was serious business.

"Yes, Sergeant Wiggers, we understand," Constable Winston Roberts replied, interrupting Wiggers's woolgathering. "We are to go to Salt Whistle Bay and interview the people working at the resort to see if any of them know anything about the French lady missing from the *Rambling Gal*. The captain of the yacht claims she disappeared there about midday on 20 October. We must check the guest register and talk to all the people working in the guest services who may have seen her. We are then to report directly back here, assuming we do not find her. If we find her, we are to arrest her and bring her here, Sergeant."

"Good, Roberts," Sergeant Wiggers said. "Constable Jones, what is this woman's name?"

Constable Samuel Jones rolled his eyes at his partner. "The name on her passport was Danielle Marie Berger, Sergeant."

"Describe her to me, Jones," Wiggers ordered.

"White female, age mid-twenties, with blond hair and blue eyes, darkly tanned, about 5 feet 6 inches tall, slight build, native French speaker; speaks fluent American-accented English," Jones said.

"Very well. Off with you two, and remember, you go straight there and do your job and come straight back. No joyriding in the patrol boat," Sergeant Wiggers said, shaking his head as the two young men saluted smartly and left his office.

"Who keep us in line when old Wiggers retire, Sammy?" Constable Roberts asked, as they made their way to the town dock.

"Don' know, Win, but I bet they got another old man lined up. Prob'ly nobody we know," Constable Jones said, watching the rigid inflatable patrol boat rising and falling rapidly with the swell that was running in Clifton harbor.

He dropped to one knee and untied the painter as Roberts jumped aboard, timing his leap with practiced ease. Once Roberts had the twin 80-horsepower outboards sputtering, Jones made his own graceful leap, and Roberts backed the boat away from the dock.

They idled out of the harbor, looking at the pleasure boats at anchor behind the reef. Now that hurricane season was winding down, the yachts were coming back. The town of Clifton would wake up again for another winter of hosting tourists, and that meant there would be more to keep them occupied.

Once clear of the anchored vessels, Roberts shoved the throttles forward and the patrol boat surged up onto a plane. He picked a comfortable, 25-knot cruising speed and swung around the end of the reef, heading for Salt Whistle Bay on the neighboring island of Mayreau.

As they opened their view into the Salt Whistle Bay entrance, both men noticed that the anchorage was jammed with yachts of all nationalities. Most of them looked to be private cruising boats.

It was a little too early in the season for the charter yachts. To the islanders, charter yachts were easily distinguished from long-term cruising yachts. The cruising boats usually only had a couple aboard, and they were equipped to be self-sufficient for longer periods, sporting solar panels, wind turbines, and more elaborate shade awnings than the bareboat charter yachts.

The bareboats weren't as well equipped, but they often carried water toys, like kayaks and windsurfers, and they were typically shared by several couples on holiday. They were an important source of revenue for the local vendors, as the people on the bareboats spent like the proverbial drunken sailors.

The larger, crewed charter boats called here as well, but their purchases were usually services, such as dive excursions, rather than trinkets and meals and drinks ashore. The people aboard the professionally crewed yachts were less likely to interact directly with the islanders than the folks from cruising yachts or bareboat charters.

The Salt Whistle Bay Club, a resort hotel, was the major tourist business on the tiny island. Besides resident guests, the bar and restaurant at the club served people from visiting yachts in the anchorage right off the beach.

There were usually a few vendors with stalls set up in the shade of the trees separating the beach from the resort area, selling T-shirts and local handicrafts. Mayreau was a small island, only about 1.5 square miles in area, with a permanent population of around 300 people.

If the Berger woman had spent much time ashore, she would

have been noticed, unless she had checked into the resort. In that case, the guest register would tell them.

If, however, she had stayed among the yachts, she could be long gone, and no one would know. She could have quietly left *Rambling Gal* and boarded another yacht, and by now, she could be hundreds of miles away and in another country.

Constable Roberts eased the patrol boat through the confusion of anchored yachts, careful to avoid the people swimming and snorkeling. He ran the bow of the boat onto the beach near the head of the trail to the resort.

Their first stop would be with the guard at the beginning of the trail. Roberts and his partner leapt ashore, hats in hand, careful to land on the hard, dry sand above the wavelets, so as not to spoil the spit-shine on their regulation oxfords.

Settling his hat squarely on his head, Roberts, the senior man, took the lead as they walked up to the guard shack and called, "Wake up, Jeffrey!"

"Hey, Win! Whatchew do heah, mon?" Jeffrey responded.

"Lookin' fo' a little blond French gal, 'bout so tall, dark for white gal," Roberts responded, extending a hand to indicate her height. "Mebbe heah las' Thursday, we t'ink."

"We all lookin' fo' one a them, no?" Jeffrey asked, grinning.

"Yeah, mon, but this p'lice bidness. She lef' the boat she come on, don' check out with immigration or nothin'," Roberts elaborated. "Speak English like American, she. Now she missing."

"Okay, okay. Mebbe I see she, then. Gal like that here las' week. Gimme she bag to watch. She go back to a big, green schooner wit' the British flag, then she swim around to see the other yacht people. Bye 'm bye, she come back with a man in a dinghy, get the bag she lef'.

"Then they go. I don' know where," Jeffrey remembered the fancy phone in the drawer in front of him as he was talking. "Le's see, Win. She los' she phone, I t'ink. Later it ring, an' she picture on the front, but batt'ry die," he explained, as he took the phone out of the drawer and handed it over to Constable Roberts.

"Okay, I take the phone. Thanks, Jeffrey," Roberts said, slipping the phone into his pocket. "The man in the dinghy? What he look like?"

"Like all the white men on yachts, Win," Jeffery shrugged. "Nothing special 'bout he, or he dinghy."

"Okay, Jeffrey. Tha's good. Thanks." Win Roberts turned to his partner. "Le's go, Sam. We check the gues' register, jus' in case, like old man Wiggers say do."

As they suspected, there was no evidence that Danielle Berger had registered at the resort, nor did any of the desk staff or the bar and restaurant staff remember encountering a woman fitting her description last week. They took the patrol boat back to Clifton harbor to make their report to Sergeant Wiggers.

"THIS IS A CELLPHONE, YOU SAY, ROBERTS?" Wiggers asked, doubt in his voice. "It doesn't look like a cellphone to me. Just smooth glass — no buttons, except this one at the bottom, and it doesn't do anything."

"Yes, Sergeant, it's called an iPhone. I've seen them on the Internet and on television. They don't sell them here yet."

"Well, turn it on, then," Wiggers said, handing the inert device back to Roberts.

"The battery is discharged, Sergeant. It won't come on, but the guard says when it's working, there is a picture of the Berger woman on the screen," Roberts said. "I have a charger at home for my iPod that I believe will work for this phone. Then we can see what is here. Pictures, her personal telephone and address book, where she has called. There is much we can learn from this, I think."

"Very well, Roberts. Take it home with you and charge the

battery tonight. We will see what there is to learn from it tomorrow morning. Now, I must call the Chief Super and tell him what we have discovered, so far. Have a good evening, Roberts, Jones. Good work."

Safely out in the hall, with the door to Wiggers office closed behind them, Roberts and Jones began to chuckle.

"He sound more British than the Brits, Win." Jones laughed. "You, too, when you talkin' to he."

"They had to speak the right English when he join the force, Sam. My father, he tol' me about them days. No patois on the job. Guess habits hard to break, after 30 year. No need to vex the ol' man 'bout how we s'pose to talk," Roberts said, a little defensively.

7

JEAN-PIERRE BERGER WAS REVIEWING THE PERFORMANCE OF HIS investments when the ringing of his telephone distracted him. He was annoyed that his secretary had failed to answer it until he glanced at the clock on the wall of his office and saw that it was 7 p.m. As the display on his desk phone showed Danielle's cell-phone number, he answered with a cheerful tone of voice.

"Hello, my dear. How are you?"

"Excuse me, sir," a deep, sonorous male voice said. "This is Sergeant Wiggers from the police in Union Island, St. Vincent and the Grenadines. May I please know to whom I am speaking?"

"Yes, certainly. This is Jean-Pierre Berger. Why are you calling from Dani's phone? What is the matter?"

"Mr. Berger, could you tell me, what is your relation to Ms. Danielle Berger, please?" Wiggers asked.

"I am her father," J.-P. said.

"Sir, your daughter appears to have lost this phone at Mayreau, the next island to the northeast. We are trying to locate her. You left her a message several days ago, so we thought perhaps you knew where we could find her," Wiggers said.

"No, Sergeant, I haven't heard from her recently," J.-P. said, worry in his voice. "Have you checked with the owner of the yacht *Rambling Gal*? She was crewing aboard. I believe the owner is a Nigel Smythe."

"Yes, sir," Wiggers said. "Mr. Smythe claims that she left *Rambling Gal* unexpectedly on 20 October, in Mayreau, and took her belongings with her. We have a report that she was last seen in the company of an unknown man in a dinghy, in Mayreau. She came with him to claim her belongings, which she had left with the guard at the resort there. We were hoping that she had called or perhaps emailed you."

"No, Sergeant, I haven't heard from her, nor has her mother. I got a call from her mother earlier today, quite upset that Danielle had not called her on her birthday a few days ago. That is the first time Danielle has ever failed to call to wish her mother a happy birthday. She's quite worried."

"I see, Mr. Berger. I hope that my call doesn't cause more worry. I'm sure everything will be all right once we find your daughter," Wiggers said. "If you should hear from her, please call me as quickly as you can." Wiggers rattled off his office number, and J.-P. read it back to him.

"Yes, Sergeant, I will. What are you doing to locate her?"

"Well, we have a recent picture of her from this cellphone. Mr. Smythe has confirmed that it is of Danielle, so we are sending out circulars to the immigration police in all the islands. We have her passport information as well. We think she probably moved to another yacht in Mayreau, Mr. Berger. Mr. Smythe said she was vexed with him, but he did not know why. We will find her when she checks in at some other island. It happens down here."

"Will she be in trouble over this?" J.-P. asked.

"Not to worry about, sir. At most, it is a small matter of not checking out with immigration if she left our country. If she is staying here, we will require a bond of some sort for her eventual departure, to be sure she does not become a burden on the state, you see. Nothing more. We have already reached a similar resolution with the captain of *Rambling Gal*, as it is his responsibility to see that she is able to leave, since he brought her into our country. We only wish to protect our government from any immigrants who might become a public burden, and it does not appear that your daughter is such a person."

"Certainly not." J.-P. snorted. "I am more worried that she is missing. You are treating her as a missing person, are you not? Surely your government must be worried that something has happened to a guest in your country."

"Yes, sir, tourism is most important to our economy. Our islands are quite safe. I'm sure you have nothing to worry about. I'm sorry to have upset you, Mr. Berger."

"It's all right, Sergeant," J.-P. said, calming somewhat. "I'm sure you are right, and I thank you for your concern."

"You are welcome, Mr. Berger. Please call me if you hear from her, or if you just need to talk some more," Wiggers said, imagining how he would feel if his daughter were the one missing. "I know what it is to be the father of a beautiful young woman."

"Thank you, Sergeant. Have a good evening," J.-P. said, hanging up the phone.

He lit a cigarette as he gazed absently out of his office window. He had to call Marie and let her know this latest development, and she would be hysterical over Dani's disappearance. She would blame him for it, without doubt.

He was not comforted by Sergeant Wiggers's assurances, either. He knew his daughter, and this was unlike her. It would be quite in character for her to jump ship; he knew she wasn't happy with her lot aboard *Rambling Gal*.

She was experienced in the ways of the yachting world, though, and not likely to do anything that would cause trouble with the authorities. He would have expected her to take the initiative to get herself on the crew list of another yacht within the same country to avoid just this kind of problem.

That she had not done so told him that she was in some difficulty. That, and the loss of her phone. She would sooner part with an arm than lose her iPhone. As she often said, her whole life was tucked safely away in those data bits in that little glass slab. If she had inadvertently left it behind, she would have moved heaven and earth to retrieve it.

She was in trouble; he was certain of it. He knew the islands well, from his own yachting adventures, as well as from some of his earlier forays into business. He could call upon old friends down that way who would be much more able to find Danielle than the authorities would be. First, though, he must call Marie. He stubbed out his cigarette, clenched his teeth, and picked up the phone.

PHILLIP DAVIS WAS ENJOYING a ti punch on the veranda of his villa in the hills overlooking the quaint little town of Ste. Anne, Martinique. As the rum soothed his sore muscles, he made a resolution to work out more often.

He wasn't old enough to be feeling this whipped after running a few miles, even in the hilly terrain around here. As his heart rate settled, he reflected on how the town had changed in the last decade, becoming more of a tourist attraction and less of a fishing village.

It was an unlikely place for a retired American soldier to end up, he reflected. But he wasn't a typical retired American soldier. He hadn't been a typical soldier even before he retired, or a typical American, either.

He recalled some of his escapades picking up "packages" offshore near Ste. Anne, running without lights in a very low, very fast boat — a boat carefully designed to offer almost no radar signature for the French Customs cutters to spot. They were less of a problem to him in those days than the other smugglers were. Most were trying to land illicit cargo in Martinique from places in the western Caribbean, and their unlighted, fast-moving "fishing" boats were a serious hazard.

Phillip had different objectives from the other smugglers. He was moving certain shipments that originated in France to places in the western Caribbean or to mainland South America. Aside from flowing in opposite directions, the two types of cargo had some similarities. Neither was sanctioned by the governments of the destination countries. Both types caused a great deal of mayhem and unrest once they were landed in their destinations. The techniques involved in moving them were similar, and the people who delivered them were well compensated for the risks they ran.

Some people dealt in both types of cargo, but not Phillip. He had refused to ship drugs, even when that had been his assigned mission back before he retired from the military. In fact, it had been his adamant refusal to participate in some of the drug-related black ops that had forced his retirement.

He had seamlessly left the military and become a civilian contractor, able to choose cargo consistent with the dictates of his conscience. His compensation had increased substantially once he left the military, too.

Now he really was retired, enjoying the fruits of 25 years of high-risk activity. The expatriate life suited him well, allowing him to distance himself somewhat from the hypocrisy and foolishness that passed for government in the U.S. these days.

The ability of his beloved country to endure the machinations of recent administrations was indeed a testament to the structure put in place by the founding fathers. The U.S. was the greatest nation on earth, despite its elected officials.

The chiming of his cellphone interrupted his thoughts. "Hello," he said, softly.

"Phillip? It's J.-P."

"J.-P., how are you?"

"I'm well, personally, Phillip. And you, my friend?"

"Not bad for an old soldier. What's on your mind? Coming down here for a holiday? I'll show you how to catch some fish."

"I wish I could, but you know how it is. Some of us don't know when to quit."

"That's what marriage does to you, J.-P. Especially when you keep doing it, over and over."

"Yes. That is more true than you can know, my friend. Please, I need your help. Dani has gone missing in St. Vincent and the Grenadines."

"Dani? I thought she was crewing on yachts these days."

"She is, or was. But she left the yacht she had been on for months, and no one can find her. Marie is frantic, and I am a little worried myself. She's a professional sailor, Phillip. She jumped ship without doing any of the paperwork and just disappeared. That is not like her. She would not cause trouble for herself that way, unless something was wrong. And she left her iPhone at a beach resort in Mayreau and never tried to recover it."

"Well, that's a bad sign. When she was through here a few months ago, I thought that thing was some sort of growth on her palm. She showed me all the stuff she had in it — music, books, finances. Pretty amazing what she could do with it. If she left that behind, I'd have to agree with you that something is rotten. Never mind the other stuff."

"You know your way around the islands better than anybody I can think of, Phillip. Will you find her for me? I'll cover your expenses, and pay whatever you wish."

"J.-P., you know I'll find her for you. Hell, she's like my little sister. I'm offended that you think you need to pay me."

"Forgive me, Phillip. You can imagine I am upset. I will be forever grateful."

"Okay, J.-P. Rest easy. Fax me whatever information you have from the police in St. Vincent, and her passport details. I'll get right on it. I'm going to pack a bag now, while I wait for your fax. I'll find her. Don't worry, and tell her mother I'm on it, too."

"Thank you, Phillip." J.-P. sighed as he hung up the phone.

8

Mike stared deeply into her eyes as the waitress set his espresso in front of him on the trestle table. When he had ordered, he had been focused on the overall impression of stunning beauty, missing those eyes, the green of clear, shallow water over a white sand bottom. He was mesmerized.

"*Excusez-moi, parlez-vous anglais?*" he asked, hoping to keep her there for a moment.

"But of course," she said, with a dazzling smile. "Why do you ask?"

"Because my French is so poor, and I would like to talk with you, if you don't mind."

"What do you wish to talk about? You have questions about the menu?"

"No," he said. "About you. You are the most beautiful woman I have ever seen. Do you come from here, originally?"

"Yes, from Fort-de-France," she said. "And you? You are from a yacht, I think, yes?"

"Yes, yes I am," he said, falling ever farther into those emerald pools that were so wonderfully set off by her creamy, caramel-colored skin, pale enough so that the freckles on the bridge of her nose made her look like a school girl. "I've just come from Grenada. Spent the hurricane season down there."

"And, so now you are in Martinique," she said, settling on the bench across the table from him, resting her forearms on the table and leaning forward, smiling as she saw his eyes inevitably drawn to the view as her spaghetti-strap top fell away from her ample bosom.

He glanced up guiltily, realizing that he had been caught, and her smile became a grin as she batted her heavy eyelashes at him.

"You are alone on your yacht, I think."

She sat up a bit and pushed her shoulders back. He looked around at the empty restaurant, realizing that they were alone. No one would be calling for her attention. Luck was with him today.

"Yes," he said, transfixed by those eyes again.

The fabric of her top rippled as she rolled her shoulders a bit. He felt like a horny teenager, knowing that she was playing him, letting it happen. This was easier than he had expected it to be.

Is she a pro, preying on lonely sailors? That would be all right, but it wasn't his normal taste in female companions. She was enough of a prize to justify an exception to his normal criteria.

"So you will stay here a long time?" she asked.

"I have no real schedule, but I'm headed for the Virgin Islands. I work there for a few months every winter," he said.

"And do you go directly there, or do you stop some along the way, perhaps?"

"Oh, I'll be stopping every night, somewhere. I'll probably spend a few weeks getting there."

"Will you stop, perhaps, in French St. Martin?"

"I always spend some time there, in Marigot. It's a favorite place of mine," he said, wondering where she was taking this conversation.

"Perhaps our meeting was meant to happen," she said, looking pensive. "I am planning to move there, myself, to Marigot. It is a beautiful little town, no?"

"It certainly is that," he said, gazing into those eyes that held his so steadily. "When are you moving there?"

"As soon as I find a yacht to take me. I can sail, and cook, and do many other things to be useful on a yacht," she said, her eyes flashing with a hint of mischief.

THE MORRIS'S boat was tied up at the Customs dock at Jolly Harbour, Antigua, as they began the paper chase involved in clearing in. Each island was different in its paperwork requirements, and people who enjoyed traveling by yacht learned to enjoy dealing with local officials. Most of the officers were pleasant and professional, and the ones in Antigua were no exception.

Jim was sure that the local bureaucracy was focused more on full employment than on efficiency, though. There were three separate officers to be dealt with in sequence, in three separate offices. The offices were next door to one another. The first one was at the left end of the small, one-storey building facing the Customs dock. The last one was at the right end, but after finishing there, it was necessary to go back to the first office to complete the process.

He and Joann were veterans at this. They each took a couple of forms and sat on the porch in the shade to fill in all the blanks. Jim had completed his stack of forms first and was killing time while Joann finished. He was reading the postings on the notice board outside the first office when a photograph of Dani caught his eye.

"Joann," he said. "Look at this. The police in St. Vincent are looking for Dani!"

"Who?" she asked, distracted. "What are you talking about, Jim?"

"This poster," he said, reading as he spoke. "They say she was last seen on the *Rambling Gal* in Mayreau, on 20 October."

"Who, Jim?" Joann asked, paying more attention now that she had finished her share of the paperwork.

"Dani. You know, Dani and Mike, from *Sea Serpent*," he explained.

"The police want her?" Joann asked, puzzled. "Why? Do we know *Rambling Gal*?"

"It says she left her crew position on *Rambling Gal* with no notice on 20 October, in Mayreau. She hasn't been seen or heard from since. Anyone with information is asked to contact the local police." Jim paraphrased the notice. "When did we meet them in the Tobago Cays? Can you remember?"

"No," Joann said. "It'll be in our log book, though. We were only in the Cays for one night, remember."

"Well, let's finish up here. Once we're anchored outside for the evening, we'll check. I'm beat, and it'll be getting dark soon. We can tell the police tomorrow, when we come in for groceries," Jim said, fatigue in his voice.

PHILLIP DAVIS WAS PERSPIRING by the time he got through with customs and immigration at the airport in Union Island. The LIAT flight from St. Vincent had been late, and the few passengers had to stand around in the hot, airless arrivals area while the pilot went in search of the officers, who were on their lunch break.

The pilot eventually found them outside, under the shade of a jacaranda tree, finishing their picnic lunch. The gate agent who kept the passengers corralled was good-natured about the jibes offered by one of the frequent travelers, obviously a local businessman.

"You know, LIAT stands for 'Leaves Island Any Time,'" the businessman said to Phillip in a stage whisper. Phillip smiled, but said nothing, rolling his eyes at the frazzled-looking gate agent.

Once the officials appeared, things moved quickly. Phillip was soon walking out of the front door. He politely declined the offer of a taxi, preferring to stretch his legs on the five-minute walk to downtown Clifton.

He entered the police station at a little after 2 p.m., to find a woman mopping the floor in slow motion. She was careful not to disturb the constable who was sleeping with his head on the desk behind the counter. Clifton was not a busy place, and Phillip could certainly understand what a big lunch and a sedentary job in a warm, quiet office would do to a man.

He stood silently in front of the counter, not wanting to start off on the wrong foot. The woman set her mop aside and raised her eyebrows at him. He nodded at her, and she nodded back, gently touching the sleeping constable on the shoulder as she whispered something that Phillip couldn't hear.

The man awoke gradually, first opening his eyes and looking around, his head still on the desk. Spying Phillip at the counter, he sat up quickly, pushed his chair back and stood up. Tucking in his uniform shirt as he walked to the counter, he looked sheepishly at Phillip.

"Good afternoon, sir. Sorry you had to wait. How may I help you?" he asked, looking at Phillip with a groggy expression on his face, a crease down one side where it had been pressed against the edge of the blotter on his desk.

Phillip, with his best poker face, said, "Good afternoon to you, too. No problem waiting; I just got here. I was hoping to see Sergeant Wiggers."

"Is he expecting you, sir?" the man asked, his professional demeanor returning.

"Yes, but my flight was late," Phillip said.

The constable picked up the telephone. "Sergeant Wiggers, a man is here to see you."

Phillip could hear murmurs from the phone.

"I don't know, Sergeant. He said you were expecting him, but his flight was late." The constable spoke into the phone, turned slightly away from Phillip.

More murmurs hissed from the handset as the constable nodded in understanding. He hung up and turned his attention to Phillip again.

"Ah! Then you would be Mr. Davis. Please, sir, come with me," the man said.

He opened the gate through the counter and led Phillip down a long corridor past several closed doors. They went out through a marked exit. Pausing at the door to an adjoining building, the officer entered a combination into the push-button lock.

He ushered Phillip into a chilly, air-conditioned foyer, where he knocked smartly on the doorframe of the only occupied office and announced Phillip. The man who had been sitting behind the desk stood and greeted Phillip, offering a firm handshake.

"I'm Sergeant Reynold Wiggers, Mr. Davis. Please sit down." He gestured Phillip to one of the guest chairs in front of the desk. "May I offer you a cup of tea? Or coffee?"

"No, thank you, Sergeant. I'm fine for now, but you go ahead, if you wish."

Wiggers shook his head dismissing the sleepy constable with a gesture. "Thank you, Constable Johnson."

He closed the door to his office and said, "The Chief Superintendent spoke highly of you, Mr. Davis. I'll do anything I can to help you. We obviously want to find Ms. Berger, as quickly as possible."

"Thank you. Sergeant. The Chief Super and I have some mutual friends, as it turns out, from when I was still doing business down this way."

"I see. What sort of business did you do in the islands?"

"Well, I did a little of this, and a little of that, you know. I've been retired so long that it's mostly faded from memory, but I'll never forget the Chief Superintendent. Did he explain that I represent Danielle Berger's father?"

"Yes, sir, he did, and he made it clear that I should share everything we have with you. To make it easy for us both, I've made a complete copy of our file on the matter for you," Wiggers said, as he handed over a thin, buff-colored folder.

"Unfortunately, there's probably not much there that you don't already know. I did, however, get a call from a colleague in Antigua this morning with some fresh information. It's too new to be in the file. A couple on a yacht which cleared into Antigua late yesterday saw one of the notices we circulated. They reported to the police there this morning that they met Ms. Berger in the Tobago Cays on the evening of 20 October. She was aboard an American-flagged yacht called *Sea Serpent* with a man named Mike. Unfortunately, we have no last name for him, nor do we have any record of a yacht of that name being in our waters during that time."

"Still, that's real progress," Phillip said. "We can find out who owns *Sea Serpent*, if she's a U.S. documented vessel. Do you have the details on the couple who reported this? If they're still in Antigua, I'll fly up there and talk to them. Maybe they'll remember more about meeting Danielle if I'm sitting across from them."

"Quite possibly, Mr. Davis. I trust you understand that a poor little country like ours can't afford that kind of follow-up, although my heart goes out to Mr. Berger. I told him, I know how I would feel if my lovely daughter were the one missing."

"Yes, certainly, Sergeant. Mr. Berger told me how sympathetic you were, and we both appreciate that. You see, I'm an old family friend, and Danielle is like a younger sister to me. Mr. Berger is reasonably well off, and we will spare no expense to find her, but we certainly understand what is reasonable and unreasonable from St. Vincent's perspective. We appreciate the efforts that you have made already."

"Thank you, Mr. Davis, for understanding our limits."

"Oh, Sergeant, I almost forgot. About Danielle's phone..."

"Yes. I discussed that with the Chief Super. We feel strongly that we should retain such a critical piece of evidence, as you are not officially in law enforcement."

"I absolutely agree, but what about the data contained in the phone?"

"Ah! I should have explained. In the file, you will find two DVDs. One of our computer boffins did what he calls a 'dump' of the data in the phone. Everything is there — even some music and videos and photographs, apparently. That's all somewhat beyond an old man like me." Wiggers chuckled to himself, thinking that Constable Roberts would want a pay increase if he knew he was a computer boffin.

"Excellent, Sergeant," Phillip said. "I'll be sure to tell the Chief Super what fine people he has in Clifton. If you hear any more, or think of anything, please call me. My cellphone number is on my card. I'll call you as soon as I've talked with the people in Antigua."

"Yes, thank you Mr. Davis. Let me call my colleague in Antigua and get the information on that couple. Can you wait a moment while I ring him? He should be in his office this afternoon."

"Yes, please. I'll just start working my way through this while you call him," Phillip said, opening the folder on his lap as Wiggers picked up the telephone.

9

Jim and Joann were busy squaring away *Morris Dancer*, getting ready for the first wave of children and grandchildren. It had become an annual family event for each of their two married children to bring their families to Antigua for a couple of weeks.

The Morris's son and his family would be arriving in a couple of days. Jim had several maintenance jobs to wrap up before they were ready for company aboard. Jim and Joann had rented a storage locker at the marina to offload some of their things to make room for visitors. They had spent the better part of yesterday ferrying extra sails and such ashore, after making their report on Dani and Mike to the police officer at the Customs and Immigration building.

Joann had just returned from a provisioning expedition to the gourmet grocery store and was fixing lunch while Jim serviced the primary winches. He washed out the old, hardened grease and salt with gasoline and packed the bearings with fresh grease, making them ready for another season of hard use.

He was cleaning up after himself when Patrick, the dock master from the marina, brought his big dinghy alongside. He was accompanied by a tall, darkly-tanned, fit-looking man in casual attire. To Jim's eye, the passenger looked more ready for the golf course than for a boat ride.

"Hello, *Morris Dancer*," Patrick said, over the rattle of the idling outboard, as he brought the dinghy up to the boarding ladder hanging off the port side. "I bring you some comp'ny, if it's okay."

"Good morning, Patrick," Jim said, eyeing the overdressed visitor in the bow of Patrick's dinghy. "I'm Jim Morris. How can I help you?" he asked.

"Good morning, Mr. Morris," Phillip said. "I'm Phillip Davis, and I represent Jean-Pierre Berger, Dani Berger's father. I understand from the police that you met her aboard another yacht down island some days ago, and I was hoping I could ask you a few questions. We're worried about her, and I'm helping the authorities a bit. May I come aboard?"

"Certainly, Mr. Davis. Come on up. You, too, Patrick."

"No, thanks, captain. I got to get back to the dock. You call me on the VHF when Mr. Davis is ready to come back ashore." Patrick touched the bill of his baseball cap in salute as he pulled away.

"Beautiful boat," Phillip said, as he settled into the cockpit. "Halberg-Rassy, from the '70s?"

"You have a good eye for boats, Mr. Davis. You a sailor?" Jim asked.

"Well, yes, but not full time. Please call me Phillip. I live in Martinique, and I keep a boat in Marin, at the marina there."

"Great, and I'm Jim, by the way. This is my wife, Joann," Jim said, as she emerged from the companionway. "We're just getting the boat ready for a visit from our grandchildren. They're flying in tomorrow."

"Pleased to meet you, ma'am." Phillip rose to his feet as Joann put three glasses and a pitcher of iced tea on the foldout table.

"Likewise," Joann said. "Please, sit back down and have some tea. What can we tell you about Dani and Mike?"

"Well, anything would help," Phillip said. "All the police told me was that you met them on a yacht called *Sea Serpent*, down in the Tobago Cays on October 20. That's as much as I know. Anything you can add would help; like, where did they meet, where were they going, how well did they seem to know one another.

"I'm a friend of the family, and since I live here in the islands, Dani's father asked me to help look for her. The local authorities don't have a lot of resources to spend on tracking down missing yachties, especially when there's no sign a crime was committed.

"Her parents were disturbed when she missed calling her mother on her birthday, and then her father got a call from the police in Union Island. They were looking for her because she jumped ship from a British yacht called *Rambling Gal*, in Mayreau, on October 20. Seems they found her cellphone at the resort in Salt Whistle Bay. That's the last place anybody saw her, until you turned up."

"Oh, I can understand how her parents must feel," Joann said. "Mike and Dani were anchored near us in the Tobago Cays late that afternoon on October 20. We were the only two boats in the anchorage. We both got in about the same time. Once we got the hook down, Jim and I were riding around in the dinghy, doing a little sightseeing. They waved us over and invited us up for sundowners. We spent maybe an hour with them; that's all, but they seemed to know one another — not like they just met. That's hard to judge, though, since we didn't know either of them before."

"But we did run into Mike a few days later, in Rodney Bay." Jim picked up the story. "We invited them over for cocktails that evening, but when Mike showed up, he was by himself. Said Dani wasn't with him anymore, that she had some stuff to do. He said the time in the Cays was like a trial run for them, and he was hoping she would decide to join him for a longer cruise. Sounded like he expected to hear from her in a few days, but I don't think he really said."

"He was on *Sea Serpent* in Rodney Bay?" Phillip asked.

"Yes. We saw the boat anchored across the bay from us when we were coming back from the grocery store," Joann said. "Jim zipped over and invited him for drinks, while I put the groceries away."

"Have you seen him or *Sea Serpent* since then?"

"No," Joann answered. "We left early the next morning for St. Pierre, Martinique. It was around dawn — just enough light that we could see *Sea Serpent* was still there. I don't think he said where he was going next — just working his way north, I guess, like everybody else this time of year."

"Okay, that's all helpful," Phillip said. "Could you give me a description, and maybe a last name for Mike, and do you know if he owns *Sea Serpent*, by any chance? I clearly need to talk to him."

"He sure acted like he owned her, but who knows," Jim said. "I'm pretty sure we never got to last names. You know how it is in this yachting crowd. He's Mike on *Sea Serpent*. Nobody needs a last name, down here."

"Right," Phillip said.

"Wait!" Joann said, jumping to her feet. "I think we took a picture or two of them. Let me get the camera."

She disappeared down the companionway, emerging in less than a minute with a digital camera.

"Yes, I thought so. Two pictures of them and a good shot of *Sea Serpent*."

She squeezed in beside Phillip, leaning over so that he could see the display on the camera as she scrolled back and forth through the photographs, which showed a nondescript man, probably in his 40's, with an arm draped around Dani's shoulder and a drink in his other hand. *Sea Serpent* was a graceful old yawl, but Phillip couldn't tell any more about her from the picture.

"Perfect," Phillip said. "Any chance I can get a copy of those shots?"

"You bet," Joann said. "Let me just fire up the laptop and I'll burn you a CD."

"Thanks, Joann. While you're at it, could you please jot down your email address in case I need to reach you later?" Phillip asked.

"No problem," she said, ducking below again, leaving the men to make small talk about sailing in the islands. She copied the pictures to a CD and taped a calling card with *Morris Dancer's* picture and their personal contact information to the envelope.

While she was below, Phillip borrowed Jim's handheld VHF radio and called Patrick for a ride back ashore.

PHILLIP CAUGHT a late afternoon flight back to Martinique, and he was home in time for a late dinner of leftovers from his refrigerator. As he worked his way through a bowl of warmed-over pasta, he thought about his next steps.

He would go online as soon as he finished eating and look up *Sea Serpent* in the U.S. Coast Guard's national vessel documentation database. If she were indeed U.S.-flagged, that would disclose the owner's name and address. Even in this age of fanaticism about privacy, the database was still in the public domain. Many vessels, though, were registered to privately held corporations, which meant he might have a little bit more work ahead to find out who this Mike character was.

Phillip wolfed down his pasta, a habit from his working days, when food was nothing more than mission-critical fuel. He rinsed, dried, and put away his bowl and utensils.

Settling himself in front of his computer, Phillip discovered that *Sea Serpent* belonged to Michael Reilly, of Green Cove Springs, Florida. He recognized the street address as a mail forwarding service — one that he had used himself in his peripatetic days. That likely meant that Mike Reilly lived on his boat.

It had only been a couple of days since the Morrises had seen Reilly in St. Lucia. Unless he was in a hurry for some reason, he could still be there.

One of Phillip's former business associates in St. Lucia had a brother who worked in customs at Rodney Bay, but it was too late to call. He would do that first thing in the morning.

Even if Reilly had moved on, he would have had to list his next port of call on the clearance documents. There was nothing to stop him from deviating from his plan once he was at sea, but there was no reason to think that he would.

Tired from two days of puddle-jumper flights around the islands, Phillip decided to get some sleep, but first he called J.-P. Berger to bring him up to date.

10

Phillip was sitting at a shaded table just off the sidewalk on the main street of Ste. Anne, having a mid-morning espresso with a *pain au chocolat* at his favorite *patisserie*. His conversation last night with J.-P. was on his mind.

They were both frustrated with the lack of information. Phillip's thoughts were racing through possible scenarios seeking a benign explanation for Dani's disappearance. His cellphone interrupted him. Glancing at the display, he saw that it was his friend in St. Lucia.

"Good morning again, Cedric," he said, putting the espresso cup in its saucer with his left hand.

"Good morning, Phillip. I have news." Cedric's gravelly voice greeted him. "My brother is working today, and he tells me that this yacht you asked me about earlier this morning cleared out a couple of days ago, for Ste. Anne, with only the captain aboard."

"I'll be damned," Phillip said. "That was quick. Thanks, Cedric. I owe you."

"You already owe me a fishing trip. You're too busy for me to collect, these days. Call me when you are retired again."

"Yeah, okay. Thanks again, Cedric," Phillip said, pressing the disconnect button.

He thumbed the keys to bring up his phonebook and called his girlfriend. Five minutes later, he left a handful of coins on the table and ambled back to his house.

As he walked, he pondered what he had just learned from his girlfriend, Sandrine, who ran the French customs office at the marina in Marin.

Sea Serpent had cleared into Marin a couple of days ago, just as he would have expected. Yesterday, *Sea Serpent* had left, bound for Prince Rupert Bay, Dominica, but this time, there were two people aboard — Mike Reilly, and Michelle Devereaux, who had a French passport.

The French passport was a stroke of luck. Since Martinique was a department of France, Sandrine had access to the database of French passports. For the price of a late afternoon lunch with Sandrine, he would have the particulars on Michelle.

Sandrine had already tried to pull up the details of her passport, but had been frustrated by computer problems. She had suggested that they get together later.

Maybe she just misses me. Phillip smiled to himself as he opened his front door.

Sandrine was the first woman he had dated seriously since before he had joined the Army years ago. It seemed to have been a while since he had seen her, but it had only been a few days. He felt as if he were looking at time through the wrong end of a telescope. Things that happened before he started looking for Dani seemed prehistoric. He recognized the phenomenon of time passing at warp speed when he was absorbed in a problem. It was a carryover from his working days.

When he had been on a mission, survival depended on living in the present, with all his senses focused on immediate stimuli. The intensity of his focus had seemed to accelerate his experiences. Maybe it was just the effect of adrenaline — some natural reaction of the human body to being constantly attuned to trouble.

Phillip didn't quite have that sense of danger now, but he did feel as if he were back in the field. He tried to convince himself that it was because he was renewing so many acquaintances from the era when he lived life on the edge of violence. Still, he felt uneasy about Dani's situation.

He settled into the hammock on his veranda, thinking that a nap would be just the thing before meeting Sandrine. A late lunch with her could turn into a late evening, after all. He might need his strength.

Just as he was about to drop off, Phillip realized that he had forgotten to call his old crony in Portsmouth, Dominica, to find out if *Sea Serpent* was in the anchorage at Prince Rupert Bay. Reluctantly, he went back inside and sat down at his desk to make the call.

Phillip was about to give up when his call finally connected. He smiled as he listened to the singsong greeting.

"Hey. This Sharktooth water taxi. I ready if you ready. Whatchew need, mon?"

Phillip heard the roar of a speedboat in the background. He pictured the dreadlocks flying in the breeze as Sharktooth drove his boat across the waves.

"Sharktooth, this is Phillip. How you been, mon?"

"*Irie*, Phillip, ev'yt'ing good, mon. You good?"

Irie was patois for all right, but the word had a somewhat broader meaning than its English counterpart. Phillip liked its connotation that everything was not just all right, but was exactly as it should be.

"Yeah, pretty good. You see a yacht called *Sea Serpent* there in the last day or two?" Phillip asked.

"Yeah, mon. They here. Dive trip today, wit' Simon. Then tomorrow, they got islan' tour wit' Robert. Prob'ly stay for some days yet, I t'ink. Why you ask?"

"I need to talk to the captain. I'll fly up there in the morning and catch a taxi to Portsmouth. Should be there about 11. You busy?"

"Yeah, mon. I busy meet yo' taxi at 11. You wan' jus' *talk* to the captain, or you gon' have some serious talk? He got a lady wit' he on the boat, if you t'inkin' to get serious wit' he," Sharktooth said.

"Nothing too serious. I just need to ask him a few questions."

"Okay, mon. Later, then. Blessings to you, Phillip." Sharktooth ended the call.

Phillip chuckled at the abrupt termination of the call, thinking how little Sharktooth had changed over the years. When he was finished with something, he moved right on with no hesitation.

Sharktooth still seemed to be on top of everything happening in the harbor at Portsmouth. Philip smiled at the notion of "serious talk."

If you had a "serious talk" with Sharktooth, you were lucky if you could walk away under your own power. Almost seven feet tall and weighing just under 300 pounds, dreadlocks to his waist, and a bald crown, the man was scary, although he had a gentle disposition — except when he didn't.

Phillip called his travel agent in Marin and booked an early morning flight to Dominica for the next day, with a return on the last flight that evening. More relaxed now, he went back to the hammock and found the nap that had eluded him earlier.

"Phillip, when I see the picture of this Michelle on my computer, I understand that I know this woman," Sandrine said, as she wiped her fingers. She was well into the *moules frites* appetizer, and was reaching for a sip of wine.

"You know her?" Phillip asked. "Is she a friend of yours?"

"No, no. Not precisely a friend. How do you say it in American

English? Someone you know, but just a little bit, maybe to say, good morning?" Sandrine was forever working on improving her grasp of colloquial American English, to be better able to deal with the Americans checking in with her at the *Douane*.

Americans spoke such slang-riddled English that even the Brits weren't sure what they were saying half the time. Phillip was sympathetic, having been on the other side of the problem early in his traveling days, when he discovered that American English was not universally understood by other English speakers.

"You mean, 'a casual acquaintance,' perhaps?" he asked.

"Yes, I think so. I think I am having a casual acquaintance with Michelle Devereaux. Is that how I say it, Phillip?" she asked, pursing her lips as she reached into the steamer for another mussel.

"Yes, Sandrine, or you might say, 'She's not really a friend; more of a casual acquaintance.' That would be a common way to express the relationship," Phillip said.

"Thank you, Phillip. She's not really a friend; more of a casual acquaintance. I will see her in the mornings, when I go to the restaurant on the quay across from my work at the *Douane* to get my espresso and pastry."

Sandrine took a sip of wine. "She is working there for some months before she leaves in this yacht, the *Sea Serpent*. After I know her from the picture, I go there to be talking with the manager to learn about Michelle Devereaux. Will this be helping, Phillip?" Sandrine plucked another mussel from the broth in the steamer and looked up at Phillip.

"Yes, Sandrine, thank you very much. And what did you learn from the manager?" Phillip asked, helping himself to a mussel and some fries.

"The manager, he is telling me Michelle works there for some months. Maybe more than six months, but not as much as a year. She is with a boyfriend who is doing the drugs. This boyfriend, he is always not being nice to her, but in the last days, the boyfriend, he is gone. Nobody knows where, but Michelle — he calls her Michie, sometimes — is alone now, and the manager, he is saying that she is happier. She has decide that she will be living in St. Martin, because she always want to go there, and now, there is nothing for her to stay in Martinique. She is the only daughter of two dead people. How is that called?" Sandrine paused for a sip of wine.

"An orphan," Phillip said. "So she had no other family in Martinique?"

"Yes, that is correct, no more family, anywhere. She is alone in the world, and then, in the restaurant, she is meeting this man from the yacht, the *Sea Serpent*, and she will sail with him to St. Martin. So, she is quit her work there, and the manager, he is need her because the busy season comes, and he has no waitress now, unless he finds someone else soon. Look, Phillip, the *lapin*!" She finished her story as the waiter brought their main course, the grilled rabbit steaming on a bed of rice.

As they enjoyed the rest of their meal, Sandrine quizzed Phillip about his interest in *Sea Serpent*. He told her the story of Dani's disappearance, and that led to a bit of the story about Dani's family, which intrigued Sandrine.

She couldn't understand why a girl from such a wealthy family would choose to live the life of a vagabond sailor. Phillip tried to explain to her that some people were just drawn to the sea, willing to live as they must to spend as much time as possible in the embrace of blue water, far from the distractions of life ashore.

"I can understand the appeal," he said, "but it's not a life that I would choose. There's nothing more beautiful than the open ocean on a nice day in the tropics, with a good boat under you and a steady breeze in the sails. It's like being the only person in the world, I think, and some people like that."

"Not me," Sandrine said, shaking her head. "I think the ocean is beautiful, but I will see it from the beach, or perhaps from your veranda, Phillip, high up on the mountain there," she pointed in the direction of his villa. "Perhaps we will go there to watch the sunset, for maybe the flash of green," she said, a mischievous look coming over her face.

Phillip excused himself to settle the bill for their meal while she went to the ladies' room.

11

DANI HAD BEEN DRIFTING IN AND OUT OF CONSCIOUSNESS FOR A while. During one period of lucidity, she overheard two women talking. She had no idea how long ago that had been; she had no sense of time. They were outside her room, probably next door, and were speaking Spanish. Dani was a long way from fluent in Spanish, but she'd been able to get an idea of what they were saying.

She spent enough time in Miami as a child to pick up basic conversational Spanish. Mario Espinosa, her godfather, was a pillar of the Cuban exile community, and most of his family were bilingual. When Mario and her father were working together, J.-P. had often parked Dani at Mario's. Her exposure had been to Cuban Spanish, so she recognized that the women were Cuban, or of Cuban extraction.

Dani had dropped off to sleep as she wondered where she was. Her first thought had been Cuba, because of the women's dialect. But how would she have gotten to Cuba? Her memory was hazy, and her head ached. She'd felt the lump on her head and the stitches and guessed that she had a severe concussion.

She'd been knocked unconscious enough times to recognize the symptoms, but she'd never had a concussion this bad.

As *Sea Serpent* rocked gently at anchor, Mike Reilly gazed out over the lush, green hillside of Dominica, watching sugarcane swaying in the breeze. He was pleasantly fatigued from a day of reef-diving. At a distance, the motion of the cane mimicked the ebb and flow of the ocean swells outside the harbor.

Sipping his rum punch while Michelle bustled about the galley making a Creole gumbo for dinner, Mike reflected that life didn't get much better than this. He couldn't remember feeling so content since before Andrea, his ex-wife, had left him, years ago.

Her departure had ushered in a long period of solitary existence. Until he met Michie, he had felt no interest in company. Ten years was a long time for a man to spend completely by himself, he reflected, although he had been content to be a loner. He had a lifetime of practice.

He vividly remembered his loneliness as an only child with a mother who discouraged any association with other children. She, herself, avoided other adults. He learned at her elbow to trust no one, and to shun all contact except with her and his father.

When he strayed from their backyard, she chased him down and dragged him home, cursing under her breath. Safely home, she would switch him vigorously with green bamboo, freshly cut from the backyard hedge for the occasion.

By the time he was three, he had learned not to leave the safety of his backyard, but the switchings had remained his mother's preferred method of discipline for his many other transgressions. He could still feel the sensation of the tiny, hair-like fibers that covered the surface of the green cane cutting into the skin of his legs.

After he had gotten a little older, he had discovered that the bamboo hedges offered a refuge, of sorts. In the corners of the hedge that bordered the backyard, there were caverns that opened within the growth. Those caverns, large enough for a small boy to creep into and shut himself off from the rest of the world, were the site of many adventures.

He would sit, hidden within the bamboo, for hours, imagining all sorts of experiences that seemed real to him. When he tired of his imaginary pursuits, he studied the bamboo itself.

It looked so graceful and inflicted such pain. In some ways, it was just like his mother. Like all little children, he thought his mother was beautiful. She was also a source of pain, and she certainly kept the rest of the world at bay, just like the bamboo.

He had learned from the nuns at school that seven years old was the age of reason, the age at which you could begin to know right from wrong. He had learned to tell the difference before that.

Right was keeping to yourself and not getting punished. Wrong was mixing with other people who might find out that you had to be switched regularly because you were bad.

"Mike, the gumbo, it is ready now," Michelle announced, ending his dark recollections and bringing him back to the present.

"Let's eat in the cockpit. Sunset's in a few minutes," Mike said.

She came up the companionway ladder, balancing a tray with two bowls of gumbo and a bottle of white wine sweating in the humid air. She set the tray on the bridge deck next to Mike and went back below, returning quickly with two wine glasses. Mike poured them each a glass of the dry white French table wine.

"To another rotten day in paradise," he said, handing Michelle a glass as he raised his in a toast.

"Yes, thanks to God," she responded, clicking her glass against his before raising it to her lips. "This is so wonderful, this life. I was never imagining that people on the yachts, they could live like this."

"It's better with you here, Michie," he said. "Much better than all those years I was alone. I hope you will stay with me after we get to St. Martin. I don't know what I'll do if you decide to stay there."

"You will find another lady, Mike," she said, a pensive look on her lovely face. "I am not believe that you have had no one with you since this foolish Andrea, she leaves you for ten years."

"I haven't wanted anyone, Michie. It was too painful to think of becoming attached to someone who might leave me like she did."

"But surely you have other people on this yacht, some ladies, while ten years," she continued to probe. "Someone, maybe, just for a little while? Why you keep that cabinet clear, if no one is use it?"

"The guest locker? I kept it empty just for you," he said, teasing her.

"I am not believe you, Mike, but is okay. I am happy to be with you, my love."

"So, will you stay with me, please, Michie?" Mike pressed for commitment.

"But of course! I am with you now. I will be with you tomorrow. Let us enjoy, and each day we will maybe enjoy more. I am learn not to demand more from life than is offer. You must do, too. It is a long time before we are in St. Martin. Do not worry so, my love. Look! It is almost to be the flash of green."

Michelle pointed at the horizon, where the sun appeared to bounce as its lower rim touched the surface of the glassy Caribbean. As it settled beneath the cloud-free horizon, they saw the brief green glow that came and went so quickly that if you blinked, you missed it. "It is beautiful," she said.

"Like your eyes," he said.

"Thank you for yesterday, Phillip," Sandrine said, kissing his cheek as she slid out of his car in the parking lot at the marina. "Call me when you are returning from the trip, please. I know you must rush to the airplane. I hope I am not to cause you being late," she tossed over her shoulder as she sashayed around the corner to the *Douane* office.

Phillip smiled, shaking his head as he watched the show, thinking that he had been a fool for not seeing her more often over the months since they had met. He drove to the airport, leaving himself plenty of time to check in for his flight.

LIAT, unusually, was on time. Phillip boarded as soon as his flight was called, and after he buckled his seatbelt, he attempted to study the file on Dani's disappearance. His mind kept wandering back to Sandrine even as he paged through the printout from the passport database. He had never had the luxury of trying to form a lasting relationship with anyone.

When he was in the military, he had been on call virtually all the time. That had been his choice. He liked the excitement of the special ops world, and he had not believed that he could balance commitment to his career and a commitment to a wife.

When he finally left the military, Phillip found himself drawn into an environment that was even less conducive to a happy marriage. After a close call with eternity about three years ago, he realized that he had enough money to live well without risking his life.

He had bought the place in Martinique and chilled out for a couple of years, just drifting through days without structure. Now that he was looking for Dani, his life had purpose again.

The difference was that he chose his own direction now, instead of pursuing goals set by others. He realized that he could finally manage a relationship with a woman, and Sandrine certainly appealed to him. He needed to pay more attention to that part of his life.

At 42, he wasn't too old to start a family. He had some financial stability, thanks to the lucrative nature of his activities as a civilian contractor to certain nameless agencies of the U.S. government.

His plane landed on time, and Phillip cleared customs and hailed a taxi. After a ride through Dominica's lush countryside, he paid off his taxi at the bridge over the Indian River, just outside of Portsmouth.

Phillip walked down to where the Indian River tour guides hung out. They waited for customers on the front porch of the building on the point, their boats tied off to a collection of odd bits and pieces of riprap that lined the shore. He spotted Sharktooth resting his huge frame on a beer crate in the shade, a frosty bottle of locally brewed Guiness in hand.

Not only was Guiness served ice-cold down here, but it also had nothing but the name in common with the brew from Saint James Gate in Dublin. The fine print on the label said, "Brewed under license," and Phillip had often wondered just how broad the terms of the license were.

Sharktooth saw him out of the corner of his eye and stood up, setting his empty bottle carefully aside. Someone would collect it for recycling. Nothing was wasted here. Even non-refillable bottles were used to package locally produced salted nuts, among other things.

"Hey, Phillip," Sharktooth said.

"Good morning." Phillip smiled, bumping fists with Sharktooth, Rasta fashion. "Life has been good to you."

"Yeah, mon, pretty good," Sharktooth agreed, patting the hard belly which made up a little more of his bulk than it had the last time Phillip had seen him. "My wife, she been feedin' me plenty good. Mebbe too good, hey, Phillip? You lookin' the same, mon. Ev'yt'ing good wit' you?"

"Everything's good, Sharktooth, irie," Phillip agreed.

"Come, Phillip. We go in the boat to get some lunch. They got a big pot of goat water over at the place on the beach. We eat, then we sit and watch the yacht, *Sea Serpent*, 'til they come back from islan' tour wit' Robert. Okay, mon?"

"Okay, Sharktooth. Let's go. I'm hungry," Phillip said, heading for Sharktooth's brightly painted speedboat. He noticed that it had a new paint job, in red, green, and yellow. Sharktooth's trademark, the dried cartilaginous jaws of a big mako shark, still held pride of place on the foredeck.

12

Phillip and Sharktooth, replete with a heavy midday meal of goat water with rice and fried plantains washed down with icy local beer, sat in the open-air restaurant, looking out over the anchored yachts. They were nursing after-dinner rum drinks and reminiscing about their adventures of days gone by.

"Phillip, you 'member the night I got this?" Sharktooth asked, raising his T-shirt to expose an ugly scar that spanned his solid-looking gut. "That mon, he was wild."

"Yeah, he was, Sharktooth. Maybe it was because you had just pulled his ear off," Phillip said, grinning at the memory. "He was just threatening to shoot us until you did that. Then he got so angry he threw the gun at me and went after you with the razor."

"How come you so slow to shoot, Phillip? He cut me good befo' you stop he."

"Well, I thought it was just a little disagreement until he cut you. Then I was afraid you were going to kill him before we got to ask him about the shipment of machine guns that went missing. I figured if I shot him in the knee you'd let him live. Never knew you to hurt a cripple," Phillip said, teasing the big man.

Sharktooth's big frame shook with laughter. "That the troot, mon," he said. "Look! Robert comin' wit' the folks from the yacht. We bes' pay Armand and get back to the boat."

They settled up with the giant behind the bar — Phillip thought he must be a relative of Sharktooth's — and strolled out onto the rickety dock. Sharktooth's boat sat bobbing in the wakes from the water taxis that were suddenly crisscrossing the anchorage, returning people to their yachts after excursions ashore.

Boarding Sharktooth's boat, they cast off from the dock and idled through the anchorage.

Sharktooth took his time approaching *Sea Serpent*, letting Phillip get a good look at the couple scrambling aboard from Robert's water taxi.

"'Allo, *Sea Serpent*," Sharktooth called, as he eased his boat up alongside. "You need some fresh fruit? Maybe cold beer? Restaurant for dinner?"

"No, thanks," the man said, pleasantly enough, as Sharktooth turned his most engaging smile upon the woman in the string bikini.

"Your lady, I bet she come from Martinique," Sharktooth said, gold teeth gleaming.

"How do you know this?" she asked.

"Because, except for my wife, the mos' beautiful ladies in the islands, they all come from Martinique." Sharktooth grinned.

"Excuse me for interrupting," Phillip said, directing his attention to the man. "My name is Phillip Davis, and I'm hoping for a word with Mike Reilly. I'm betting you're the man himself," he said in a friendly tone.

"Sure am," Mike said. "What can I do for you, Phillip?"

"Well, I just spoke with Jim and Joann on *Morris Dancer* the other day. They told me that you knew Dani Berger," Phillip paused.

"Mm," Mike said.

Who the hell is this guy? Mike remembered his encounter with the folks on *Morris Dancer*. Except for what he'd learned from Jim and Joann, he still had no recollection of this Dani woman.

What could this guy want? Mike couldn't lie; he didn't know the truth, so fabrication was dangerous. If he made up answers to questions about Dani, he might dig himself in more deeply. Maybe he'd already gotten himself in trouble with what he had told the Morrises. *I gotta be real careful with this.*

Phillip waited, his gaze fixed on Mike.

"She was just aboard for a little while," Mike said. "That's when we met Jim and Joann. I can't really say I knew her."

Phillip was picking up a discordant vibe from Mike, watching the fingers of the man's right hand fidgeting. Glancing at the woman, Phillip saw that she was looking strangely at her companion. There was a question in her green eyes.

"So how long did your 'trial run' last with Dani?" Phillip asked, trying to provoke a reaction, sensing that Mike was not going to offer much in the way of information.

"Trial run? I don't understand." Mike shook his head, looking at Phillip with genuine confusion.

"When you saw Jim and Joann in St. Lucia, you told them that Dani was just aboard for a trial run, and that you hoped she would join you for an extended cruise. At least, that's what they told me."

Phillip watched as Mike's eyes shifted erratically from side to side. The woman, presumably Michelle, was looking at him as if he had just sprouted horns and a tail.

"I don't remember saying that. I don't know what you're talking about. None of this is making sense. Who are you, anyway?" Mike's voice rose in pitch as he spoke. He looked at Phillip, bewildered.

"I'm a friend of Dani's, and her family is worried. She's disappeared, and you seem to be the last person with whom she was seen. The police from St. Vincent are looking for her, too, to ask her some questions about her departure from *Rambling Gal*. She left unexpectedly in Mayreau on October 20, the same day the Morrises saw the two of you in the Tobago Cays. I was hoping you could at least tell me where you put her ashore after that," Phillip said, holding Mike's gaze.

"I don't have to talk to you. I want you to get away from my boat, now," Mike said, trembling.

Phillip sensed Sharktooth shifting his position, getting ready for aggression. Phillip gestured behind his back for him to back off. They had gotten as much from Mike Reilly as they were going to get. There was no point in making a scene that would involve the local police at this stage, even if Sharktooth was solidly connected.

"I'll leave," Phillip said, "but I have a feeling that we have more to talk about. Fair winds until I see you again," he said, releasing his grip on *Sea Serpent's* toe rail.

Sharktooth's boat began to drift away; Sharktooth blew a kiss to the woman as he turned to start the outboard.

"WE GO BACK LATER and take he fishin', Phillip? Without the lady?" Sharktooth asked, as they tied the boat to the dock at the restaurant where they had eaten lunch.

Sharktooth led the way back into the open-air restaurant, which appeared to be closed, now. He sat down and motioned for Phillip to do the same.

"The man mus' know somet'ing, the way he act."

"Maybe," Phillip agreed. "Maybe not. He was shaken; that's for sure. But I don't think he was lying to us. More like he thought he should know the answers to the questions we were asking, but he didn't. I'm going to find out everything I can about him while I keep looking for Dani down island. He was evasive and upset, but I'm pretty sure he doesn't know what happened to Dani."

Phillip had visions of Sharktooth making fish bait out of

Reilly; he wanted to calm Sharktooth down a bit. It wouldn't be the first time Sharktooth had taken independent action after getting involved in a situation like this with Phillip.

"If he put Dani ashore somewhere, why he don' jus' say it, Phillip?" Sharktooth wondered. "You see the way the lady look at he?"

"Yes. I think that's why he was so upset, Sharktooth. There was something going on with that lady, too — her name is Michelle Devereaux, by the way. He didn't want to talk about Dani in front of her. I could see that right away. I just wanted to push him a little and see what happened.

"I don't think he knows where Dani went. As you said, it would have been too easy just to tell us, 'She spent a few hours aboard and I dropped her back at Mayreau,' or whatever. That would have been a bulletproof answer. All we could have done was say thanks and go looking where he said he left her. I almost felt like Dani bailed out on him, and he didn't have a clue about where or why. That Michelle's another puzzle, too."

"Michelle? She a puzzle? Why? Wait. Thirsty. I be right back."

Sharktooth went around behind the empty bar and dredged two cold beers out of the icebox. He popped the caps off the bottles using his teeth and planted one on the table in front of Phillip.

"She worked in the café near Sandrine's office for months. Then a few days ago, she stopped showing up for work." Phillip told Sharktooth what he'd learned from Sandrine about Michelle. The two of them tried to make sense of the information that Phillip had gathered.

If Reilly had been truthful with Jim and Joann Morris, then what was he doing with Michelle aboard? It could be that Dani was planning to join him at some later date. Or maybe she'd decided against cruising with him.

Phillip had more questions than answers from his encounter with Reilly, but his impression was that Reilly didn't know anything about Dani's whereabouts. Maybe he just made up the 'trial run' thing to explain her unexpected disappearance to the Morrises. The more Phillip thought about it, the more likely this explanation seemed to him.

"Did you catch the look on that Michelle girl's face, when you ask he 'bout Dani?"

Sharktooth's question brought Phillip's attention back to the people on *Sea Serpent*.

"She gone give that man some trouble, now. She one unhappy lady 'bout the whole Dani t'ing, I t'ink."

"Yes," Phillip said. "I think you're right. I was watching her when I could. I don't think she knew anything at all about Dani. Did you get a different idea?" Phillip asked.

"She look like the new wife, jus' find out the husband, he already married to some other lady. Tha's what I t'ink. She don' know they been another lady in he life, least not lately. I t'ink he been tellin' she some tale."

"I think you're right, Sharktooth," Phillip said, looking at his watch. "I've got time to catch the last flight back to Martinique."

Sharktooth ran Phillip back into town in the boat, and called a taxi to take him to the airport. He agreed to talk to his cousin at the customs office in Portsmouth and give Phillip a call with all the details when *Sea Serpent* left Dominica.

MIKE WAS NURSING A COLOSSAL HEADACHE, and Michelle was not helping.

"Why do you tell me you have no one, when only last week, you have this Dani on the yacht in the Tobago Cays?" she asked, her voice shrill.

Mike's vision was wavering in time with her rising inflection. "Michie, what difference does it make?" he asked, in a pleading tone. "I can't even remember her. She must have been aboard for a few hours, because those people saw her, but she left somehow without me knowing, I guess. Nothing happened. I don't even know her."

"Is exactly, Mike. She make no difference to me. She is not now. Is very strange, this story you tell about alone, and about not remember. It make me to be some frightened that you do not wish me to know about her. Why have you go around the way to tell me what is not true? So, now you tell me how many other lady have been sailing on this yacht with you in the years you are being alone."

Michelle was a keen student of human nature. Her hard-won ability to read people had been essential to her survival thus far in her young, colorful life. She wasn't distressed that there had been other women in Mike's life, but she was alarmed that she had been so taken in by his pathetic tale of loneliness. This lapse in her powers of observation infuriated her.

She couldn't believe that he could lie so effectively, and over such an extended period, without a single tell. This ability of his was unique in her experience.

She found herself falling for this idiot, only to discover that she was being misled. Her fury aside, she was relieved that she had found him out before she made a complete fool of herself with him.

Mike was in shock. His beautiful new companion had turned into a virago, and someone had connected him to this Dani woman's disappearance. He couldn't think, let alone respond coherently to Michelle.

He felt the waves of stress washing over him as physical pressure. He imagined his brain was throbbing, pressing rhythmically against the inside of his skull, threatening to force his eyes from their sockets. This raging woman, with her broken English, was stepping up the already intolerable pressure.

If only he had the strength to shut her up; but it was too late. He sensed that he was leaving, somehow. He thought that soon, he would find peace in oblivion — this physical torment had to be self-limiting, surely.

When Michelle saw Mike's eyes glazing as he appeared to slip from consciousness, her rage was amplified. She would not be ignored. As she rose to her feet, her right foot lashed out at him, seemingly of its own volition, making solid contact with his shoulder and knocking him from his perch on the cockpit coaming.

The sound of his head hitting the deck resonated like a coconut dropping on concrete, bringing her down from her fury. Michelle worried that she might have killed him as she watched the slowly spreading pool of blood beneath his head. Not that he didn't deserve to die, but she didn't know enough to sail this boat to St. Martin by herself.

Much calmer, her perspective restored somewhat by the physical release of striking him, Michelle dropped to her knees beside him to assess the damage. She discovered a small cut above his hairline on the right side of his head.

His head had struck the sharp edge on the genoa sheet block mounted on the track along the deck near where he lay. Michelle knew scalp wounds bled profusely; she had seen plenty of them at close hand. She felt his pulse and checked his pupils, deciding that he would be all right once he regained consciousness.

Michelle tried to lift him, thinking that she should take him below and put him on one of the settees in the main cabin, but he was heavier than he looked. She rolled him onto the seat cushions in the cockpit and stretched him out, to try to make him comfortable.

She went below and rummaged in the lockers in the head until she found first aid supplies. Taking them back up to the cockpit, Michelle cleaned Mike's cut and spread antibiotic cream over it, closing it with butterfly strips. Taping a gauze pad over the wound, she decided he would be all right where he was for the night.

Not knowing what kind of mood he would be in when he came to, she went below and locked herself in the forward cabin. Her rage had subsided, but she didn't trust this man.

The teak door wouldn't withstand much of an assault, but it would at least wake her up if he tried to open it while she slept. She collapsed on the double berth, and drained by her angry outburst, was soon asleep.

13

Mike Reilly was in that strange state between sleep and wakefulness. He knew he was dreaming, but the images in his mind were vivid, real to him, and he couldn't banish them. All he could do was watch them unfold, feeling the emotions they evoked. He'd had this dream before; he knew it well. But he couldn't stop it, couldn't find peaceful sleep.

The dream was a recurring one that went back to his childhood. He'd been little — maybe four, or five. His favorite uncle had surprised him with a puppy. Mike's mother had been surprised, as well, and she didn't like dogs.

Mike had been ecstatic, enamored of the puppy, feeding it and cuddling it. He'd named it Randolph, and he managed to sneak it into his bed that night. He had fallen asleep holding it.

When he woke up the next morning, the puppy was gone. Upset, Mike had run outside in his pajamas to ask his mother about it.

"Mama! Mama, where's Randolph?"

In his dream, he could still feel the sense of panic.

"That nasty dog? I gave him to the egg man. He'll be happier on that chicken farm. Get yourself inside and get dressed before somebody sees you. You know better than to come outside in your pajamas." She turned from hanging the laundry on the clothesline and pulled a fresh piece of green bamboo from the hedge. She grabbed his wrist with her other hand, dragging him inside. The sting of the switching she'd given him was as real in the dream as if it had just happened.

The old black mood was heavy upon him as Mike roused himself. He looked around, wondering why he had slept in the cockpit last night. Sitting up, he smelled the mingled aromas of coffee and bacon wafting up from the companionway.

Who's cooking?

Alarm replaced his feeling of profound loss. Did he have company aboard? He looked around, recognizing the anchorage in Portsmouth, Dominica. It was early morning, gray and misty as it often was in Portsmouth until the sun came over the mountains to the east of the harbor.

"HIS REACTIONS WERE STRANGE, J.-P.," Phillip said.

He'd gotten in from Dominica late last night, too late to call J.-P., given the time difference between Martinique and Paris. Impatient to hear his report, J.-P. had called him a few minutes ago, while Phillip was getting his first cup of coffee. He paused to take a sip.

"What do you mean, strange, Phillip?"

"I don't think he knew what I was talking about when I asked him about Dani," Phillip said.

"But the Morrises said they saw her on his boat," J.-P. said. "Why would they say that, if it were not so?"

"Oh, I think they saw her on *Sea Serpent*, all right. But there's something wrong with Reilly. He was upset and confused. I think Dani was on his boat and he has no recollection of it. That's the only way I can reconcile his behavior with the facts that we have. Either that, or he's a far better liar than I've ever run across."

"What about this Devereaux woman?" J.-P. asked. "Where does she fit in?"

"I think she just hitched a ride to St. Martin on *Sea Serpent*. Maybe she hustled Reilly in the bargain. Everything about her is consistent with what we learned from her former boss. Her reaction when I questioned Reilly about Dani was interesting, though."

"Why is that?" J.-P. asked.

"We'd have to know more about her relationship with Reilly to be sure, but I think she was surprised that Dani had been on the boat as recently as a week ago. Maybe even pissed off with Reilly. Devereaux only met Reilly a day before they left Martinique. I'm thinking he might have told her something that was inconsistent with Dani having been on the boat," Phillip said.

"So Michelle Devereaux heard from you that Dani was aboard last week, and this upset her? This is what you think?" J.-P. asked. "Why would that be so?"

"I can imagine that she might have asked him about recent girlfriends, or guests, maybe," Phillip said. "And he might have told her there had been none."

"You think maybe that's a reason for Reilly to lie, Phillip? To hide a relationship with Dani from his new woman?"

"It could be. That might explain the Devereaux woman's reaction. But, there were no tells from Reilly, no sign he was lying. I think Reilly believes that Dani was never aboard his boat."

"So, this adds nothing to our understanding."

"Not so, J.-P. It's confusing, all right. But I don't think Dani was on *Sea Serpent* when Reilly left St. Vincent and the Grenadines. Reilly's reaction to my questions tends to confirm what we've learned. If he were trying to hide that, he could have told me things that would have taken us in a different direction, but he didn't. As it stands now, we know Dani's not with him, and that he probably doesn't know where she is. It's still possible that he had some role in her disappearance, but if he did, we won't learn about it from him."

"What if you and Sharktooth worked on him a bit?"

"J.-P., I understand how frustrated you are, but trust me. If I thought Reilly knew something and just wouldn't talk, Sharktooth and I would get it out of him, one way or another. My read on Reilly is that we could take him to the edge of death, and he still couldn't tell us anything. If he were lying, all he had to do was say, 'Yeah, she spent a couple of days on the boat with me and went ashore in Bequia,' or wherever. He didn't use the easiest way to get rid of me, so I think that's one more indication that he believes what he told us."

"Okay, Phillip, what you have said makes sense. Where do we go from here?"

"I think we need to learn as much as we can about Mike Reilly. Now that I've defended him to you and Sharktooth, I have to say there was something a little off about him. You still have your contacts in Miami, right?"

"Phillip, you're the one who is retired. I'm still working, remember? I'll put Mario to work on it. I will let you know what he finds."

"Okay, J.-P. While you're doing that, I'm going back down island and check out the grapevine. I'll see if anybody has heard anything that might give us a lead. You still haven't heard anything to indicate that one of our old competitors might have kidnapped Dani, have you? Or thought of any reason why she might want to disappear for a while?"

"No, Phillip, neither of those things. I have been involved in a project in South America, but I am in a partnership with the people you are talking about. Times have changed. It is better for them to work with me instead of competing, these days. It is harder to make money than it used to be. They would be hurting themselves as much as me with a kidnapping.

"Nobody I can think of who could kidnap Dani would stand to benefit. I have searched my soul over that. Besides, if somebody had kidnapped Dani, there would have been a ransom demand by now. As for Dani herself, who knows? She's gone off our radar before, but not like this. She has always sent some signal to let me know not to worry. True, she has lost her phone, but she's resourceful. She would have another by now, unless she is where she can't communicate. I don't like to think this way..."

"Nor do I, J.-P.," Phillip said. "Nor do I. We'll find her. I'll send you a fax with my itinerary, once I work it out."

"*Bonjour*, Mike," Michelle said, as she balanced a breakfast tray in her left hand. She emerged gracefully from the companionway and folded out the cockpit table, placing the tray on the table, careful to avoid sloshing coffee from the mugs.

She looked at Mike for a few seconds, watching him, not sure what to expect. Michelle had decided to pretend nothing unusual had happened between them last night. That seemed to be her least risky option. She noticed that Mike was gazing at her with open curiosity on his face, almost as if he didn't know her. That puzzled her, but at least he didn't seem angry.

"Good morning," Mike said, bleary eyed. He wondered who this angel with the dazzling green eyes could be, and how she came to be cooking breakfast on his boat. At the same time, he felt drawn to her, as if she were an important part of his life.

I'm in love with her. How can that be? I can't remember her name, but I know her. Who is she? Does she belong here with me, somehow?

"Are you have sleep okay? I worry that you are not comfortable, but I can not to make down the ladder with you, last night," she said, smiling at him as she planted a brief kiss on his forehead.

"I'm okay," he replied, probing gingerly at the bandage on the side of his head. "I'm afraid I can't remember what happened."

Maybe she'll give me some clue, if I just stay cool.

"You are stand up and fall, last night, and hitting the head on the thing there," she explained, pointing at the deck, where Mike noticed a bloodstain around a sheet block.

So she was here last night. Who could she be? Where did she come from?

"Mine?" he asked, touching the bandage with one hand and pointing at the bloodstain with the other.

"*Oui!* You are bleeding when you fall. I am scare at first you are die, but then I see you are alive but not wake up, and I make the bandage, but I am not enough strong to move you to the bed, so you are sleeping here."

"I see," he said, taking a gulp of coffee to wash down a mouthful of bacon and eggs.

"Are you feeling good now, Mike?" she asked, concern on her face.

"Better and better," he said, truthfully. Food and coffee were a miracle cure, it seemed.

"You are not swim today, because the bandage," she said, looking worried.

"No, not today." *Were we going swimming?*

"When Robert is coming soon, I tell him that we snork at the reef tomorrow, maybe, when you are better, instead not today."

"Yes, I think so," Mike said, drinking more coffee.

Mike was beginning to piece together some of his recent history, now. He had been in Dominica for a few days, playing tourist with this beautiful girl.

What was her name? It will come to me. His gaze caressed her bikini-clad body. Those curves seemed quite familiar.

Have I been sleeping with her? We argued last night. Something about another woman, maybe.

But he couldn't remember any other women. Not since his

wife left him. There was that woman those Morris people had asked him about, but he didn't think he actually knew her.

What did Jim Morris call her? Dani. Dani, that was it. Somebody asked me about her yesterday.

I don't remember anything about a woman named Dani. But this girl was angry last night. Something about Dani being on the boat. Why do they all keep asking me about Dani?

One of the colorful water taxis pulled alongside, interrupting Mike's thoughts.

"Good morning, Mike, Michie," the man in the water taxi said.

Mike gave an absent-minded wave as the woman responded. *Michie. She must be Michie.*

"*Bonjour*, Robert," she said. "We are wanting to not snork today the reef, but in the next morning. Mike has injure on his head that we must wait, okay? Tomorrow, yes?"

"Sure, Michie, tha's okay," Robert replied. "You need anything fo' the head, Mike?"

"No, Michie fixed me up, Robert. Thanks, though," Mike said, pleased that he now knew the woman's name.

Michie — Michelle Devereaux! I remember her now. Martinique. She's from Martinique.

His head was clearing, now.

"Okay, then, I come tomorrow, an' we go snorkel on the reef 'roun' the point." Robert started the big outboard and idled slowly away, making a call on his cellphone as he waved goodbye.

Michie took the breakfast dishes below and started cleaning up the galley as Mike sipped more coffee, sorting through his scrambled memories.

We quarreled about Dani, whoever she is. Those men — who were they? They came out to the boat. They were asking about Dani, said someone had seen Dani aboard Sea Serpent. And then Michie got pissed off at me.

He had told Michie about being alone ever since his wife left him, years ago. Michie was angry because he hadn't told her about Dani. He had been upset already because he wanted Michie to stay with him permanently, and she wouldn't agree. That was before the two men brought up this whole Dani thing. He shook his head.

I had the puppy dream last night.

He'd spent enough time with shrinks when he was in foster care to know that the recurring dream was triggered by fear of loss. The shrinks didn't quite get it, though.

Yes, it was about fear of loss, but it was a warning to him from his subconscious; one that he had learned through painful experience to heed.

In taking the puppy away, his mother had taught him a valuable lesson. If you let yourself care about something, you made yourself vulnerable.

And here I am, in love with Michie.

She seemed to reciprocate his feelings, but she still wanted to leave him, to move ashore in St. Martin.

I gotta watch it. Michie hasn't mentioned our argument. Maybe she hopes I've forgotten about it. Does that mean that she wants to put it behind us?

I'll just wait and see. Gotta be careful, though. If she thinks she's gonna leave me, I'll have to deal with it.

14

AFTER HE FINISHED TALKING WITH PHILLIP, J.-P. BERGER PAUSED for a moment before he called Mario Espinosa, his old friend in Miami. J.-P. had last seen Mario five or six years ago, when he and Dani had visited the states on a holiday. Old enough to be J.-P.'s father, he had been J.-P.'s friend and partner for many years, now.

Mario had worked with J.-P.'s father in the bad old days, not long after Castro's revolution. J.-P. was far too young to have known Mario then, but he remembered his father's tales about how Mario had napalmed Cuba's sugarcane fields for weekend entertainment when he was a young man.

WHEN J.-P. CALLED, Mario was sipping a *colado* at his favorite café on Miami's Lincoln Road, smoking a big, illegal Cuban cigar. He was sharing lies about his golf game with his friends when his cellphone began to vibrate in the right front pocket of his open-necked, white linen shirt. He opted to ignore it.

It was too early for any of Mario's people to be calling him, and he didn't want to interrupt his cronies during their weekly get-together. The phone stopped vibrating just as Manny Fernandez finished telling a long, convoluted joke about an Anglo, a goat, and his sister-in-law. Mario chuckled politely with the other men at the table.

He was about to make his own contribution to the conversation when the phone began to vibrate again. Thinking it was his wife, he sighed, made a gesture excusing himself, and fished the phone out of his pocket. He turned away to read the caller ID before he pressed the connect button. His eyebrows arched in surprise when he saw the caller's name, flashing in time with the humming of the phone.

"*Hola, Jean-Pierre,*" he said. "*Comment allez-vous?*"

"*Buenos días, Mario. C'est bon, merci. Cómo está usted?*"

"Not so bad for an old man, J.-P., but not like I used to be, either. How is my beautiful goddaughter?" Mario asked.

"That is why I am calling you, my friend. Dani is missing, somewhere down in the islands. The last man with whom she was seen is from Florida, so I am hoping you could make a few inquiries."

"Certainly, J.-P., I will do that. So, have you spoken with Phillip Davis yet?"

"Yes, he's helping me down there, Mario. You know how he feels about Dani."

"Yes. There's not much that I can offer down island that Phillip can't do, but if he can use my help, he has but to ask. You tell him this for me, please?"

"I surely will, Mario. Thank you, my friend."

"It's nothing, J.-P. Now you will send me a fax with what you know about this man in Florida, yes?"

"Yes, Mario. As soon as we finish this call."

"Okay, J.-P. It is good to hear your voice again. We will find Dani, and we will make someone very sorry if he has harmed her even just a little bit. Don't worry. I will call soon."

"Thank you, Mario. Take care, old man."

"*Tu, tambièn, J.-P.,*" Mario said, disconnecting and turning back to his friends.

Of the five other men at the table, all but one knew Phillip and J.-P. and had at various times been involved in some of their nefarious dealings. They listened attentively as Mario recounted his conversation with J.-P.

Paul Russo was the newcomer to the group. Paul was retired from the Miami Police Department, where he had served as a detective running the homicide department. While he had never been involved in business dealings with the others, he knew Phillip Davis by reputation from Phillip's days working for various government agencies. Paul had been the MPD's liaison for several interagency working groups over the years, and Phillip was known to several of them for his covert activities on behalf of the DEA, among other, more secretive organizations.

Since his retirement, Paul had heard enough war stories from the rest of the men at the table so that he felt as if he knew J.-P. Berger, as well. By now, Paul had been part of the weekly gathering for long enough to gain the trust of the others. Early in his tenure, they had been somewhat guarded in telling their tales, but as they got to know Paul, they had taken him into their confidence.

He was one of their own kind, willing to do what was right whether the lawyers agreed or not. Paul spoke up when Mario paused in his recitation.

"Mario, this is something I can help with, if you'll let me."

"You sure, Paul?" Mario asked. "I appreciate your offer, but I could hire a private detective. It's no problem. The money doesn't matter, and you're retired."

"Retired, and bored. This could be interesting — it's what I always liked best. I'm not offering to save you and your friend money. I'm offering because I'm the best, and I would enjoy doing it. Besides, I'd like to meet this J.-P., after all the tales you've told about him. Not to mention Phillip Davis — he was well known by a lot of people in law enforcement, back in my working days. Almost like a folk hero in South Florida and Latin America. I understand if you aren't comfortable letting an old cop get too close, though. Just an offer. Your call, Mario."

"Okay, Paul, you're on. I think we're all on the side of law and order here, anyway. No conflicts for an old cop in this one, the way I see it. I'll call you when I get J.-P.'s fax."

Paul nodded, smiling and shaking hands all around, as the group broke up.

PHILLIP SAT on his veranda drinking coffee, pondering how best to search for Dani down in the southern Windward Islands. He had spent the early morning calling his old contacts, asking them to be on the lookout for her.

The people he spoke to in the local police forces had seen the notice that Sergeant Wiggers had circulated. Phillip encouraged his friends outside the law enforcement community to get a look at the poster the police were using until he could provide a better description.

He explained to everyone that his interest in this was personal and that he was working with Dani's father. Phillip didn't want to fuel rumors about who might want to find Dani. After all, there were some places down island that catered to people seeking anonymity, and he didn't want anybody to misunderstand his motivation. If they thought he was just being nosy, some of them might try to help Dani remain invisible.

Phillip felt the compulsion to act, now that he had worked his way through his list of contacts. He knew that he wouldn't find Dani by sitting on the veranda, waiting for his phone to ring.

The most he could expect from any of the sources he had

enlisted would be a cold lead. Those people couldn't drop what they were doing and go looking for her. He was prepared to wait; he had certainly done his share of that.

But Phillip was sure that he would uncover more information if he became part of the world he was studying, as opposed to remaining an observer. He was thinking that he should stock up his boat and go sailing for a while.

He would learn more from the yachting community as a participant than as an outsider. Phillip wondered briefly if he should ask Sandrine to go along. Being part of a couple would be useful in social settings, but it would be impractical for her. She had to work, and he didn't have a specific itinerary. Nor would he be keeping to a schedule.

Phillip pulled a duffel bag out of his closet and began tossing a few items of clothing into it. Most of what he would need was already permanently stowed aboard *Kayak Spirit*, his old 40-foot Carriacou sloop.

He smiled as he thought about the good times he'd had on the classic wooden boat, and the number of folks who had asked about the name, which had nothing to do with the lightweight paddle-driven boats that it suggested. In the Grenadines, Kayak was the local term for a native of Carriacou, the second most populated island in the country of Grenada.

The town of Windward, on the reef-strewn northeastern corner of Carriacou, had been a boat-building center for hundreds of years, producing fine, fast, wooden hulls for the inter-island trading fleet. Many of the larger ones were still hauling freight up and down the island chain, having been converted from sail power to diesel during the last half of the 20th century. Some of the smaller vessels like *Kayak Spirit* had been spruced up for pleasure use.

Carriacou sloops all shared the beautiful traditional, sweeping sheer line, with a relatively high bow and low sides.

The sloops were raced competitively in the islands, and they invariably attracted attention from the locals when they pulled into a harbor.

Phillip was depending on *Kayak Spirit* to serve as his calling card during his search for Dani. The vessel's pedigree would open doors among the islanders, and her American flag and yacht club burgees would serve a similar purpose among the yachting crowd.

He put his duffel bag in his car and drove to the marina in Cul-de-Sac Marin, just a few minutes from his house in Ste. Anne. After he parked, he walked over to the *Douane* office and told Sandrine what he was planning.

As he had hoped she would, Sandrine wanted to go along on his adventure. But as he expected, she couldn't find a way to fit the loosely planned trip into the demands of her job. They agreed to stay in touch by phone and email. Perhaps she could join him for a few days at a time, flying in and out as their schedules permitted.

To soften the disappointment, he invited her to lunch at the open-air restaurant across the way. She agreed to meet him in an hour, giving him time to buy groceries for his trip. Sandrine stamped the paperwork for his outbound clearance to Rodney Bay, St. Lucia, and accepted a kiss on the cheek as he left the office.

"You kiss all the captains goodbye when they clear out with you?" he asked.

She smiled and shook her curly head as the door closed behind him.

Phillip strolled down the dock to *Kayak Spirit*, unlocked the companionway, and opened all the hatches to air her out while he unpacked his duffel bag. He stowed his clothes in the lockers and set about doing an inventory of the galley.

He would eat dinner ashore most nights, in hopes of joining

the crowds in the restaurants and bars that catered to yachties. He might run into someone who had seen Dani.

HOPING she would be alone for a while, Dani opened her eyes just far enough to make sure that there was no one in the room with her. She sighed with relief, pleased that she'd managed to pass for being unconscious when the women came to check on her.

Before the last woman came in, Dani had been eavesdropping again, as two women chatted outside her room. She heard them on previous occasions, too.

During an earlier lucid period, she recognized their colloquial Spanish as Cuban. She wondered then if she was in Cuba.

She remembered several interludes of consciousness; she was glad of that. Otherwise, she would have mistaken the women for people who wanted to help her.

Today, the women were discussing how much longer 'Big Jim' would wait for 'the girl' to wake up. One of them had wondered if Big Jim would sell her while she was still unconscious, but the other one disparaged that idea. She said that it cost Big Jim nothing to keep 'the girl,' and that she would bring a much higher price once she recovered.

As their conversation ended, one of the women unlocked the door into Dani's room. Dani didn't want the woman to know she was conscious, so she focused on relaxing, slowing her breathing. She felt herself drifting away as the woman picked up her wrist to check her pulse.

When the door slammed, Dani felt herself jerk, startled. She'd dozed off while the woman took her pulse, but had she managed to fool the woman? She'd know soon enough.

Now that the woman was gone, Dani began to ponder her

situation. She wondered where she was and who this Big Jim might be.

He seemed to hold her fate in his hands, or at least the Cuban women thought he did. Dani intended to change that, but she wasn't able to fend for herself yet. And she didn't think she was in Cuba. The name 'Big Jim' had an American sound to it.

As she puzzled over that, she drifted off to sleep again.

15

Phillip had stowed his groceries aboard *Kayak Spirit*, and he and Sandrine had enjoyed a leisurely lunch at the restaurant on the dock in the marina. She kissed him goodbye as she left to go back to work, leaving him to imagine what wonderful company she would be if only she could join him on his cruise.

Shaking his head and grinning ruefully, Phillip settled the check with the cashier and walked down the dock. He stepped aboard *Kayak Spirit* and started the diesel, letting it warm up while he cast off the dock lines. There was a light breeze blowing off the dock. Phillip let it carry the boat into the fairway.

Once clear of the dock, he put the transmission in gear and opened the throttle a bit, motoring through the mooring field off the marina until he was in the channel that led past the point, out into Cul-de-Sac Marin. In the open water off Club Med, Phillip centered the tiller and took the transmission out of gear, allowing *Kayak Spirit* to coast while he went forward to the mast and made sail.

As the three sails flogged, he scrambled back to the cockpit, pulled the tiller to the windward side, eased the main, and sheeted in both headsails. The boat heeled the least bit and surged forward on a beam reach, the bow wave like a bone in her teeth.

Phillip shut down the engine and leaned back against the leeward cockpit coaming, his bare right foot resting on the tiller to counteract the boat's slight tendency to round into the wind. Savoring the glorious day, he settled into the rhythm of the boat and the sea.

Once out of the protection of Pointe Dunkerque, a long-period ocean swell made itself felt beneath the two-foot wind chop. Spray was flying from her bow as *Kayak Spirit* sliced through the blue-green water, and all was right in Phillip's world.

It was hard to think about anything unpleasant in his current circumstances, and he fully understood why people like Dani chose to sever their ties to life ashore. Who wouldn't enjoy this feeling of freedom combined with the sense of oneness with nature?

To complete the postcard-perfect Caribbean day, a school of dolphins began to play in the bow wave, crisscrossing *Kayak Spirit's* path. Occasionally, one leapt from the water right beside Phillip, splashing him before dropping gracefully back into the sea.

The thought of Dani tugged at Phillip, and he forced himself to contemplate the work ahead. His plan was to backtrack along the route that he assumed Reilly would have taken when *Sea Serpent* was northbound from Grenada to St. Lucia. He sought some trace of Dani, or some additional information about *Sea Serpent* and Reilly.

While there were many possible stops along the route, most yachts traveled in daylight, and they moved at roughly the same speed, so they often stopped in the same places. Reilly had stopped at Rodney Bay, St. Lucia, after a trip from St. George's, Grenada.

That was three days of easy sailing with stops to anchor overnight. The Morrises had met Reilly and Dani in the Tobago

Cays, and Dani had jumped ship from *Rambling Gal* in Mayreau. The Tobago Cays and Mayreau were only a few miles apart.

Most yachts would have broken the trip from St. George's northbound at one of those two places, or at Union Island, which was only a few miles from either of the other two. It was possible to make the trip from that area to Rodney Bay in a long day, but it was around 80 miles.

To break such a long sail, Bequia made a convenient stop. Phillip knew that some yachts would anchor for the night in a country where they had not checked in with customs. The typical routine was to hoist the yellow "Q" flag, indicating that they had not yet cleared customs, and move on early the next morning.

While the legality of this was open for debate, the authorities generally didn't make an issue of it. Phillip strongly suspected that Reilly had stopped for a night in Bequia, although he had never officially entered St. Vincent and the Grenadines.

Kayak Spirit rounded Pigeon Island on the northwest tip of St. Lucia and made Rodney Bay at dusk. Phillip anchored off the Sandals Resort and stowed his sails, settling in for the evening. By the time he had squared away *Kayak Spirit*, it was too late to clear customs.

He was pleasantly tired from the exhilarating sail across the St. Lucia Channel, and not particularly hungry after his big farewell lunch with Sandrine. He opted for a cold beer and a sandwich in the cockpit. Sated, he took a quick shower to cool off and crawled into his berth, making an early night of it.

PAUL RUSSO HAD GATHERED extensive information about Michael Carroll Reilly in a short amount of time. He had started with a former co-worker at the Miami Police Department who checked the driver's license and motor vehicle registration databases, using the mailing address that Phillip Davis had unearthed.

Reilly didn't own a car, and he had gotten his Florida driver's license 25 years ago, surrendering a Georgia license that he had gotten at age 18. He had been born in Savannah, Georgia.

Armed with that information and a history of addresses, Paul made use of several databases to fill out his dossier. He was amazed at how much he was able to find using online searches. Quite a bit more information was available now than when he had been chasing crooks for a living.

Paul discovered two things that were of interest. The first was that Reilly had been orphaned at the age of thirteen. He had downloaded an article from the Savannah Morning News describing the house fire that had claimed Reilly's mother's life.

The article referred to his father's death from a heart attack just a few months before his mother's death. Young Michael had been "camping out," in the back yard and had been awakened by the fire. He had gone to the next-door neighbor's house to call for help. Paul wanted to know what happened to Mike in the aftermath of the fire.

He found the second piece of information in a newspaper article in an online database as well. It was more interesting and of more recent origin. The article was from the local newspaper in Fort Lauderdale, Florida. It described the mysterious disappearance of Andrea Reilly, Mike's wife of 13 years.

According to the article, Mike Reilly had worked in the yachting industry in Fort Lauderdale. The article said that he was well known in the community. He had been on a yacht delivery from Nassau to Fort Lauderdale with another local man, and he had returned home after several days to find that his wife was gone.

The Reillys had made their home aboard a yacht named *Sea Serpent*, moored at a private dock in one of the many canals in Fort Lauderdale. Paul wondered if that was the same *Sea Serpent*. He would check that.

Their nearest neighbor, the man from whom they rented the

dock space, reported that he had not seen Andrea around the boat since before Mike left for the Bahamas. Nor had he noticed anyone else on or around the boat while Mike was absent.

The neighbor had assumed that Andrea was with Mike, since he knew that she often accompanied him as a cook when he took work as a delivery captain. He thought nothing of her absence until Mike returned and asked if the neighbor had seen her. Mike had called the police and reported her as missing.

The strange part of the story was that all her clothing and personal belongings were missing as well. Paul thought it sounded like she had enough of the guy, picked her time, packed up, and left.

There was a Fort Lauderdale detective quoted in the article, a Sergeant Donald Funk. Paul figured Funk could shed more light on Andrea's disappearance, if he was still around.

He decided that it would be worth a drive up to Fort Lauderdale if he could track down Donald Funk. Paul called the Fort Lauderdale Police Department, identified himself, and asked if Donald Funk was still on the force.

It turned out that Sergeant Funk was now Lieutenant Funk, and Paul soon had a lunch date with him. He looked at his watch and decided to drive up a little early. There was no telling what traffic would be like on I-95 North. It was always a gamble.

LIEUTENANT FUNK WAS a pleasant man about 10 years Paul's junior. He had suggested a sandwich joint called the New York Deli, and Paul had driven them over to the shopping center that housed the place.

They were each well into hot pastrami sandwiches that were dripping grease into the waxed-paper-lined baskets that served as dishes. They both ate quickly and efficiently, a habit common to many who shared their occupation. Paul might be retired, but that kind of habit persisted. In their line of work, you never knew when your meal would be interrupted.

Paul had explained his interest in Reilly on the phone earlier that morning, so, as Don Funk finished his last mouthful, he started right in on his recollections of the case without waiting for Paul to ask.

"Now, about the Reilly case, I remember it well. You've had cases like that, I bet. Just can't let it go. I can still get worked up over this one, even after 10 years, and since you called, my mind's been in overdrive. It was the strangest case I've ever had, bar none.

"First thing you figure is she just had enough of the guy and bailed out on him while he was gone. That's what I thought at first, but she didn't touch any of the money in their joint accounts, and they had a good bit. I guess they didn't spend a lot of money compared to what they made. Anyhow, she didn't touch the bank accounts. Didn't use the credit cards. No calls on her cellphone after Reilly left for the Bahamas. Not a stitch of clothing left behind, nor anything else of hers. 'Course, we mostly had to rely on Reilly about the belongings. They were an odd pair. Both orphans, no family for either of them. Didn't socialize outside of work, either." Funk paused for a sip of iced tea.

"Sounds strange all right. What about Reilly as the perp?" Paul asked.

"Yeah, definitely the next thing you think of. We checked him seven ways from Sunday and couldn't find a thing. Most important of all, no motive that we could figure. No money issues — I told you they were solvent — and no life insurance, or anything like that. Everybody that worked with either one of 'em said they got along with one another; no outside love interests on either side that we could find. No drugs, no drinking problem, nada. Zip."

"So, what does your gut say?" Paul asked, nibbling at his cold kosher dill pickle.

"Well, I don't buy into alien abduction, and that only leaves me one place to go."

"He killed her," Paul said.

"Yeah. I'd bet my badge on it, after 30 years in this game. I just can't figure out how or where."

"The newspaper article said that she often went on deliveries with him as a cook; the landlord figured that's where she was, from what I read," Paul said.

"Yeah, that's right. We looked hard at that. He was delivering that boat from Nassau with a friend of his, so he had the guy to provide an alibi for him, except Reilly got to Nassau two days before his friend. Flew on Chalk's Airline. Remember them, with the little seaplanes? Cash for a ticket, no real records back then. He could have taken her with him; dumped her somewhere before his friend showed up. We couldn't find a trace, so what're you gonna do?" Funk asked, shaking his head. "You got anything on Reilly for your missing girl?"

"Not yet, but we're still working on it," Paul said, as they got in his car. On the way back to town, he gave Funk a thorough briefing on everything he had to date.

"You mentioned the newspaper article from Savannah," Funk said. "For what it's worth, I went up there and asked around about Reilly. I ran across an old woman who lived next door to the Reillys when he was a kid. She said he was an evil little bastard, and his mother was an oddball; didn't socialize with anybody. She said Reilly was in trouble with the juvenile authorities before the fire that killed his mother, but I couldn't get anywhere on that. It was all sealed."

"You didn't try to get a court order?" Paul asked.

"No, I didn't see that it was worth the effort. We didn't have enough to charge him with anything. But the old lady swore Mike set the house afire. No proof, just her gut feeling, because of other stuff he did. But she also said some of the other neighbors blamed him for pets disappearing. That wouldn't be inconsistent with what we suspect him of."

"Was the fire investigated?" Paul asked.

"Yeah. They put it down to faulty wiring — no sign of arson. I only mentioned the old lady because she thought Reilly was such a little shit when he was a kid. Something for you to keep in mind, maybe. You found anything off the wall about him?"

"Not really. I'd be glad to make you a copy of what I have," Paul said, as he stopped in front of the police department.

"That's all right. You're retired. You got time to chase this guy, and it sounds like the gal's old man's got the money and connections to keep looking. You know what my life is like. This one is a serious ice-cold case; not even any evidence that a crime was committed, period. I'm allowed to have an ulcer over it on my own time, but that's about all. If I spent any time on it, the chief would have my head. We got more hot cases than we got people to work 'em," Funk said.

"I know how that is," Paul said.

"I bet you do. I gotta get back to it. I enjoyed talking with you, and thanks for lunch. Hope you pin something on Reilly and put him down. Call me if you need something I got. Deep down, I know he's dirty," Funk said, as he closed the car door.

16

The gray light coming through the foredeck hatch awakened Phillip. He took a moment to savor the quiet of the early morning, broken by the plaintive cry of a solitary seagull looking for breakfast. There was nothing as peaceful as a quiet night at anchor, and nothing as good as the first cup of coffee in the cockpit to accompany the sunrise, he thought. He put a pot of coffee on and washed the sleep from his eyes, shaving while the coffee perked.

Wide awake now, he took his coffee up on deck to greet the day. The cockpit seats were damp, their crust of salt drawing the moisture from the humid air. He put his cup down and wiped a spot dry with a chamois. He settled back and took a sip of the strong, black Haitian brew as he watched the orange glow of the rising sun, its light diffused by the mist coming off the damp earth of the island.

After he finished his coffee, he would launch his dinghy and go ashore to clear in. Phillip thought that he might as well have breakfast at the marina. Maybe he would find an early riser to share his table, and he could start asking about Dani and *Sea Serpent*.

He swallowed the last of his coffee and went below. After rinsing his cup, he assembled the paperwork he would need for clearing customs. He put pictures of *Sea Serpent*, Dani, and Mike Reilly in the waterproof plastic envelope with his ship's papers.

Phillip was waiting at the door when the Customs Office opened at 8 o'clock, and he was cleared in a few minutes. He didn't bother asking about his quarry, figuring that Cedric Jones had already found out what could be learned from the officials. He sat down at a table in the restaurant downstairs and spread his pictures out to study them. The waitress soon came to take his order.

"Pretty boat." She turned the picture of *Sea Serpent* a bit to get a better look at it. "Yours?"

"No." Phillip looked up, smiling at her. "No, it belongs to this man, I think," he said, pointing at the picture of Mike.

The waitress picked up the picture of Mike and Dani and studied it, shaking her head. "Pretty lady, too." She put the picture back on the table. "Coffee?" she asked.

"Please," Phillip said.

"What would you like for breakfast? Eggs?"

"Yes, fried over well, please. Do you have any saltfish patties to go with them?"

"We do." The woman smiled. "Saltfish patty, and maybe some fungi?"

"Great, that would be fine." Phillip returned the smile, wondering if she was testing him with the offer of fungi, and if so, whether he passed or failed by ordering the dish of grits cooked with chopped okra. "I'm not used to finding fungi outside the Virgin Islands," he said.

"That's where our chef's from," she said. "You live in the islands." It was not a question.

"Yes." He figured the fungi gave it away.

"The Virgins?"

"No. Martinique."

"But you are not French. Why does an American live on a French island?"

He thought for a minute about his reply. He shrugged, mostly moving his shoulders, as he asked, "Why not?" He gave her a wry grin.

"Maybe you are some French, after all." She laughed as she left to place his breakfast order.

Phillip finished his breakfast and dawdled over another cup of coffee, making idle conversation with the waitress. By 10 o'clock, he was still the only customer in the restaurant, so he settled his tab, leaving a generous tip. He went back to *Kayak Spirit*, hoping he would have better luck at lunch.

WHILE MIKE HAD a second cup of coffee after breakfast in the cockpit and wrestled with his memories, Michelle was in the galley, doing the breakfast dishes. The more time she spent with Mike, the less comfortable she became with him.

This morning, he had behaved as though he had put their quarrel behind him. She thought he wanted to smooth things over, to encourage her to stay with him past their arrival in St. Martin.

Michelle was thankful that he was not nagging her about that any longer. No man had ever treated her as well as Mike was treating her, she reflected. What was it about him that put her off?

His behavior toward her wasn't what was making her anxious. Maybe it was the way he carried on when he was by himself that was troubling her.

Sea Serpent was 40 feet long. To most non-boaters, that seemed big. Even so, *Sea Serpent* was a classic yawl design from the 30s, and she was much smaller in terms of interior space than a modern 40-footer.

The interior design was functional at sea, and comfortable in port, but what privacy it offered was largely illusory. While two people could spend hours aboard out of sight of one another, the smallest sounds were audible throughout the boat.

As she did the dishes, Michelle realized that Mike talked to himself when he forgot she was around. His vocalizing wasn't just restricted to exclamations or outbursts of surprise, pain, or fear. She wouldn't have found that remarkable.

No, she could hear him now, conversing freely with unseen people. She couldn't make out what he was saying, and at first, she thought that he must be talking to someone in a dinghy alongside. The local vendors in Dominica would drop by an occupied boat frequently during the daylight hours, offering fruits and vegetables, local crafts, and fresh baked bread. Some were soliciting odd jobs or selling tours.

Maybe he was visiting with one of them. She didn't think much of it. By the time she had finished the dishes, she realized that she was still hearing the steady, soft drone of conversation, and she was curious. She looked out the portholes on both sides of the boat, but she saw no one alongside. Then she realized that she hadn't heard more than a single voice. She climbed the companionway ladder and joined Mike in the cockpit.

He looked momentarily confused by her sudden appearance, but he recovered quickly. "Breakfast did wonders for my head, Michie. I'm feeling much better now," he said.

"I am glad, Mike."

She remembered thinking earlier this morning when she took Mike's breakfast into the cockpit that he didn't know who she was. He had looked at her strangely, and he only called her by name after he heard the water taxi man, Robert, speak to her. His blank look passed more quickly this time.

"Are you want some juice? Anything?"

"No, no thanks. Not just yet."

Mike was gazing out over the boats bobbing at anchor.

"Will it be all right with you if we just stay aboard today, to let my cut heal?"

"But of course."

"What's wrong, Michie?"

She thought she must look worried. She forced a smile. "Mike, when I am washing the dishes, I am hear someone, talking, talking, long time, same voice. Do you hear?"

"No, Michie. I didn't hear anyone. Probably just the breeze in the rigging. Sometimes it hums. Sounds just like someone speaking. Maybe that's what you heard," Mike said, frowning.

"Perhaps," she said, shaking her head. "I am go below and read some, while it is not being hot yet. You call me if you are need something, yes?"

"Sure, Michie," Mike said, absently. "I'll do that."

Michelle went below and found a murder mystery on the bookshelf. She thought that if she worked her way diligently through the book, she might improve her grasp of American English.

She stretched out on the port settee in the saloon and began wrestling with the unfamiliar text. She had forgotten about the conversation with Mike, until she heard him start talking to himself again.

She couldn't make out his words, but she could tell it wasn't the breeze in the rigging. After a few comments, he fell silent. She turned back to the novel, and after a few more minutes of struggling with the colloquial English, she dropped off to sleep.

17

After his late breakfast, Phillip had kept busy by tackling some of the endless maintenance tasks aboard *Kayak Spirit*. Glancing at his watch, he saw that he had killed the morning. He went below and put the metal polish and his bag of rags away in one of the galley lockers.

After being the only early bird in the restaurant for breakfast, he wanted to be sure that he didn't miss the lunch crowd at the yacht club. He went into the head to wash the grime from his hands and face; he didn't need to dress up for lunch, but he didn't want to put anyone off, either.

Phillip put on a clean T-shirt with his cargo shorts and put his wallet and a Ziploc bag containing the pictures into one of the big pockets, zipping it shut. He went back up into the cockpit and locked the boat.

Tossing his flip-flops into the dinghy, he cast off the painter as he climbed down. He started the outboard, striking out across the anchorage to the beach in front of the club. As he wove through the anchored boats, he smiled at the thought of how different the club was from the image that non-sailors had of yacht clubs. It was a place for sailors, not social climbers.

He ran the dinghy up onto the beach and hopped over the side, sinking into the water up to his knees, wetting the lower part of the legs of his shorts. No one would mistake him for one of the tourists who wandered in from the adjacent beachfront hotels.

Pulling the dinghy up onto the dry sand, Phillip tied it off to a large chunk of broken concrete. He sat on the side of the dinghy and brushed the sand off his feet, slipping on his flip-flops. Ambling up the beach to the veranda of the club bar, he saw that he was early enough to get a seat, but late enough so that he would have to share a table. Perfect, he thought.

He walked over to a round table with three couples, a single man, and an empty chair. From the arrangement of the silverware and the absence of drinks, he guessed that the people had just taken their seats.

Pulling the extra chair out, he asked, "May I join you folks, or were you expecting someone else?"

"Sure, have a seat," one of the women said. "Looks like you're the one we were expecting."

"Thanks. I'm Phillip," he said, looking around the table as he sat down and slid the chair forward. "From *Kayak Spirit*."

The people at the table introduced themselves, giving only first names and the names of their boats. Phillip thought, *Who needs more identity than that?*

After Phillip had nodded his acknowledgement of the introductions, one of the men said, "We were admiring your boat out in the anchorage. She's beautiful. Built down here, somewhere?"

"Carriacou," Phillip said, smiling. "Thanks. She's a good boat."

"Ah," said the man's wife. "We were betting Carriacou, because of the name."

"You won your bet, then," Phillip said. "The name's original. She was built in the '50's. Launched at Windward in 1956, according to one of the old timers down there. He remembered helping roll her down the beach to the water on logs, when he was a young man."

"How fascinating," the woman said, "to own a boat that's part of the islands' history. Do you run into many folks who remember her like that man did?"

"Not really, but I run into a lot of folks who recognize what she is and where she came from," Phillip said. "I just got in last night, from up in Marin. I've been ashore for a while, so I'm just getting back into this life. I'm on the lookout for some folks on a boat called *Sea Serpent*. Anybody seen her recently?"

He took out his pictures and passed them around, just as a waitress appeared with an armful of menus. With her free hand, the waitress took the picture of *Sea Serpent* from the woman who was examining it.

"Who's on *Sea Serpent*?" she asked the crowd, looking around.

"None of us," Phillip said. "I was just asking these folks if they'd seen her lately. How about you?"

"Not lately," she said, "but she was here a couple of years ago. Stayed out in the bay for a couple of months. My frien', she lef' on that boat."

"Ah, so you know this man?" He passed her the picture of Mike and Dani.

"The man, yes, but not the girl," she said, handing both pictures back to Phillip. She passed out the menus. "I be right back wit' some ice water, an' take your drink order," she said, as she walked away.

Phillip put away the pictures and joined in the conversation around the table. He made sure to chat with the waitress every time that she came by, in hopes that she would remember him later.

When the lunch crowd thinned out, Phillip moved to the bar. He ordered an iced tea and waited until he saw the waitress come out of the kitchen carrying a single plate and a cold drink. She sat down at a table near the kitchen door, wearily slipped off her shoes, and started to eat her lunch. Phillip picked up his tea and walked over to the table.

"Excuse me," he said. "My name is Phillip, and I'm looking for the girl that was in that picture with the man from *Sea Serpent*. I hate to interrupt your lunch. I'd be glad to buy you dinner when you're not working, if that's better. Would you be willing to talk to me?"

"Sit down. Today finished. I only work the lunch, while my children in school. That girl in the picture, she your girl?"

"No," Phillip said, putting his glass down as he slid into the chair. "I used to work with her father. He's my best friend, and she's like a little sister to me."

"I hope she don' spend too much time wit' that mon," the woman said, as she loaded her fork with salad. "I don' like that mon one bit. He funny-headed, I t'ink."

"How well did you know him?" Phillip asked.

"Well, like I say to you before, he here for a couple of months. He come here in the club, every day. Mos' days, he come for lunch, and again at the happy hour. But he don' drink so much. Jus' watch the people."

"You said your friend left on his boat."

"Agnes. She name Agnes Saint James. We grow up over in Gros Îlet, together all the time, like sister. She don' have no fam'ly, so she stay by my mama house when she little, 'til we grown. Then I get married, but Agnes, she like to drink the rum and party, an' my mama, she put Agnes out of the house. Mama, she a church lady, like me. Christian. Not Agnes, though. She go her own way. Agnes work here wit' me, 'til she lef' on the boat wit' that mon."

"So where did she go with him?"

"I don' know, Phillip. She say he take her to Grenada, an' they gon' live on the boat, 'til hurricane time pass. Then they will come back. But she don' come back. She call me one time from Bequia. Sound scared, like, but she say she okay. She can't talk long. Say she call me 'nother time, but she no call. Tha's the las' time we talk."

"Why did you say that man was funny-headed?" Phillip asked, taking a sip of tea.

"He talk to self. All the time, when he here by self, he talk. Quiet, sof' like, so nobody hear, but he lips moving, an' if you get close, you hear he talkin' up a storm. If somebody wit' he, he don' do that."

"Did that not worry Agnes?" he asked.

"That Agnes, she don' worry. You know the song Marley sing? Bob Marley? Famous song, 'Don' worry, be happy!' Tha's the way Agnes t'ink. She want to get away from the life she got here. Sad, when somebody go to the rum like that. She don' have much life here. Hope she in a better place, now, she," she said, looking into the distance, shaking her head. After a moment's reflection, she looked Phillip in the eye, blinking back a tear. "Sorry," she said. "I t'ink Agnes gone, now, or she call me. I hope that girl in the picture, she okay."

"I hope so, too. Would you write out Agnes's full name for me?" he asked, sliding an index card and a pen to her. "I'm going down to Grenada soon. I'll look for Agnes while I'm there."

"Tha's mighty good of you," she said, forcing a smile as she picked up the pen and began to write. "I write my name and my phone number here, too. You call me, please, when you in Grenada. I don' t'ink she there, but I like to hear, jus' the same."

"Certainly, I'll call you," Phillip said, pocketing the card as he got up. "Thank you for taking the time with me."

"You are welcome, Phillip. God bless," she said. Her eyes were bright with unshed tears for her friend.

MICHELLE REALIZED that she had been asleep when she found herself trying to follow a conversation that she could no longer hear. She must have been dreaming, and the fragmentary conversation faded quickly from her memory as the fog of sleep lifted.

Or had Mike been talking to himself again? She wondered. She felt a sharp pain in her right hip and ran her hand along the upholstered cushions beneath her. Something was wedged in the crevice between the two cushions.

Michelle used both hands to pull the cushions apart. She found a woman's wristwatch. She hid the watch in a fold of her skirt, checking to make sure she was alone. She listened to the ambient noise aboard the yacht until she recognized Mike's snoring, coming from the cockpit.

She took the watch into the head compartment and put the privacy latch on the door. Michelle examined her find. It was a woman's gold Rolex with a gold bracelet. She had seen a few of these on the wrists of some of the pampered women in the marina restaurant, and she knew that it was an item of extraordinary value.

She admired it, holding it on her wrist, turning it this way and that, wondering what it would be like to be wealthy enough to wear a watch that cost more than most people made in a year. Unable to picture herself ever being in that situation, she shook her head and turned the watch over, looking at the back.

There was fine engraving on the back of the case. She held it up, so that it caught the sunlight coming through the porthole. "Danielle Marie Berger," she read.

Her blood ran cold. More worried now, she hid the watch in her makeup kit, itself stashed far back in one of the many small lockers in the head compartment. She had a stash of jewelry hidden in the bag, in case she needed funds and didn't have access to a bank, but she doubted that her whole collection was worth as much as the watch.

She returned to the settee and picked up her novel, hoping that the effort of reading the English text would calm her, but it didn't work. She now knew that the Dani woman had been on *Sea Serpent*, no matter what Mike said.

She had not only been here, she had lost an expensive watch, a piece of jewelry with her name on it. Certainly, she would want the watch back. People who had things like that kept up with them, in Michelle's experience. That man, Phillip Davis, she remembered he called himself, he had said that the Dani woman was missing, and that she was last seen on *Sea Serpent*, but Mike claimed to remember nothing about her.

Last night after their argument, Michelle had thought her way through the whole issue of Mike and Dani and the inconsistencies in his story. For a moment, she had questioned her judgment of Mike, but then she had decided that she had not misread him. She was sure he was telling the truth, at least about not remembering Dani.

She had plenty of experience with practiced liars, and she had picked up nothing in Mike's manner or words that caused her to doubt him. Yet, the man called Phillip seemed quite sure this Dani had been on *Sea Serpent*.

Mike had no memory of Dani, or of her being on the boat with him. And, he was talking to himself again, right now. She realized with a shock that he was calling out loudly, perhaps in his sleep, perhaps not. Once again, she couldn't make out his words.

She calmed herself, figuring that so far, at least, Mike had been a perfect gentleman to her. If she continued to behave normally, perhaps he would, as well. She must control herself and maintain her focus.

She would get to St. Martin and leave Mike and *Sea Serpent*. Surely, she would be able to sell that expensive watch for enough money to keep herself hidden until Mike moved on.

She tried to persuade herself that she was better off now than she had been with Frankie in Martinique, but deep down, she wasn't sure. She sensed violence in Mike, although she hadn't seen any evidence of it in his behavior so far.

Frankie had been a cokehead. She understood cokeheads well. He had been violent, but the important thing was that she could predict his behavior. When the violence had become a threat to her, she had dealt with it. Druggies were easy.

Mike was something else. What, she wasn't sure, yet. If she expected to manipulate him, she must understand what drove him.

She had dealt with violent men all her life, and she knew she couldn't allow herself to be cornered, taken by surprise. She didn't have the physical strength to overpower most men. She had to anticipate their behavior, so that she could strike preemptively, if necessary, as she had with Frankie.

She heard Mike stirring on deck. She climbed the companionway ladder to see him stretched out in the cockpit, thrashing violently in his sleep. She put a gentle hand on his shoulder.

Leaning over, her face close to his, she spoke softly, comfortingly. "Mike? Mike, my love, is all right, is all right."

His body went stiff under her hand, his muscles tensing as his eyes snapped open. He looked at her blankly, trying to sit up against the resistance of her hand on his shoulder. "M-m-m-missy, uh, Michie?" he mumbled, recognition slowly dawning in his eyes.

"Is okay, Mike. Michie is here, baby," she soothed him, pulling him to her breast as a mother would a troubled child.

He relaxed into her arms, seeming to drop off again for a few minutes, as she sat in the cockpit, rocking him and humming softly as she held him. He opened his eyes after a moment, and pulled free, sitting up and looking around, puzzled.

"I think you are having the bad dream, Mike," Michie said. He looked at her, his gaze steady, for an uncomfortably long period. She let the silence linger, waiting for him to fill it.

"Did I say anything? Cry out, or something?" he asked, finally.

"Only cries like the bad dream. Nothing I am understand," she said, hoping to keep him calm. "I am sleeping in the cabin when I am hearing you, struggle, cry out."

"Sorry," he said, looking down, avoiding eye contact. "Sorry to wake you. I can't remember...just feeling anxious, scared...no idea what I was dreaming about."

"Is okay, my love. Is happen to us all, I think, sometime."

18

Phillip finished transcribing his notes and stuck them into the file folder that Sergeant Wiggers had given him a few days ago. He was shocked when he saw the dates in the folder and realized how little time had passed since J.-P.'s first call. It seemed like forever.

He put the folder back into the drawer under *Kayak Spirit's* chart table and looked up at the clock on the bulkhead. It was early enough that he might still catch J.-P. in the office.

He placed the call on his cellphone and collected his thoughts as he waited for an answer. J.-P. was still at his desk. He had just gotten off the phone with Mario, who had called from Miami to pass on the information that Paul Russo had collected. J.-P. summarized Mario's detailed report for Phillip. "So, Phillip, what have you learned in the last day?"

Phillip quickly recited the facts he had gathered. Both men sat for a moment in silence, listening to the occasional crackle of static on the telephone as each absorbed what the other had reported.

"I think this Mike Reilly did something to Dani." J.-P. was the first to break the silence. "From what you say, he is demented. Perhaps dangerous."

"No argument on that, J.-P. I think you're right. I'm cleared out to go to Bequia tomorrow, leaving at first light. Unless you have a better idea, I'm going to keep asking questions and showing the photographs around. Somebody must have seen something. Dani couldn't have just vanished."

Phillip realized as the words left his mouth that Mike Reilly's wife had done exactly that, 10 years ago.

"I think that's what you should do, but we need another look at Reilly. I do not doubt your opinion on his truthfulness, but we should ask Sharktooth to search Reilly's boat. We have nothing to lose, doing that, and maybe we will find something. Even if Reilly does not remember her, Dani might have left something behind. I have to take some action, Phillip. You know me; I cannot wait any longer."

"I think that makes a lot of sense, especially given what we've learned about Reilly. I'll call Sharktooth tonight. He's itching to do something, anyway. I don't think he liked Reilly much."

"Thank you, Phillip. We will talk again tomorrow. Rest well, my friend."

"Not until we find her," Phillip said, disconnecting.

He called Sharktooth and relayed J.-P.'s request.

"They still here, Phillip. They stay on the boat today. The lady, she tell Robert the mon he hurt he head, so no swim today. Robert take them to the reef to snorkel tomorrow. When they go, I search the boat. Don' worry, mon. They never know about it."

MIKE AND MICHELLE left *Sea Serpent* at about 9:30 the next morning with Robert. He took them to the reef in Toucari Bay, a few miles up the west coast from Portsmouth. The water over the reef was sheltered and crystal clear. The profusion of colorful marine life made it a popular spot to snorkel.

While Mike and Michelle were enjoying the myriad of tropical fish, Sharktooth was enjoying free access to *Sea Serpent*. One of his fellow water taxi drivers had given him a ride, so that he didn't have to leave his own distinctive boat tied alongside to advertise his presence.

Sharktooth figured he was safe enough from casual notice since all the nearby yachts were unoccupied. It was the peak time of the day for tourist activities. He would have as much time as he needed to do a thorough search.

Mike and Michelle would be out with Robert until the afternoon. If they decided to come back early, Robert would call Sharktooth on his cellphone to make sure that he had time to put everything back together and depart before they returned.

Sharktooth was an old hand at searching boats, thanks to his time helping Phillip move contraband around the islands. He had been on both ends of searches, more times than he could remember.

There weren't too many places to hide things on a yacht the size of *Sea Serpent*. At first glance, all the little nooks and crannies were overwhelming, but if you started at one end of the vessel and worked your way to the outer skin of the hull, going from one enclosed space to the adjacent one, you could hardly miss seeing what was there.

Sharktooth skipped over provisions, spares, and such familiar items. He paused to examine papers, which he photographed with his cellphone. He didn't find much of a personal nature belonging to Mike Reilly, but he went through everything carefully anyway. A methodical search could tell you as much from what was not found as from what was found.

He was about halfway through with his search when he got to the locker over the forward end of the starboard settee, where he discovered Michelle's belongings. There were two tightly packed, medium-sized duffel bags.

Sharktooth went through them quickly, not really expecting to find anything of interest, but he was intrigued by the quality of her bags and their contents. Remembering from Phillip's comments that she was moving to St. Martin, he was surprised by how few things she was carrying.

What she did have was expensive, mostly designer-labeled, and none of it was counterfeit. Sharktooth had a practiced eye for counterfeit merchandise.

For a rootless girl just out of her teens, Michelle had nice things. He wondered whether that had any relevance, but he didn't slow down to think about it. He kept mechanically checking through everything in his path as he moved from the aft end of the main cabin to the forward bulkhead.

He opened the door separating the main cabin from the head compartment and the forward sleeping area. It was in the head compartment that his methodical approach paid off.

The head compartment combined a shower, a sink, and a marine toilet in a space about the size of a phone booth. That was typical on a boat the size and age of *Sea Serpent*. What was unusual was the quality and quantity of the cabinetry. It was all hand-rubbed, solid teak, an example of what a good ship's carpenter could do, given free rein and an unlimited budget.

Sharktooth felt as if he stood inside a piece of hand-carved, antique furniture. He ran his hands over the softly glowing surfaces of the teak for the pure pleasure of touching it, admiring it for a moment before he started opening all the little compartments.

The small lockers and drawers kept stored items handy but out of the spray from the shower. In most, he found the things that he would expect: shampoo, soap, extra towels, and extra toilet paper.

Tucked far back in a corner of one of the least accessible lockers, he felt a buttery-soft, leather bag of some sort. He extracted it carefully, slithering it past all the mundane things in the front part of the locker.

He put the bag on the countertop and unzipped it, noticing how smoothly the zipper worked. It was one more example of the quality that plenty of money could buy. The bag was in perfect condition, so he knew that it had not been aboard for long. Leather would mildew, tucked away in a corner like that.

The bag was filled with women's toiletries: lotions, make-up, oddly shaped little brushes, and other things that a man couldn't hope to understand. In a little, velvet-lined compartment along one side, he found a few pieces of jewelry: several pairs of diamond earrings, a modest pearl necklace, and a gold Rolex watch.

All of it was the real thing — no cheap trinkets. He was surprised again at Michelle's apparent wealth, until he saw the engraving on the back of the watch. He put aside his promise of stealth, deciding that it was more important to preserve this evidence of Dani's presence on *Sea Serpent*.

Given how deeply the bag had been buried, he thought that its removal was likely to go unnoticed. This bag was probably untouched since Dani was here, Sharktooth reasoned, revising his assumption as to who owned the bag. There was a good chance that Reilly didn't even know it was here.

Sharktooth concluded his search about thirty minutes later, finding nothing more of interest. He called his friend to come pick him up, and while he waited, he did a thorough check to make sure that he had left no trace of his activity. Unless Reilly missed Dani's makeup kit, he would never know about Sharktooth's visit.

19

Timothy Walker was 12 years old, the eldest of the six Walker siblings. His family had lived in Bequia for many generations, always along the south coast of the island, in the Paget Farm area. Timothy was out of school today; it was some sort of holiday, but he wasn't sure what he was celebrating.

He was scavenging along the rocky part of the shoreline, between Paget Farm's little fishing-boat dock and the airport. He could usually find something interesting washed up along this stretch of shoreline, something to pique his curiosity or stimulate his imagination.

He had just spied a piece of bright yellow fabric wedged in the rocks, and he was working his way carefully across the sharp-edged outcropping to see what it was. From a distance, it looked like one of those inflatable life vests that the tourists wore when they went snorkeling.

He was closer now, and he could see that it was indeed a life vest, but more complicated than the ones the tourists wore. He fished it out of the water and examined it.

It had a rip on one side, about the length of his hand, and when he blew into the orange tube that was used to inflate it, he could hear the air hissing right back out. Disappointed, he turned the vest in his hands, examining the heavy webbing straps with the shiny buckles and hardware. This was a life vest, he was sure, but not like any he had seen. He noticed that one side of the vest felt heavier than the other side.

Timothy ran a hand over the fabric and found a pouch sewn into the thick, blue canvas backing on one side. He pulled the pouch's flap free of its Velcro closure, enjoying the crisp, tearing sound that it made. He stuck it back and pulled it again, just to listen to it. His little brothers would like that.

He upended the vest, to empty the pouch and see what it contained. Timothy looked at the thing that fell into his palm, puzzled. He had never seen anything quite like it.

It was about the size of the mouse that he used with the computer at school. Made of bright yellow plastic, it had blue rubber trim all around the edges, so it fit nicely in his hand. There was an antenna-like thing sticking out of it, too. It was almost like the little handheld VHF radio that his father had, but it didn't have the controls or the channel display.

He looked at the writing on the front. "ACR," he read, and saw a round drawing, like a picture of a globe, and more letters, "GPS PLB." Timothy wondered what that meant. There were two little raised dots: one red, and one green. On the top, next to the antenna, there was a black tab. The tab had an edge that he could catch with his fingertip.

He turned his prize over in his hand, enjoying the heft, wondering what it was. There were little, cartoon-like drawings on the back. The first one showed somebody's fingers, flipping the black tab up. The next one showed red and green lights, flashing, he thought. The third one had an ear with some half-circles radiating toward it. The last one showed what looked like lightning, coming from an antenna.

Timothy pulled the black tab, flipping it all the way over, the way the picture showed. There was a snapping sound, and then the little red and green dots started to flash. The device emitted a loud, high-pitched tone for about a second. He dropped it, fearing the lightning bolt would come from the antenna, but after a while, nothing happened.

The lights kept blinking. He put it back in the pouch and struck out for home, thinking he could keep his little brothers busy all afternoon with this thing, whatever it was.

IT WAS mid-afternoon as Phillip sailed past Bottle and Glass rocks on the west coast of St. Vincent. He had left Rodney Bay at first light, motor-sailing down the coast of St. Lucia. That was to be expected, he knew.

The volcanic islands, with their steep, craggy profiles, cast a wind shadow that reached miles out to the west into the Caribbean, even as the eastern sides of the islands were subject to trade winds of 15 to 25 knots.

Once he passed the Pitons on St. Lucia's southwestern tip, the wind filled in, and he had enjoyed a fast, if rambunctious, four-hour sail across the St. Vincent Channel. In the wind shadow of St. Vincent, he fired up the diesel again. Now, as he passed to the west of Bottle and Glass, he found more breeze.

Phillip secured the diesel and hoisted his sails, relaxing into the peaceful rhythm as *Kayak Spirit* came alive. She was doing what she had been built to do. It took a little while for his ears to recover from the thrumming sound of the diesel, but he was soon back in tune with the hiss of the bow wave as *Kayak Spirit* cut through the calm water.

She rolled along, riding up and down the gentle, long-period ocean swell, still in the protection of St. Vincent. It was only a few minutes before the wind chop appeared on top of the swell. As the shoreline fell away to the east, both the chop and the breeze built, until *Kayak Spirit* was whipping along at six to seven knots, spray flying.

Phillip grinned, thinking that this was a delightful reward for listening to the diesel for all those hours. He had a couple of hours to go before he made Bequia, and by then, the sails would have worked their magic. He was sure that the world had lost something intangible, but valuable beyond price, when the age of sail had given way to the age of fossil fuels. At least occasionally, he and a few other lucky people got a special, private glimpse of the peacefulness of that bygone era.

An hour and a half later, Phillip left the flashing marker on the Devil's Table reef to his port just as the sun touched the western horizon. He was taking down his sails and lashing them out of the way when he saw the green flash as the sun disappeared over the clear horizon.

What a grand day, he thought, as he started the engine and went looking for a spot to anchor in Admiralty Bay, Bequia. Most visiting yachts anchored off Princess Margaret Beach, over on the south side of town, leaving plenty of room for late arrivals just inside the Devil's Table, on the north side of the ferry channel. Phillip dropped his anchor there.

It was too late to go ashore and visit customs, so he replaced the St. Lucia courtesy flag flying from his starboard spreader with the yellow "Q" flag, planning to launch his dinghy and clear in early tomorrow.

He went below and rummaged in his liquor locker for his bottle of Chairman's Reserve, his favorite rum from St. Lucia. Phillip reached into the freezer compartment of his refrigerator for a couple of ice cubes, and poured himself a generous tot, squeezing half of a fresh lime into the glass, and adding just a little water.

He got his cellphone out of the drawer under the chart table and took his drink and the phone back up to the cockpit, thinking he would call Sharktooth. Phillip leaned back against a cushion with his feet up, took a sip of his drink, and thumbed his way to Sharktooth's cellphone number.

"Hey, Phillip! How the sail, mon?" Sharktooth answered.

Phillip smiled, thinking that caller ID had radically changed the way people answered incoming phone calls. No more mystery, no aura of suspense.

"That's too bad. I miss that," he said, not realizing he had given voice to his thoughts until Sharktooth responded, puzzled.

"Huh? What you say, Phillip? That you, mon?"

"Sorry, Sharktooth. Guess I was still at sea. I had a great sail. Sorry you weren't along. I caught a nice tuna, about seven pounds. Tuna steaks will be on the grill as soon as I get a chance to cut it up. Did you find anything aboard *Sea Serpent*?"

"Yeah, mon, I send email, 'bout 2 o'clock. Send pictures of all the boat paper. Phillip, I find Dani's watch. Gold Rolex, her name on the back. In a bag wit' all her lady t'ings, diamond earrings, pearls, lipstick, stuff. It stuck way back in a little locker in the head. Send picture of all that stuff, too. I t'ink that mon, he don' know it's on the boat, so I take it. Okay, you t'ink?"

"Yeah, Sharktooth, I think it's okay. You're probably right about him not knowing. Maybe Dani stuck it there and forgot it, or she didn't get a chance to grab it when she left."

Phillip tried to work out a benign reason why Dani would leave her valuables behind. He dreaded the thought of telling J.-P. about this.

"Even if Reilly knows about it, he's not going to pull that out while he's got Michelle aboard, so I think you did right."

"Thanks, Phillip. I worry some 'bout taking it, but I t'ink you mebbe want to give to J.-P., yes?"

"Yeah. I think I'd rather give it to Dani, though."

"That the troof. Okay, mon, I call you if they clear out wit' the customs, okay?"

"Okay, Sharktooth. Thanks."

"Blessings, Phillip," Sharktooth said, disconnecting.

As much as he wanted to postpone it, Phillip knew he had to share this news with J.-P. before it got any later. He placed the call and took a sip of his drink as he waited for the connection. As Phillip had known he would be, J.-P. was distressed by the news.

"I gave her that watch for her birthday, the year she quit working for Marie's father. I don't know about the other jewelry Sharktooth found, but she always did like diamond earrings."

"He said he sent me pictures in an email. As soon as I get ashore to an Internet café, I'll forward the whole lot to you. Any news from Mario?" Phillip hoped to change the subject.

"No. Nothing. You are in Bequia tonight?"

"Yes, I just got in. It's late here, so I won't get ashore until tomorrow. You can expect that email in the afternoon, your time. I'm going to be ashore all day tomorrow, so don't forget that you can reach me on the cellphone any time you think of something."

"Yes. I will call when I get the email. Maybe we will both have more ideas by then. Have a good evening, and thank you for your help."

"You're welcome, J.-P. You know that. Keep your spirits up. Talk to you tomorrow. Good night." Phillip disconnected.

He sipped his drink, feeling discouraged by the news from Sharktooth.

20

A COUPLE OF HOURS INTO THEIR SNORKEL TRIP, MICHELLE mentioned she was hungry. Robert beached the boat not far from where they were swimming. He rummaged in his ice chest, passing Mike and her each a beer.

Robert lit a fire on the beach and began cooking. By the time they started a second round of beer, he served them each a heaping plate of salad, fruit, and barbecued lobster.

Michie couldn't remember a better meal or a bigger surprise. After they ate, they rested in the shade of the coconut palms until they were ready to go back into the water and cool off before returning to *Sea Serpent*.

An hour later they were back aboard *Sea Serpent*. Michelle was relaxing with a cool shower after the day's exercise.

She was pleasantly tired as she rinsed the shampoo from her hair and reached into one of the little lockers for her conditioner. She tipped the bottle up and squeezed it over her open palm, annoyed when it spluttered. *Empty!*

She kept another bottle in her makeup bag. Michelle rinsed her hands and dried them, opening the locker where she stashed it. She ran her hand into the back corner, but she didn't find the soft leather makeup bag.

She patted around in the locker, growing alarmed. The bag was there last night, when she found the watch and put it with her jewelry. She picked up the flashlight from above the sink and got to her knees, peering into the locker.

The bag wasn't there. Thinking that maybe she had put it back in a different locker, Michele went through them all.

The bag was not in the head compartment. Forgetting the conditioner in her anxiety, she toweled herself dry and put on a pair of shorts and a T-shirt.

Michelle took her towel up on deck, where she clipped it to the lifelines to dry. Mike was stretched out in the cockpit, sound asleep.

She went back below and searched the whole boat for the missing bag. When she didn't find it, her initial alarm turned into a deeper fear.

She remembered putting the gold Rolex in the bag and putting the bag back into that locker yesterday afternoon. Michelle kept the bag hidden in that dark, hard to reach corner since the first night she had been aboard *Sea Serpent*.

Bitter experience taught her to hide her valuables. She kept her passport and wallet in her purse, always to hand. There was a bankcard in the wallet, and some cash. Having been robbed more than once, she separated the make-up kit with its jewelry pouch from the rest of her belongings. It was her form of insurance.

Michelle saw Mike lock the boat when they left this morning. She watched him unlock it when they got back from snorkeling. There were no signs of intrusion that she could see. No one had been aboard in their absence.

That left only one explanation for her missing bag. Mike must have found it. This idea was profoundly disturbing to her. Why would he take it, even if he found it? He was wealthier than any man she knew.

Her few jewels could be readily converted to cash if she needed money. They were worth a lot to her, but they wouldn't mean much to a man who owned a yacht like this one. Not by her reckoning, anyway.

To her, this was further evidence that Mike was deranged. He not only talked to himself and drifted off into trances, but he secretly went through her belongings. That was creepy enough, but why had he taken the bag?

It wasn't as if she could go anywhere. While she wasn't a prisoner on the boat, she couldn't go ashore without his knowing.

Mike made no secret of his wish that she should accompany him indefinitely. They quarreled several times about her plans to leave him when they reached St. Martin.

He was possessive, but there was something off about it. She understood that he wanted her; men always wanted her. This was a weapon in her arsenal. She depended on it and used it to her advantage. But Mike didn't want her the way other men wanted her.

She encouraged him when they first met. He offered a way for her to escape from Martinique before anybody found out what she'd done to Frankie.

When she realized that Mike's interest wasn't sexual, she was confused. He wanted her to stay with him, but she couldn't understand why. The idea of her leaving made Mike angry, but he couldn't tell her the reason for his fury.

He became insistent when she put him off. While this puzzled her at first, now she found it disturbing. That he took her valuables was even more disturbing. *Did he take my jewelry to keep me from leaving?*

She was already planning where she could go with the money from the watch. *The watch!* She was so focused on the loss of her financial security that she forgot there was another dimension to the gold Rolex. Now Mike knew she found it.

Did he hide it beneath the cushions and forget it? Or did the

Dani woman lose it there, without him knowing? Either way, it didn't matter. He found her jewels, and he found the watch.

He knew that she knew about Dani, not just from the Phillip man's questions, but also from finding Dani's watch here on *Sea Serpent*.

Does he really not remember Dani being here, or is he a better liar than I've ever known?

That added new depth to her fear. A man who could lie like that, fooling even himself, he was a kind of crazy that Michelle didn't want to contemplate.

She reached for her purse and opened it. Inventorying its contents by feel, she reassured herself that she still had her identification and a little money. There was money in the bank, too — several hundred euros. She could draw on that anywhere, as long as she had the bankcard.

She would be all right without getting the jewelry back, but she wasn't ready to give it up just yet. She worked her finger through the little slit in the lining of the purse and fingered the straight razor. Frankie's razor.

It was a thing of beauty with its mother-of-pearl handles and gleaming blade. The one thing of value that Frankie had owned, it was inherited from his grandfather, a Portuguese seaman.

His grandfather loved a woman from Fort-de-France and gave up the sea for her. That was a nice story that Frankie told when his head was straight, but Michelle didn't believe it.

One time, Frankie had gone too far and hurt her. She dealt with him; he would never hurt anyone again. And she kept the razor.

The razor served her well when she severed her relationship with Frankie. Frankie's razor would free her from Mike, too. And she would use it to make him return her jewelry. She would keep the razor handy.

Their next stop would be Les Saintes, Guadeloupe. She could blend in easily there, another beautiful French girl from another

French island. There would be another yacht going to St. Martin. It was early in the season.

MIKE WAS STILL STRETCHED out in the cockpit, but he was awake now, feeling refreshed after a day of exercise and a nice, long nap. For a change, he slept without dreaming.

At least, he didn't remember dreaming, and that was a relief. Lately, he had been having the vivid dreams, the ones that disturbed him and woke him up, so that he carried their agony into consciousness.

When that happened, Mike would find himself lying awake, trying to resolve the elements of his nightmares. He would feel an overwhelming sadness, a sadness for which he couldn't account. As he struggled to find its cause, he would become angry. Angry, and frustrated.

The first time he remembered dreaming like that was after the fire. It wasn't immediately after the fire; he wasn't upset, then.

Everything had been going according to his plan in the days right after the fire. It was after the foster homes that his plans went awry, and the dreams began.

He intended to go to live with Uncle Andy after the fire. When the social worker had asked him if he had any close relatives, he had told her about Uncle Andy, giving her the address down in Jacksonville.

He worked all of that out, memorizing the address before the fire, figuring he would need it. Uncle Andy was always good to Mike, bringing him presents and spending time with him when he was little. He would go to live with Uncle Andy, now that his parents were dead, he told the social worker.

Two days later, the social worker had come to the temporary foster home again. Mike recalled in detail how he felt when she told him that he couldn't live with Uncle Andy.

"Your Uncle isn't well," she said.

"I can take care of him while he's sick," Mike said.

That was when she told him that his Uncle Andy was in a state-run mental hospital in north Florida. He would never get out.

21

Phillip finally admitted to himself that he was awake. He knew it was early; it was still too dark to see any details of the space around him. He consoled himself with the thought that he had gone to bed just after dark last night, and rolled out of the berth, turning on a light in the main cabin. The clock on the bulkhead told him it was 4 a.m. He had four hours before he could clear in with customs.

He started a pot of coffee and sat down at the chart table to think while the coffee perked. He turned on his cellphone, and in a few seconds, it chimed to let him know he had a voice mail. He retrieved the message, expecting to hear Sandrine's voice.

He listened instead to J.-P., telling him to call as soon as he got the message. "I have news of Dani!" The excitement was plain in his voice. As he returned the call, Phillip felt guilty that he had turned off the phone last night.

"Phillip! I got a call just a couple of hours ago from the U.S. Coast Guard. The Rescue Coordination Center in Miami has received notification that Dani's Personal Locator Beacon was activated several hours ago."

"That's good news, J.-P. Where is she? Why did it take them so long to call?"

They both knew the search and rescue routine. When one of the satellite beacons like Dani's PLB was activated, an earth station passed the information to a search and rescue coordination center within seconds, and a position for the beacon was established within a few minutes. When a beacon was activated, the search and rescue center would telephone the listed contacts in the registration database to verify that there was an actual emergency before starting a search.

"The position was 12 degrees, 59 minutes north, 61 degrees, 15 minutes west — on the south coast of Bequia. From the position and the altitude, they think it is ashore. It is not moving. There was some confusion with the dispatch; they said Dani had not updated her registration recently. They had the wrong phone number for me. The Coast Guard was about to put out a bulletin on her when they finally reached me. I told them I would call you in Bequia — to hold off. When I called you, I was forwarded to your voice mail, and I left you the message, and I was just about to call them back. Then you returned my call just now. They may have already started something."

"Okay, J.-P. I still have the radio direction finder that we used with those cheap tracking beacons, back when we used to put them in our shipments. It's perfect for this job — those little beacons we had used the same frequency as everything else, 121.5 megahertz. That's what the search and rescue teams use on their final approach if they can't get a visual. Just call the Coast Guard back and tell them I'm looking. They probably wouldn't send out a chopper anyway. I'm guessing they'd give this to the locals in Bequia. Probably should let them do that, just in case. I'll get ashore as quickly as I can. I can go to see customs after I deal with this; I don't think they'll give me any grief, if I explain. Let me go. I'll call you back soon. This is good news."

"Thank you, Phillip," J.-P. said, but Phillip had already disconnected.

Phillip slugged down another cup of coffee as he unpacked the RDF and put fresh batteries in it. As an afterthought, he replaced the batteries in his handheld GPS, too.

He looked at the chart of Bequia, already spread out on the chart table, and plotted the position that J.-P. had given him. It was close to the Paget Farm community dock.

It would be faster to take the dinghy around there than it would be to go ashore, find a taxi, and negotiate the mountain roads going over the ridgeline that formed the backbone of the island. Moreover, the dinghy would give him greater mobility, if he needed to search the southern coastline. The position fix was only accurate within about a mile; the search and rescue people figured that with the 121.5-megahertz homing signal and the RDF, that was good enough.

Phillip tossed his clearance paperwork, the GPS, and the RDF into a canvas briefcase. He also included his handheld marine VHF radio. He went up on deck and launched the dinghy.

Dawn was breaking as he got under way, helping him to negotiate his run to the west along the south shore of the harbor. The island of Bequia was shaped like a backwards "C," with the opening facing west, and the lower, southern, arm was much longer than the northern one. The southern arm was a peninsula, tipped by several small islands.

The harbor where Phillip was anchored was in the middle of the "C." To get to the location of the beacon, he needed to go out, around the tip of the southern peninsula, and double back along the south shore of the island. It was a distance of a few miles. In the dinghy, with its shallow draft, he was able to cut through the islands, avoiding the longer trip around the westernmost tip of land.

After about 15 minutes, Phillip turned back to the east and followed along the south shore, past the airport. Half-way between the east end of the runway and the Paget Farms dock, he throttled back to idle speed and turned on his GPS.

While his GPS went through its startup sequence, looking for satellites, he took the RDF out and did a 360-degree sweep. Phillip found no signal, which didn't really surprise him. If the beacon was indeed ashore, the craggy terrain could block the line of sight from the RDF to the beacon.

The GPS beeped. He looked down at the screen. This was the place. He did another careful sweep with the RDF, focusing his attention on the water between the shore and the string of islands a few hundred yards distant. Nothing.

He put the outboard in gear and idled along the shoreline, keeping the RDF aimed at the high water mark a hundred yards away. It was light enough now that he could visually scan the shoreline. He made two passes between the west end of the runway and the Paget Farms dock, still without finding any sign of Dani or her PLB.

He tied the dinghy to the rickety dock and scrambled ashore, canvas briefcase in one hand and RDF in the other. There were three men loading an open fishing boat. Phillip greeted them and told them what he was looking for. One of them volunteered an opinion.

"If this lady, she come ashore here, we know 'bout it. Not so many people live here, like Port Elizabeth."

Phillip thanked him, sure that he was correct, but that didn't explain the PLB signal. The fishermen all agreed with that assessment, but couldn't offer any further insight, beyond the obvious thoughts that the beacon itself had washed ashore, or that the lady had lost it, perhaps.

They climbed aboard their boat, and Phillip set off up the hill, RDF in hand. As he swept the hillside with the RDF, he thought about what the men had said.

The problem with their suggestions was that the PLB required manual activation, unlike the bigger units called EPIRBs that were designed for ships and aircraft. Those were automatically triggered, in the one case by immersion and in the other by impact.

Somebody had manually triggered Dani's PLB. Phillip hoped that somebody was Dani; that would mean that she was alive and conscious, or had been a few hours ago, anyway.

As he walked to the west along the rocky road that paralleled the coastline, he swept the uphill side, where all the little houses were, with his RDF. The sun was up over the ridgeline to the east, beginning to warm the ground, baking the water out of the soil, increasing the humidity.

Phillip was wiping the first beads of perspiration from his eyes with his left hand when the RDF let out a squawk. There was only one house that it could be; the hillside was thinly populated.

He put the RDF in his canvas briefcase and turned to climb the steep path to the house. He could hear children at play long before he was close enough to call out a "Hello, good morning," to let the people know he was coming. He didn't want his knock on the door to startle anybody, figuring that visitors were scarce.

His greeting had just faded when the door opened and a handsome, solidly built young woman came out onto the porch, a child on her hip and two more following in her wake. "Good morning," she said.

"Good morning. Excuse my disturbing you," Phillip said. He explained why he was there.

The woman frowned and shook her head, turning to look back through the open door into the house. "Timothy," she called. "Timothy, come here, please."

She turned back to Phillip and smiled. "Timothy my oldest. He know 'bout this t'ing, mebbe."

Timothy soon appeared, followed by two boys, obviously his younger brothers. One had the PLB in his hand, the lights still blinking.

"Talk to the man, Timothy," the woman said. "He ax 'bout the t'ing you find."

Fear was plain on Timothy's face as he took the PLB from his brother's hand and extended it to Phillip. "My name is Phillip, Timothy," Phillip said.

Phillip took the device from the boy and told him what it was. He explained about Dani, and how her parents were worried. Timothy's shoulders relaxed as he began to understand. He volunteered that the PLB had been with a life vest, and he dispatched the smaller of the two brothers to retrieve it. Showing Phillip the rip, and the pouch where the PLB had been, Timothy explained sheepishly that he had pulled the black tab, like the cartoon showed. "But no lightnin' come, Mistah Phillip," he concluded.

That brought a smile to Phillip's face.

"Timothy, you've done an important thing this morning, by telling me all about how you found this. It may help us to save this young woman's life. Thank you for being such a good person. I need to keep the PLB, but there is a reward for you, for finding it and giving it to me, as long as your mother approves." All eyes turned to the woman with the baby on her hip. She smiled and nodded.

Phillip reached into his pocket and took out his wallet. He opened it, and withdrew a crisp $100 E.C. bank note, handing it to Timothy, whose eyes got very big as he thought about the things that he could do with that money.

Phillip, in a hurry to call J.-P., repeated his thanks and turned back down the hill. Once he was under way in the dinghy, he called J.-P. He had to run at idle speed to hear J.-P. over the noise of the outboard, but he wasn't in a hurry. He would still get back to *Kayak Spirit* in time to have breakfast before customs opened.

"This is disappointing, Phillip," J.-P. said. "I was so sure that you would find her..."

Phillip could hear the emotion choking his friend's voice. "Yes, it is disappointing, but it's still progress, J.-P. Most likely, Dani had the vest and the PLB when she left *Sea Serpent*. We don't know how long it drifted, but it hasn't moved very far since the Morris folks saw her in the Tobago Cays. I think everything points to her being in the area, here. There's not a lot of geography to cover, nor a lot of people, between here and the Cays. Keep the faith. We'll find her," Phillip said, as much for his own benefit as for J.-P.'s. "I'll call tonight."

"Yes. I'll talk to you then." J.-P. sounded dejected as he hung up the phone.

WITH TIME TO spare before he could clear in, Phillip returned to *Kayak Spirit* and called the Coast Guard's Rescue Coordination Center to tell them about the PLB. The Coast Guard immediately started broadcasting a bulletin requesting all vessels in the area to keep a watch out for Dani.

After that, he ate breakfast and cleaned up the boat from yesterday's sail. By the time he was through, it was a little after 8 o'clock. Phillip gathered his paperwork and took the dinghy ashore to clear in.

Leaving the government building after he took care of the entrance paperwork, Phillip ambled down the waterfront. There was a personal matter he needed to handle. He followed Port Elizabeth's Front Street until it came to its uncertain end. The first impression was that the street turned into a parking lot; then again, maybe it was a beach. It was hard to say.

Phillip walked into the open-air restaurant at the end of the street. The proprietress spied him as soon as he entered.

"Welcome to Bequia, Phillip," she said, opening her arms, inviting a hug.

"You're looking well, Mrs. Walker," he said, as she released him.

She put her hands on his shoulders and leaned back to study his face. "And you. It's been too long since you've come to visit. What brings you here?"

"I'm afraid I'm bringing bad news. Dani's missing, and J.-P. asked — "

"Missing? My Dani? What do you mean, Phillip?" She led him to a table in the corner.

When they were seated, Phillip gave her all the details. She listened without interruption.

"So she's in this area, then," she said, after Phillip finished.

"She was a few days ago, anyway."

"I need to call J.-P.," she said. "That poor boy must be beside himself with worry."

"I'm sure he'd welcome hearing from you," Phillip said. "He wanted me to tell you about this, face to face."

"And thank you both for that, Phillip. J.-P. is as much family as my own boys. I practically raised him, you know."

"I know you're close. And with Dani, too."

"Close? Yes, Dani's like my granddaughter — my only grandchild. If anyone's harmed her, I'll see that they pay."

The cold look in her eyes sent a chill down Phillip's spine. She and Phillip had known one another for a long time. Her husband, Lowell, had been a business partner of J.-P.'s during Phillip's early days in the islands. Lowell had passed away several years ago.

"I didn't realize you'd known J.-P. that long," Phillip said.

"Known him? I remember when he was born. Lowell and J.-P.'s father were in business together from the time they were teenagers."

"I knew you took care of Dani when she was little," Phillip said. "But not J.-P."

"I did, yes. Both of them. Well, I know you'll find her, but don't forget that I'm still in touch with Lowell's crowd. I may be old, but I'm able, and if you need anything, you ask."

"I will, Mrs. Walker."

"And now let me feed you."

"If it's not too much trouble," Phillip said.

"Pah! I'll be right back; let me sort out the kitchen help. It's almost lunchtime. Excuse me."

A waitress brought Phillip a cold beer. "Mrs. Walker say she be a few minutes," the woman said.

"Thanks," Phillip said, taking a sip.

Not for the first time, Phillip wondered how old Mrs. Walker was. Until just now, he would have guessed she was in her 60s, although she didn't look it. Based on her comments a few minutes ago, he added a couple of decades to his estimate.

Still a striking woman, she must have been stunning when she was young. She was an amalgam of the best of Bequia's diverse gene pool. The bone structure in her face and the straight, black hair came from the nearly extinct Caribs, her skin from Africa, and her green eyes were pure leprechaun. No doubt, there was more beneath the surface.

Meanwhile, he was enjoying being in Mrs. Walker's place. It felt like home, and she was like a favorite aunt.

There was a couple in the opposite corner of the room engaged in an intense argument about which of them was to blame for their decision to come to Bequia. They were the only other people in the place, and given that they were almost yelling, Phillip couldn't help overhearing.

They had just come from St. Vincent, on the ferry. The woman was berating her husband about the experience thus far, complaining about the heat, the filth, and the crowded, dirty, noisy ferryboat.

"And this place, it's not even air-conditioned. And that black woman who seated us acts like she owns the place," she ranted. New York, Phillip thought, listening to the accent.

"She does act that way," Mrs. Walker said, softly, smiling as she put Phillip's lunch down in front of him. "They surely are vexed. Wait until they find out that they have to wade along the waterfront to get to their hotel."

"And it's not air-conditioned, either," Phillip said, with a smile. Mrs. Walker chuckled quietly, shaking her head.

"I have some pictures of Dani with the man we think may have been the last one to see her." He handed them to her. "His boat's named *Sea Serpent*."

"May I keep these for a little while, Phillip?"

"Of course. As long as you like."

"I'll show them around a bit this afternoon, and ask if anyone's seen the boat. I have some nice pork chops for dinner this evening, if you plan to eat ashore. Maybe I'll have some information for you by then."

"I wouldn't miss your pork chops for anything. See you about eight?"

"Yes. I'll see you then. Enjoy your lunch. I need to talk with a few people, if you'll excuse me."

He rose from his seat as she smiled and nodded pleasantly at him. He helped her from her chair and then sat down to finish his meal.

THAT EVENING, Phillip had taken another set of his pictures to the happy hour at the bar down the beach and socialized with the boaters there, but to no avail. No one had seen *Sea Serpent*, though several remarked that she would have made a lasting impression, with her classic lines.

He was enjoying the peaceful ambience of Mrs. Walker's after the raucous crowd at the other place. Phillip had finished a bowl of conch chowder, and he was about to cut into a juicy looking pork chop when Mrs. Walker joined him.

"Is the meal to your liking, Phillip?"

"Yes, ma'am. It's perfect," he said.

"I'm pleased that you are enjoying it. I have some information, but I'm afraid it won't be especially helpful."

She explained that *Sea Serpent* had spent a good bit of time in Bequia over the past few years, and the skipper was known to most of the folks who did business with visiting yachts. He was remembered because he was a loner, and more than one person had remarked that he talked to himself. He had kept company for a while a couple of years ago with a woman named Sylvia Defoe, who had been working as a waitress at one of the resort hotels.

"She was what we used to call a 'loose woman,'" Mrs. Walker said. "She came here from Kingstown, St. Vincent, and she worked at the hotel most of that winter, until the man on *Sea Serpent* left for Grenada. Some people think she went with him; some think she went somewhere else. She told one of the other women at work that she was going to Grenada with him and live on *Sea Serpent* for the hurricane season. But she often told lies, so not everyone believed her about that.

"She said she planned to come back and work at the hotel again, but no one ever heard from her after she left. *Sea Serpent* came back after the hurricane season. The boat spent a few weeks in the harbor, and the man was seen in the usual places, but he had no one with him.

"I have as much information as the people at the hotel knew from the Defoe woman's employment records." She put a manila envelope down, placing it to the side of Phillip's food. "It's all in here with your pictures. I hope this helps you to find Dani."

They talked about the old days while Phillip finished his dinner, recalling how Lowell Walker had entertained Phillip when they weren't working, teaching him to fish like the locals. After coffee and dessert, Phillip returned to *Kayak Spirit*.

Back aboard, he sat down at the chart table and brought his file up to date. He had talked with his friend, the Chief Superintendent of Police for St. Vincent and the Grenadines, by telephone this afternoon.

The Chief Super had put his minions to work on a records search at Phillip's request. Phillip had asked them to check the clearance documents for *Sea Serpent* for the last three years, to see when Reilly had entered and left the country.

Further, he had requested the passport details of any passengers or crew aboard the vessel. He wanted to know specifically if *Sea Serpent* had come here after leaving St. Lucia, two years ago, and if so, whether Agnes Saint James had been aboard. He made a note to ask Cedric Jones whether she had been on the vessel's outbound paperwork when she left St. Lucia, too.

Now, thanks to Mrs. Walker, he had another name to check. He would ask the Chief Superintendent about this Sylvia Defoe when they spoke tomorrow. The similarity between Defoe's story and what Agnes Saint James had told the woman in St. Lucia was uncanny.

His notes up to date, Phillip called J.-P. and shared what he knew.

22

After breakfast, Phillip had spoken to the Chief Superintendent of Police in St. Vincent. The records checks he had requested were in progress, but results weren't expected until tomorrow. Rather than waiting in Bequia, Phillip decided to try his luck in Mayreau, where Dani had parted ways with the yacht *Ramblin' Gal*.

He raised the sails, allowing them to luff in the early morning's gentle breeze. After he retrieved the anchor by hand, Phillip sheeted in the sails, and *Kayak Spirit* made way slowly on the port tack. As the boat cleared the anchorage, Phillip fell off the wind a bit and eased the sheets.

The boat came alive, picking up speed on a close reach. As he left Whale Cay, the rock at the southwest corner of Bequia, off his port quarter, Phillip came up on the wind, putting a little more south into his course.

Phillip planned to start his search in Mayreau's Salt Whistle Bay, where Dani's phone had been found. He planned to show the pictures of Dani, Reilly, and *Sea Serpent* to the people working at the resort there.

Sergeant Wiggers's men had already shown everybody there a

picture of Dani, but Phillip wanted to see if anyone remembered Reilly, or *Sea Serpent*. Besides, the police had been using a passport picture. Someone might recognize Dani from the more natural looking snapshot that he had of her with Reilly.

It was a short trip to Mayreau. Phillip would be anchored in Salt Whistle Bay by mid-afternoon, leaving him time to ask his questions before it got too late.

He planned to call the Chief Super again tomorrow morning. Depending on what he learned from the records checks and from his efforts this afternoon, he might clear out at Union Island tomorrow and go down to Carriacou, or perhaps Grenada.

Meanwhile, he decided to get a lure in the water. The tuna were running, and with a little luck, he could have sashimi for lunch while he was underway.

THE PAIN in his arms was excruciating. Mike couldn't imagine what was causing it. He forced his eyes open, dazzled by the glare from the slick surface of the sea. He looked around slowly, trying to get his bearings. He was looking up at sails, hanging limp in the calm, flapping as the boat rolled in the swell. *I'm on Sea Serpent. But where?*

He started to sit up in the cockpit, but when he put his weight on his left arm, his hand slipped out from under him, and there was a new surge of pain from his forearm.

Deck's slick. Arms hurt. He rolled onto his back and raised his left arm to look at it. The gorge rose in his throat when he saw that his forearm was sliced open from elbow to wrist; the tendons were exposed, and the blood flowed freely. *Cut. Cut bad. What happened?*

Gotta get a bandage on that. Mike rolled to a sitting position, focused on getting below. Crouching to maintain his balance as the boat rolled with the swells, he worked his way to the companionway. Placing his right hand on the sliding hatch cover, he saw that his other forearm and hand were drenched in blood, too. *Damn. Hurts; bleeding. Need the first aid kit.*

Once below, he wedged himself into the head compartment. He retrieved the first-aid kit from the big locker over the sink and sat down on the toilet, opening the zippered, foldout case on the counter beside him.

Mike washed the cut on his left arm, using disinfectant solution from the first aid kit. He turned on the shower, which was more like the sprayer found at a kitchen sink, and rinsed the wound. He dried his arm as best he could, using paper towels from the roll hanging on the bulkhead. Wrapping the arm with gauze, he tried to close the wound.

Need stitches. Not now, though. Just stop the bleeding. Gotta stop the bleeding. Mike felt nauseated and cold. *Going into shock. Hurry.*

He washed and wrapped the right arm. Still seated, he bent over, sitting with his head between his knees, clinging to consciousness.

Mike wasn't sure how long he sat there, but at some point, he became aware of the boat's motion changing. He heard the wind, and the sails started rustling. Then he felt the sails fill, and the boat heeled, accelerating gently.

She seems happy enough. Must have the wind vane set. I'd better go take a look, see where the hell I am?

Mike stood tentatively, making sure that he wouldn't faint. He looked down at the bandages on his arms. The gauze was blood-soaked, but the blood was beginning to dry. Maybe he wasn't losing as much, now.

Feel better. Not dizzy anymore. Hurts like hell, though.

He followed the trail of his blood back to the cockpit. *Sea Serpent* was sailing along, perfectly balanced, with the wind vane holding her close-hauled on the starboard tack. He scanned the horizon. There were no other boats in sight.

There was a cluster of islands a few miles off his port side and a much larger island well behind them. There was another good-sized island off the starboard side. Mike glanced down at the compass in the steering pedestal. His course was east northeast. He could see the dim outline of a low island on the horizon off the bow.

Okay, nobody around. I'm okay for a minute.

He went back below. Leaning against the galley counter, Mike checked his bandages and decided they were all right for the moment. He lifted the lid of the refrigerator compartment and fumbled out a pint container of orange juice.

Gotta keep the blood sugar up. Let's see where the hell we are.

He turned to the chart table. There was a chart held to the surface with spring clamps. It was labeled "Guadeloupe to Martinique." Right in the middle was the island of Dominica.

I was just there. Dominica, that's right.

He looked at the GPS. His position was 15 degrees, 44 minutes north, 61 degrees, 29 minutes west. Picking up a pencil, Mike made a small 'x' at his position on the chart. He was right in the middle of the Dominica Channel, midway between Dominica and Les Saintes, the cluster of islands off the south coast of Guadeloupe.

About 15 miles to Marie Galante. That's what I'm seeing out there off the bow.

Climbing into the cockpit, Mike stretched out on the seat with his orange juice. He needed to think about this. He had been in Dominica, but he didn't remember leaving. He couldn't have been out here for long; he hadn't come very far.

He must have set a course for Marie Galante, although that didn't sound right. He usually went to Les Saintes from Dominica, or on to Deshaies, if he was in a hurry.

Am I in a hurry?

He couldn't remember. Maybe he had set up the wind vane for Les Saintes, and the wind had clocked.

That's probably it. Wind died. No wind when I woke up. Then it clocked and put more east in the course. Good thing, too. If I'd stayed on course to Les Saintes, I'd have hit the rocks before I woke up.

Mike shook his head and took another sip of the orange juice.

I'll just go to Marie Galante. Not as many people. Clinic there can stitch me up. Probably less hassle than Les Saintes.

As he felt less disoriented, Mike began to wonder more about the cuts. There was blood all over the cockpit. He really sliced himself on something. Both arms, too.

Was I fishing?

He looked around. *No tackle; no filet knife.* He shook his head. Mike couldn't think of any part of the boat that was sharp enough to do that kind of damage.

A puzzle.

He drank the rest of his orange juice. Mike began to wonder about clearing in with customs in Marie Galante. Was there even a customs officer there? He couldn't remember. He would go below and check his cruising guide. He could check his paperwork, too, and make sure he was right about Dominica. He scanned the horizon for any boat traffic, and then went below. Mike got another orange juice out of the refrigerator and sat down at the chart table.

PHILLIP SAILED into Salt Whistle Bay a little after lunchtime. He was hungry, his expectations of sashimi while underway having been frustrated by uncooperative fish. Once he got the anchor down, he took his dinghy ashore, thinking he would find a sandwich at the Salt Whistle Bay Club. He stopped at the guard shack and pulled out the photographs.

"Good afternoon," Phillip said. "I know the police probably asked you about this a few days ago, but these are new pictures, and I'm trying to help this young lady's parents find her. Would you please take a look, and see if you recognize either person, or the boat?"

The guard studied both photographs carefully. "The people, I see here, like I tol' the constable. The boat, I cannot say. Sorry." He shook his head.

"Is this the man who brought the girl ashore to pick up her bag?" Phillip asked.

"Yes. Tha's the mon. The constable, he don' have a picture of the mon. But that mon, he the one wit' the girl. The p'lice, they tell you 'bout the phone?"

"Yes, they did. Thank you very much. Does the bar serve food this time of day?"

"Sure, mon. They got the roti, mebbe some burger, sandwich. The big lunch finish in the rest'rant. You miss that, one time. Dinner start at six this evening. Must wear shoes for the rest'rant. Don' need for the bar. I hope you enjoy," the guard said, looking as if he meant it.

Phillip was reminded that the farther south you went in the islands, the slower the pace of life became. The people weren't necessarily friendlier than their neighbors to the north, but they took more time to visit with strangers, especially in places like this. Mayreau didn't get much tourist traffic, other than a few people coming to the tiny resort.

"Thank you. I'm sure I'll enjoy it," Phillip said. He nodded at the man and walked into the bar.

23

WILLIAM CLINTON HAD A BELLYFUL OF LIFE ON THE *ERZULIE FREDA*. He regretted the day that he had first seen the rusty little ship. She had been loading a cargo of bananas in Rouseau, Dominica, and he had been working the docks.

He had struck up a conversation with the ship's engineer and discovered that the ship was short-handed. They needed a hard-working, healthy man for deck crew. William had just split up with his long-time girlfriend, and he was ready for some excitement.

Work was scarce in Dominica, and many able-bodied men went to sea when they could. William's father had worked the island schooners in his younger days, and William had grown up wishing he could experience the adventures that his father still recounted.

If he shipped out, he could save his money, too. Food would be provided, and he could give up the apartment that he shared with his friends. When he was home for a few days, he could just stay with his parents. They would like that.

If he saved his money, he could afford to get married and

settle down. He had been keeping an eye out for an opportunity like this, but seafaring jobs were scarce.

He asked about pay, and the engineer explained that the crew worked for shares, each man getting a set percentage of the profit from each voyage. When William wanted to know how much he would make on a trip, hauling several tons of green bananas down island, the engineer laughed and wouldn't answer him.

"We make most of our money going the other way," was all he said.

He induced William to come aboard and meet the captain, a jovial, back-slapping, one-eyed rogue who was busy getting drunk on jackiron rum. After sharing a few shots with the captain and the engineer, things looked promising to William.

He never got an answer to his questions about what he could expect to earn, but as the rum did its work, he realized that even if he made nothing, he would still be fed. Loading green bananas on a piecework pay scale when work was available didn't offer even that much security.

When he woke up sometime later with a terrible hangover and a roaring in his ears, he was in a grimy berth just off the engine room. As he fell while climbing out of the berth in his hurry to find somewhere to throw up, he recognized the engineer, tinkering with something at a workbench.

William had become a merchant seaman. He didn't remember it, but he had gone home and gotten his passport, packed a few belongings and rejoined the party. Sometime after he had passed out, they had left Rouseau.

Life aboard *Erzulie Freda* was not what William had expected. He did get fed, after a fashion. There was food available, and a galley that he could use, but the provisions were often spoiled, and he and the two other deck hands made do with what they could pilfer from the cargo, for the most part.

"It's okay, mon. We eat less than the rats," one of them had explained, when William had asked him about whether they would get in trouble for breaking open a case of corned beef in the hold one afternoon. "Jus' don' mess wit' the women or the dope," the man said.

William kept his mouth shut and his eyes open, but he didn't see any sign of women — passengers, he assumed the man meant — and he figured that dope traveled in the other direction. He wasn't sure the man was even serious about that, but he knew dope moved from south to north. Everybody knew that.

Now, two years later, William was somewhat wiser. He had indeed managed to accumulate a small amount of money, but he was disappointed. He could support himself for a few months, but that would break him.

He had finally figured out that the captain and the engineer split the real profits, which came from smuggling women and dope, but mostly dope. Women were apparently much more difficult cargo.

As William pieced together what was happening, his conscience started to trouble him. The dope didn't bother him too much. He didn't use dope, and he rarely drank rum.

The one time he had tried smoking pot, he didn't inhale, and he had been teased about it ever since. He didn't want to waste his money that way, but he figured that if other people did, it was their own business. They had recently had several narrow escapes from DEA patrols, though.

At first, he figured that even if they were caught, he and the other deck crewmen could play dumb, and not get in too much trouble. Now, he was less confident about that. Last month a man he knew had been shot during a DEA raid on another inter-island freighter.

Just an innocent crewman like William, his friend had been trying to stay out of the way when a stray bullet killed him. That was a wake-up call for William. The danger from being around drugs, and the misery of the women who were their human cargo — both of those things finally got to him.

He was watching Dominica come over the horizon, thinking this was his last voyage. The last one on the *Erzulie Freda*, anyhow. He shook his head at the irony of the name, which he had learned was Haitian Creole for "Spirit of Love," a Voodoo goddess.

When the ship docked in Rouseau, he would be gone. He didn't plan to say goodbye, either. One of his fellow crewmen had tried to leave the ship in Grenada, and Julio, the one-eyed, drunken captain, had beaten him severely. Julio had told that man that if he ever got off the ship, it would be when he was wrapped in chain and tossed over the side. William figured he knew too much for Julio to let him quit, so he had a different plan.

When Julio put the bow against the quay, William would leap ashore with the mooring lines in hand, as he usually did. Instead of securing the heavy lines to the bollards on the quay so that the crew could warp the ship alongside, he would throw them in the water and take to his heels.

The gusty offshore wind would blow the ship away, and Julio would have to circle and make another approach, this time one man short on deck. By the time Julio and the others got the ship tied up, William would have vanished into the rabbit warren of Roseau's back streets that he knew so well.

This was his home, not theirs, and they couldn't stay here for very long to look for him. Once the ship left, William planned to go to the authorities and report Julio and the engineer. He was sure he had enough details to put them in jail for a long time. Drugs weren't always taken seriously, but human trafficking was, and he had quietly gathered all the details of Julio's dealings.

KAYAK SPIRIT ROLLED GENTLY with the swell in the anchorage off Ross Point, just south of the entrance channel to St. George's, Grenada. Phillip had made a quick stop in Union Island that morning, securing his outbound clearance from St. Vincent and the Grenadines to Grenada.

He had phoned the Chief Super in St. Vincent, and Cedric Jones in St. Lucia. Both men had answers to the questions Phillip had asked the day before.

The Chief Super told Phillip that *Sea Serpent* had indeed cleared into St. Vincent and the Grenadines two years ago, coming from Rodney Bay, St. Lucia. Agnes Saint James had not been aboard.

This tracked with what Phillip had learned from his early morning call to Cedric. Agnes had not been shown on *Sea Serpent's* outbound paperwork from St. Lucia, either.

Phillip saw two explanations: either Agnes didn't make the trip, or Reilly didn't list her on his documents. Phillip figured that Reilly didn't list her, given her friend's statement, and her comment about Agnes calling from Bequia.

Phillip had started a list of missing women, women who were connected to Reilly. So far, they included Reilly's wife, Andrea, and Dani, in order of their disappearance. He inserted Agnes Saint James's name in between Andrea and Dani. The Chief Super had found that Sylvia Defoe did leave Port Elizabeth, Bequia, on *Sea Serpent* that winter, bound for St. George's.

He also reported that Sylvia had a police record in St. Vincent, with arrests or cautions for possession of controlled substances, prostitution, and public drunkenness. Phillip made a note to check with George Castle, his contact in the Criminal Investigation Department of Grenada's national police force, to see if either woman had entered the country during the period of *Sea Serpent's* visit two years ago.

Three women missing was an unlikely coincidence. A fourth would add some certainty to the notion of Reilly's involvement in their disappearances. Phillip would know in the morning whether Sylvia Defoe made it to Grenada.

It was too late in the day to pursue further inquiries. Besides,

Phillip was tired from his sail down and the rush to clear customs when he arrived in St. George's. He wanted to get that done, and he only had 30 minutes after his arrival before the office closed. He took *Kayak Spirit* in to the fuel dock at the yacht club.

There were customs and immigration officers on duty at the club, and going to the dock saved him the time of assembling and launching his dinghy. He had taken advantage of being at the dock to top off his fuel and water tanks before moving to his present spot in the outer anchorage.

He liked it better out here than inside the harbor. It wasn't as protected from bad weather, but it offered much more privacy, plus a breeze, and the water was crystal clear. Phillip had seen a dinner-plate-sized starfish on the bottom in 30 feet of water as he watched the anchor settle into the sand. He was also entertained out here by sitting in the cockpit and watching the commercial ships come and go.

Tomorrow, he would call George Castle to see what he could learn from Grenada's records about *Sea Serpent's* visits over the last few years. Then maybe he would move *Kayak Spirit* around to the south coast, where most of the yachting community was scattered over three or four well-protected bays.

He knew there would be a few hundred boats in that area, and he was planning to make the rounds with his pictures. There were innumerable social activities down there: happy hours, organized excursions, potlucks, and less structured gatherings. By making the rounds, he might uncover new leads on Reilly and Dani.

The sun had set, and Phillip had eaten a sandwich. He was starting to feel sleepy when his cellphone chirped.

"Hello, J.-P."

"Good evening, Phillip. Are you still in Mayreau?"

"No. Mayreau is still a one-day town, unless you just want to sit on the beach. There may not even be as many people there now as there used to be when you were in the islands."

"It is nice to hear that not all of the islands have been overrun with development. Where are you?"

"I'm in Grenada," Phillip said, giving J.-P. his news about Agnes and Sylvia. "I'll do some follow up on both of them tomorrow morning with George, once he's in the office."

"Thank you, Phillip. Please call anytime you have something new," J.-P. said, his desperation beginning to show.

"I will, J.-P. Good night," Phillip said, disconnecting the call.

24

MIKE SAT UNDER THE AWNING OF THE *PATISSERIE* ON THE MAIN street in Grand Bourg, Marie Galante, sipping his *café au lait* and watching the girl at the table with him. She was picking pieces of the pastry from her *pain au chocolat*, nibbling at the crumbs, making it last.

When he had first noticed her, on the beach at Marie Galante, he had thought that she was a child. She was a small girl, but, on closer examination, no child. She had been sunbathing alone when he had walked by on his way to his dinghy after a follow-up visit to the clinic. He'd gone in when he arrived yesterday to have his arms stitched up.

She had appeared to be sleeping, face down on a beach towel, the top of her bikini untied, the strings out to the sides, so as not to mark her back with tan lines. She had rolled over and come to a sitting position as he passed, casually leaving her bathing suit top on the towel. That was when he saw that she wasn't a child.

She had smiled up at him invitingly, and he had stopped in his tracks.

"*Bonjour. Je m'appelle Liesbet,*" she said, looking him squarely in the eye, smiling again as she watched him struggling to keep his gaze on her face.

"Sorry, I don't speak French," he had said, flustered.

"It's all right," she said. She had a touch of a British accent. "I'm happy to speak English. My name is Liesbet Chirac, but most people call me Liz. Where are you staying?"

"Oh, I'm here on my boat." He pointed at *Sea Serpent*, dancing at her anchor a hundred yards off the beach.

"She's beautiful," Liz said, staring at the vessel critically, her eyes moving along the lines and taking in detail. She looked at the boat as only a sailor would look at a boat. "A Concordia yawl?"

"Yes," he said, impressed, knowing the boat was at least twice as old as the girl.

"Was she built in the States? Or by Abeking and Rasmussen?"

"She's German," he said. "One of the last before they started building the 41-foot version. Would you like to come aboard?"

"Oh, yes, very much. Could I?" she asked.

And so, it had begun. Liz was in love with *Sea Serpent*, and Mike thought that he was in love with her. They had spent that first afternoon sailing back and forth off the beach at Marie Galante, carrying a beam reach on the port tack to the southwest a few miles, coming about and reaching on a starboard tack until they were in the shallow water off the beach again.

Liz had quickly taken over sailing *Sea Serpent*, as the nurse practitioner who had stitched up his arms had cautioned Mike not to use his muscles any more than necessary. He was happy to ride, enjoying the obvious pleasure that Liz took in feeling *Sea Serpent* come to life under her small, callused sailor's hands.

"Where is your home?" he had asked her, that first afternoon. "Do you live here, on the island?"

"Oh, no. I grew up in Belgium. I'm just visiting Guadeloupe. I've been here for nine days, now."

"And how long will you stay? Are you on holiday?"

"Well, yes, a sort of holiday. More of what you Americans call a sabbatical, I think." She smiled at him as she trimmed the mainsheet. "I was working for the E.U. in Brussels on a contract, doing some financial analysis. When my contract was finished, they wanted to hire me, but I was cold, so I came here. When I want to be cold again, I will go back to Europe. Or maybe the States. I think maybe I could find work in a warm part of the States."

"What about your family?" he had asked.

"Hmm. I have no one, really. When I was very small, my mother died of cancer. My father brought me up. When I was older and away at school, he remarried, but I was too old to bond with my stepmother. Now, just last year, my father died. I keep in touch with my stepmother occasionally, but just as a friend. How about you, Mike? Do you have family in the states?"

"No. No one. I was an orphan," he said. "Should we get you back ashore for dinner?"

"Okay. Yes," she said. "Would it be all right if I invited you to join me? I would buy your dinner, to thank you for the wonderful sail, if that's agreeable."

Time passed quickly in her company. Mike had never met a woman like her. Besides sharing his love of boats, she was intelligent and independent. He had not felt attached to anyone in this way since his wife had left him. Not that he spent much time with women.

He'd had little interest in women after Andrea, but Liz made him feel young, and excited to be alive. They rented scooters and toured the island. In the evenings, they ate in a little Creole restaurant in Grand Bourg, and most days, they sailed for a few hours.

Mike had never known a woman who so fully shared his love of sailing. He was still surprised that she knew the Concordia yawls, but she had explained that odd bit of knowledge at his urging.

Liz's father had loved sailing. Although he never owned a yacht, he often sailed with other people, and he had taken Liz whenever he could. He had always pointed out a Concordia yawl that someone kept in the harbor where his friends kept their boat. She had grown up thinking that the Concordias were the ultimate evolution of the wooden yacht.

They had decided that she would move aboard *Sea Serpent* with him and sail to the Virgin Islands, once he was able to stand watches.

"Why not?" she asked, with a Gallic shrug. "We get along well, you and I and *Sea Serpent*."

"WHERE AM I?" the girl asked Rosa, her eyes searching her surroundings.

"You are all right. You are in a safe place, for now. You must be calm. You've been unconscious for some days, now. We have worried about you. It is good that you are awake, but you must not worry. It will take some time for you to understand things, maybe."

"How did I get here?" she asked.

"Some men on a ship found you, floating in the water near St. Vincent," Rosa said. Seeing the uncertainty in the girl's eyes, Rosa paused for a moment. "You know St. Vincent, the island?"

"No," the girl said, eyelids drooping.

Rosa adjusted the sheet over the girl's slight, wiry frame. At least she's coming out of the coma, Rosa thought. That's good. If she's awake, we can feed her and make her healthy.

She doesn't need to remember. Maybe it's better if she doesn't. Better for her, certainly, but maybe better all around. Some men might pay extra for a beautiful girl who didn't know what was happening.

She would be easier to manage than most of the street-savvy girls Rosa got in this place. She thought about the Anglo men that she had known in Miami, with their "dumb blond" jokes.

This one might be the ultimate dumb blond, she thought, shaking her head as she went to find Big Jim.

She knew that Big Jim would be relieved that the girl was regaining consciousness. Not that he cared about her personally, but the girl represented a windfall. Rosa knew that they would get a good price for this one. She was beautiful, clean, and drug-free. No tattoos, blond with blue eyes; perfect furniture for some sheik's *pied-à-terre.*

Big Jim told Rosa about his negotiations with that drunken pig, Julio. They laughed at the notion of splitting the price for this one with Julio. They would give him $5,000, maybe even $10,000 — nothing, compared to what they would get for her.

She was quite different from their normal stock. Rosa wondered how Big Jim would go about finding a customer to buy this girl. None of their regulars would be able to afford a fine specimen like this one. Mostly, they only cared that they got girls, or the occasional boy, that were disease-free, lighter-skinned, and young.

Fat, skinny, deformed, there was a market for everything. This one, she would be special. Worth maybe 20 of their regular ones. That was four or five shipments — say, six months of business. Maybe they should focus on finding more like this one. Fewer, more expensive women would reduce their risk quite a bit, although she knew they would be harder to acquire.

25

Phillip sipped at the morning's first cup of coffee in the cockpit. He had just gotten off the phone with George Castle, who said that he could find what Phillip wanted in the Customs and Immigration records in time to share his results over lunch at the yacht club. That left Phillip with a couple of hours to kill.

He was tired of scrubbing and polishing, and it was a beautiful morning. He decided to relax until lunchtime, and he was getting into it, thinking that he might fall asleep. He was contemplating setting an alarm to wake him up for lunch when his cellphone rang. He glanced at the display as he picked it up.

"Good morning, Sharktooth. How are things in Portsmouth?" Phillip asked.

"Morning, morning, Phillip. They gone," Sharktooth said.

"Reilly and *Sea Serpent*? Today?"

"No, Phillip, they lef' the day before. Sorry I let them slip out like that, but the customs, they change the rules. You know 'bout the two weeks?"

"No. What two weeks, Sharktooth?"

"You stay only two weeks, one time you clear in an' out, same time. I don't know this. I look in the harbor las' night for *Sea

Serpent, and there they were, gone. I ask my cousin at the Customs this morning, and he look. He say to me that *Sea Serpent* do the 'two week in and out.' Tha's the firs' I know 'bout the two week t'ing. My cousin, he say they change the rule a few months ago, make it easy for visiting yachts. Good for business, I t'ink."

"Okay, so they left yesterday sometime. Do we know where they're bound?"

"Les Saintes. That's on the paper. They s'pose to come back to Customs, they change they mind before they leave, but they don' do that. So they mus' still go to Les Saintes."

"Okay, Sharktooth. Thanks."

"Sorry I miss that, Phillip."

"No problem, Sharktooth. Don't worry about it. We're in good shape. I'll call Sandrine, and she can find out if they cleared into the Saintes. Thanks again."

"Wait, Phillip! Where you at, mon?"

"Grenada. I'm meeting George Castle for lunch. He's been checking up on *Sea Serpent* for us."

"Say hello to George fo' me."

"I'll do that. Talk with you later." Phillip disconnected and called Sandrine.

He told her what he needed, and Sandrine promised to make a few phone calls to her colleagues in the *Douane* in Guadeloupe and get back to him. She explained that while they were using identical software, they had two separate computer systems, so that she couldn't just look it up herself. Phillip could hear the frustration in her voice.

"It's all right Sandrine," he said. "A couple of hours won't make much difference."

"It is not on the point, Phillip! Is that the right words?"

"Close. You might say, 'that's not the point,' or 'that's beside the point.' I think that's the phrase you want."

"Yes, thank you, Phillip. Besides the point, these computer people, they are the idiots. Why do we not have one way to do this, in all the French Customs? Is the same, the laws, the forms, everything, but I can't see. I must call someone else to see. Besides the point, exactly. I call you back soon. You miss me?"

"I do miss you. Maybe you can come to Grenada, if I'm here long enough. I'll look forward to hearing from you in a little bit, Sandrine."

He looked at his watch and decided he had just enough time to rinse his coffee mug and clean the coffee pot before his lunch appointment.

PHILLIP SAT in a rattan chair on the veranda of the yacht club, looking out over the lagoon, sipping a glass of cold beer as he waited for George Castle. He was studying the fancy new marina that had sprung up across the way.

There was little space for anchored boats in the inner harbor now. The sprawling docks of the marina took up almost the whole lagoon. There was a face dock for megayachts along the point at the south entrance; the deep-water berths were in the place where a wide, shallow reef had been.

Until the marina had been built, there had been a dogleg channel through the wide reef, which protected the inner harbor from the west, but that appeared to be gone, now. The developer must have removed the reef to make room for the megayachts. Phillip wondered what the next hurricane would do to the new docks.

"Hello, Phillip, my friend." George Castle interrupted his musing.

"George." Phillip stood, clasping his friend's huge hand. "It's been a few years."

"Yes. A few years too many. Welcome back to the Isle of Spice. You shouldn't stay away so long. Where are you staying?"

"My boat. I sailed down from Martinique."

"Ah, so you are one of the rich men with yachts, now. What sort of fine vessel did you buy?"

"She's a fine vessel, but I don't think many rich men would want her. You remember *Kayak Spirit*?"

"Yeah, mon! The one old man Rochelle used to sail from Carriacou, when he was running the jackiron rum into Martinique under the noses of the *Douane*. That *Kayak Spirit*?"

"The very same one."

"I'd like to see her. He was special, that old scoundrel. We miss him. I think the French Customs miss him, too."

"I imagine they do."

The waitress came by the table and spent a few minutes flirting with George, who was obviously a regular customer. She left without asking what they wanted, and when Phillip commented on that to George, he said, "What she brings us will be the best, Phillip. She knows, mon. Don't worry. Do I look like I go hungry?"

Phillip smiled and shook his head.

"Okay. Business before the food comes," George said. "First, *Sea Serpent*. She has come here for the hurricane season every year for the last four years. The owner, this Michael Reilly, he brings her in, and she stays in our waters from early June until late October. One year until mid-November.

"From his visa extensions, I think that he stays with the boat, but maybe he flies somewhere for a few days or a couple of weeks during the summer. I have all those dates printed out for you, and where he cleared for.

"This woman, Agnes Saint James, we have no record of her ever coming to Grenada. Same with the other one, Sylvia Defoe. Sorry I can't help you with them. It's possible that they came with him, but they both had E.C. passports, so it would have been no problem for him to show them on his paperwork.

"No reason he would have smuggled them in, that I can see. I traced the passports, by the way. That's something new that we can do. Neither of them has been used to cross any borders in the last three years. That's as far back as I could go.

"So, Phillip, if those ladies are not in their home countries, I think that they are missing. I take it you thought that anyway, from what you told me about J.-P.'s daughter. Sorry I can't tell you more."

"That's all most helpful, George. We get a little piece of information here, a little piece there. Soon, two pieces will fit together, I hope."

"I hope so, too, Phillip. I'm sorry for J.-P. How is he bearing up?"

"Well enough, I think. He wanted me to let Sharktooth have a 'serious talk' with Reilly, though. His patience is wearing thin."

George chuckled. "Sharktooth still got the dreads down his back?"

"Yes, all the way to his waist, now, but he's gone bald as an egg on top, George. It looks strange, but please don't tell him I said so. He says hello."

The food came and as George had promised, their waitress knew what was good. They finished the meal, mostly in silence, and when they parted, they agreed to meet for lunch again the next day, if Phillip stayed anchored nearby.

George went back downtown to the Criminal Investigation Department offices near the market square, and Phillip returned to *Kayak Spirit*. He figured he would sleep off the heavy lunch and go to the 5 o'clock happy hour at the bar at the new marina. He had heard an announcement about it on the cruiser's radio net this morning. It would be a chance to show his pictures around, at least.

BEFORE HE HAD LEFT to meet George for lunch, Phillip rigged an awning to shade the back half of the boat. In the tropics, shade was almost as good as air-conditioning, especially if you were on the water with a breeze.

The temperature ashore might be in the 90s, but the shade and breeze combined with a seawater temperature in the low 80s made *Kayak Spirit's* cockpit a pleasant place. He rigged a hammock under the awning, climbed in, and dropped off to sleep.

The insistent ringing of his cellphone pulled him from his dreams. He had just been telling Sandrine why he liked Grenada so much, when the ringing woke him.

He looked over, expecting to see her in the other hammock, but there wasn't another hammock. Maybe next trip, he thought, hopefully, shaking off the dream as he reached for the phone.

"Hello, Phillip," Sharktooth's voice rumbled in his ear.

"Hello, Sharktooth. George was just asking about you at lunch."

"Okay. George must wait, Phillip. I got news, mon. My cousin in the customs, he tell this to me. You ready?"

"Talk to me, Sharktooth."

"Okay, this mon, he name William Clinton. Bill, we call him. He is in Rouseau, Phillip."

"Is this a joke? Bill Clinton's old news, Sharktooth."

"No. You let me tell it. This mon, he from Rouseau, an' he been sailin' on a freighter from Haiti, all over the islan' fo' the las' two year. The captain, he smuggle drugs, but he smuggle women, too. The drugs from south to north, the women, he buy in Haiti and Venezuela, an' he sell to a man on Baliceaux, dungda by Mustique. You hear me?"

"Yes, I'm with you so far. Keep talking."

"Okay. This mon, Bill Clinton, he don' like the captain. He worry 'bout the DEA catch 'em wit' the drugs. A frien' he had get shot in DEA raid, make he t'ink, see. An' he don' like the selling of the women. Nobody dungda the islan' like that. To be selling people is ver' bad t'ing, you understand?"

"Yes, Sharktooth. Go on."

"Okay, Phillip. Bill Clinton, he jump the ship in Rouseau yesterday. He hide 'til the ship leave las' night. Today, he go to p'lice. When he at p'lice he see the picture of Dani on the wall, from St. Vincent. He know this lady, he tell p'lice. They find she in the sea some days ago, between St. Vincent and Bequia. She got life vest on, but she out cold. They pick she up. They on the way to Baliceaux to unload some drugs, and this Bill, he say the captain leave Dani at Baliceaux. Prob'ly he sell she to the mon at Baliceaux, but she never wake up, this mon t'ink."

"Okay, Sharktooth. Good work. Do we know how long ago they took her to Baliceaux?"

"He t'ink mebbe one week. They go Baliceaux to Haiti, then Haiti to Venezuela, then to Baliceaux, then to Rouseau, now back to Grenada wit' fruit. He say he hear the captain ax the Baliceaux mon 'bout the girl, an' the mon tell the captain she still out cold. That mean she alive an' she on Baliceaux day befo' yesterday."

"You're right. That's great news. You say they're coming to Grenada? The ship?"

"Yeah, mon. They leave las' night, mebbe stop in Kingstown, today, load more fruit. Prob'ly Grenada tomorrow, late. My cousin, he check the papers. Grenada, tomorrow, 1800, it say."

"What's the name of the ship, Sharktooth?"

"Name *Erzulie Freda*. The goddess of love in the Haiti Voodoo."

"Okay, Sharktooth. Can you catch the next flight down here? Tonight, if it's not too late. We need to have a serious talk with that captain, and I have a feeling I'm going to need your help."

"I hope you say that, Phillip. The plane leave in 30 minutes. I am at the airport, already have the ticket. I get to Grenada at 1930."

"Good. Thanks, Sharktooth. Take a taxi to the new marina across the lagoon from the yacht club. I'll meet you in the bar. I need to call J.-P. and give him the good news. See you in a little while."

"Blessings, Phillip," Sharktooth said, and disconnected.

J.-P. was delighted by the news, listening with rapt attention as Phillip translated Sharktooth's tangled report.

"Baliceaux?" J.-P. asked, when Phillip finished. Phillip could picture the uncertainty on his face.

"Yes. Baliceaux."

"That would make a good transfer point," J.-P. said, "but I did not know anybody was using it. I do not think anybody ever thought of it. I want to check with my partner in Buenos Aires, Phillip. Perhaps he has heard something about Baliceaux, and who is using it. You and Sharktooth go ahead and have your talk with the captain tomorrow, and then we will talk again. Perhaps I can discover who these people are by then."

"Okay, J.-P. Talk with you tomorrow." Phillip pressed the red disconnect button, but before he could put the phone down, it rang again.

"Hello, my love." Phillip hoped as he said it that his blind faith in caller ID didn't embarrass him.

"'Allo, Phillip. I have talk to the man in Pointe-à-Pitre. The *Sea Serpent*, she is not showing in the computer with customs in Guadeloupe. My friend, he says *Sea Serpent* is possibly clear into Les Saintes, or to Marie Galante, or perhaps somewhere else, and they are not using the computers. They are send the paper by fax, to someone with the computer, so, they are maybe there, or maybe not. There is no way to know for some days. Sorry. You still love me, Phillip?"

"You know I do, Sandrine. Thanks for checking." He told her about Sharktooth's discovery, and she wanted to know what they would do next. He gave her a rough outline of their plans, and was saying his goodbyes, when she interrupted.

"Phillip, I forget to tell you. My friend in Pointe-à-Pitre, he sets the trap in the computer, to know when the *Sea Serpent* comes."

"What's that, Sandrine? The trap?"

"He makes the computer so that it must tell him, when the *Sea*

Serpent, she is clearing in. Then he calls me with the information."

"Ah, okay. That's great, Sandrine. I'll be thinking about you until we talk again."

"Yes, Phillip. You and Sharktooth are having care. Bye-bye." And she was gone, leaving Phillip with a foolish smile on his face.

26

Phillip could smell meat frying as he woke up. He had made a grocery run late yesterday afternoon, knowing that Sharktooth started every day with a big breakfast.

Bacon and sausages, eggs, grits, several slices of bread fried in butter, and plenty of coffee were necessary to keep the big man going until "deenah," which was another big meal, usually a curry or stew of some sort, with peas and rice, eaten in the early afternoon.

With such fortification, Sharktooth usually didn't need any more food until the evening meal, eaten sometime shortly after sunset. Phillip imagined that he could hear the sound of his own arteries clogging, just from smelling the grease.

He reminded himself that he shouldn't try to keep up with Sharktooth's food consumption, no matter how wonderful it smelled and tasted. Sharktooth was big, but he didn't have much fat over the hard slabs of muscle.

Phillip had never known him to exercise, either, so he figured it had to be genetics that accounted for his friend's physique. He rolled out of his berth and squeezed past Sharktooth, reaching for a cup and pouring himself some coffee.

"What we do today, Phillip, after we eat?" Sharktooth asked.

"We've got some extra time, I think. *Erzulie Freda's* not due in until 6 o'clock, according to what you said. I figure they'll anchor right out there off the entrance channel and go into the terminal early tomorrow. Most of those guys don't want to pay the overtime to go in and unload after hours."

"My cousin, he say that what they do in Rouseau, too. Prob'ly you right, Phillip."

"We'll just sit out in the cockpit this afternoon and watch for them, then. If they anchor, we'll board them tonight. If it looks like they're going in, I'll call George Castle and we can stage some sort of customs search so you and I can get a shot at the captain by himself. What was his name, again?"

"Julio Garcia," Sharktooth said, around a mouthful of eggs. He was eating his breakfast from the skillet.

"Plates are in that locker over the stove," Phillip said.

"Have to wash the plate, Phillip. Already have to wash the skillet. Don' waste water; don' make extra work."

"Okay, suit yourself. Anyhow, if they anchor out there, we'll just take the dinghy over for a visit late tonight, don't you think?"

"Yeah, mon. That sound good. We go dungtung to the market this morning? Some good fish market in St. George's. Vegetable, too." Sharktooth had inventoried Phillip's provisions, and found them wanting.

"We can go downtown to the market, if you like. We should try to get some rest this afternoon, in case we have a late night. We just need to be back by late afternoon to watch for *Erzulie Freda*."

"After deenah be plenty of time," Sharktooth said, as he began to scour the skillet. "Got to eat, Phillip. Keep up the strengt', mon."

J.-P. HAD CALLED his partner in Buenos Aires as soon as he thought the man would be awake this morning. He was expecting a callback in a few hours. The man had known nothing about anyone using Baliceaux as a transshipment point, but he also expressed surprise that no one had thought of it before.

J.-P. was impatient to act. He had built his empire by leading from the front lines, not by managing from on high, and he was frustrated by the distance and time difference that separated him from the action.

He knew, though, that he had been out of the field too long to be on the front lines. His value was back here, working his contacts for information. The man in Buenos Aires would be better able to track down information from Venezuela or Colombia, but J.-P. thought that Mario might have something to offer in terms of the islands themselves. He owed his old friend in Miami an update, in any case.

"J.-P., good morning." Mario listened quietly as J.-P. brought him up to date.

"So, this is good news, J.-P. Phillip and Sharktooth are going to Baliceaux?"

"Yes, but I want to know what to expect there. We have no idea who these people are, nor do we know what we may find on the island. The freighter is due in Grenada this evening. Phillip and Sharktooth will question the captain before they go to Baliceaux, but the captain probably only knows enough to do his job. Do you know what I mean?"

"Sure. I understand. You want me to ask around? I still got some friends down in the islands. You know, from some of my other product lines — the stuff that you don't carry these days."

"That would be helpful," J.-P. said. "I would be grateful if you could do that."

"I'll call you back soon." Mario disconnected from J.-P. and immediately placed a call to St. Vincent. He had a cabinet level contact there, and he agreed to wait on hold until the man could take his call.

Most of Mario's dealings were legitimate, these days, as were J.-P.'s. They had both cut corners when they were younger and hungrier, but the times had been different.

While they had made their fortunes doing some things that were illegal, they had both had their limits. They had relied on their consciences to guide them.

The laws they had broken had been politically contrived rules that had been bought and paid for by people whose business interests were at odds with their own. Now that Mario had a son who was practicing law in Miami, he knew that there was a legal concept that described most of their criminal activities.

His son had explained that many, if not most, illegal acts were covered by the term, "*malum prohibitum*," literally meaning that they were only bad because they were prohibited by law, as opposed to those acts that were "*malum in se*," or bad in themselves.

His son had joked that Mario had spent a quarter of a million dollars on his legal education so that he could explain the difference well enough to keep his clients out of jail.

"Papa, it's no different from me asking you when I was about six why I shouldn't do something that seemed perfectly harmless to me. You would say, 'You shouldn't do it because I said you shouldn't. I'm your Papa, and I make the rules.' Same thing. That's *malum prohibitum*. When you told me not to kill my little sister, that was an example of *malum in se*. It would have still been wrong for me to kill her, even if you hadn't told me not to do it."

Mario thought the distinction was plain, and so did his business associates. They had never worried much about what he now knew were *malum prohibitum* activities. They were only wrong because their competition had outbid them when it came to buying politicians. He was virtually certain that politicians were *malum in se*, now that he thought about it.

The cabinet minister picked up the phone. Mario was careful to ask his questions in a way that didn't put the man in an awkward position. Mario knew that he was talking to one of the good guys.

The minister made it clear that he understood Mario's hidden questions, and he was a skillful politician, so he was able to couch his answers in terms that sounded as vague and innocuous as Mario's questions. The real answer came toward the end of the conversation, in the form of the man's closing comment.

"Well, Mr. Espinosa, I'm afraid I haven't been very helpful to you. It seems that I have told you only what you knew to begin with. Sorry I couldn't offer a different perspective."

If he hadn't already known that this guy was a lawyer, Mario would have guessed it. The minister had roomed with Mario's son when they were both learning those fancy words for things.

PHILLIP AND SHARKTOOTH HAD FINISHED "DEENAH," and were sitting in the shade in the cockpit, letting the heavy meal settle. Sharktooth was sharpening a wicked-looking filet knife that he had purchased at a fisherman's supply across the street from the fish market.

"They don' let you carry on the plane, Phillip."

Phillip had not asked Sharktooth any questions about the knife. He could guess what Sharktooth had in mind. Before they had gone to town, Sharktooth had asked if Phillip had weapons on board. Phillip had rattled off his inventory of firearms.

"From the old days, Sharktooth. Just a habit, you know."

He had gone on to voice the opinion that he didn't think they should carry firearms tonight. There was too much risk of trouble, in his view.

"But Phillip, you know the captain, he mus' have a gun. Prob'ly the engineer, too."

"We'll slip aboard and do what we need to do, Sharktooth. If we get into a gunfight, who will go get Dani? Maybe you'll get a chance to shoot somebody in Baliceaux. If we let that happen here, we'll be tied up with the police for days before we get it straightened out."

Sharktooth had nodded, seeing Phillip's point. He had settled for the new filet knife and a machete about two feet long, reasoning that those were tools that many people in the islands used. They wouldn't attract attention.

Phillip was reading as Sharktooth shifted his attention from the filet knife to the machete. The ringing of Phillip's cellphone startled both of them.

"That was J.-P.," Phillip said, after he hung up. "He sends you his best."

Sharktooth nodded, running a thumb over the edge of the machete, testing it.

"He says the people on Baliceaux are part of a gang from Venezuela. People call it El Grupo, but nobody is quite sure who's in charge. Some people think it's some crooks that are high up in the government, but that's mostly rumor. Whoever it is, they've got the fix in with somebody in St. Vincent, so he says not to bother trying to get the local authorities involved. It would just make trouble for the honest people, and we probably wouldn't get much help. Also, nobody seems to know about the women. The word was that the fix was in for drugs and money. If they're running women, nobody will be too upset about us shutting them down. The word J.-P. got was that the guy running Baliceaux could be trafficking in women on the side, without the higher-ups knowing. The crew on the island is usually small — probably no more than six people. They feel safe, because nobody knows they're there, so their security is loose. It should be pretty easy for us to snatch Dani."

"So what we want wit' the captain, Phillip? Just see what he know?"

"Yes. He can probably tell us how many people are there. Who's the boss? What's the layout? That kind of stuff."

"We gonna let he go when we through wit' he?"

"We'll see. We need to make sure that he and the engineer don't warn the people on the island. I haven't figured out how to do that. If we could keep them locked up for a couple of days, that might do it, but I don't see a way to do that. You got any ideas?"

"The captain an' the engineer, they drunks, Bill Clinton say. Mebbe they both get drunk an' kill the other one."

"Maybe. We'll watch what they do when they get anchored. We need to get the deck crew out of the way. That's for sure. No point in them getting hurt, from what you said. There were two men in the crew?"

"Yeah, mon. Unless they pick up somebody in St. Vincent to replace Bill Clinton."

Phillip placed a quick call to his friend the Chief Superintendent. Explaining that it was urgent, he waited on hold for about 10 minutes. "Four men, total. Captain, Engineer, two deck crew. That's it," he told Sharktooth when he disconnected.

"Here's what I think we should do," Phillip said, after a few minutes of thought. "I'll put on a black dive skin and some face paint, so I won't glow in the dark like a white man. We should be able to drift the dinghy out to them, because they'll be downwind. That way, we won't have the noise of the outboard to worry about. I've got a big magnet. We'll stick that to the hull and tie the dinghy off to it. We'll both scale the side together. We'll go about 3 a.m. Everybody should be asleep by then. I doubt they'll have anybody on anchor watch in a place like this. If we see anybody on deck, I'll take out the first one and you back me up. Then you take the next one. If nobody's on deck, we'll work our way forward. If *Erzulie Freda*'s like most of these old rust buckets, the deck crew's quarters will be in the forecastle, don't you think?"

Sharktooth nodded.

"If the two men are in there, we'll take them first, both at the same time, if we can. Knock them out; zip ties, duct tape. Right?"

"Mm-hmm," Sharktooth said.

"Then we'll work our way aft. The captain's cabin is probably up aft of the bridge. The engineer probably bunks down amidships. I'll go up and take the captain; you take the engineer. Once he's tied and gagged, bring him along. Come find me on the bridge and we'll see what he and Julio can tell us about Baliceaux. Okay so far?"

"Okay."

Phillip sat quietly, thinking. Sharktooth waited.

"I think your idea is the best, Sharktooth. They got drunk, and argued. The captain shot the engineer, then realized what he had done and shot himself. Happens sometimes, yes?"

"Yes, mon."

"I've still got one of those cheap little .38s. Remember them?"

"Argentina?" Sharktooth raised his eyebrows.

Phillip nodded. "We'll take it, just in case the captain doesn't have a gun. Better if he uses his own gun, but if he doesn't have one, we'll lend him one. I'm sure those cheap .38s are still scattered all up and down the islands, so it won't look out of place on a crappy little freighter."

Sharktooth went below and came back with two cold soft drinks, knowing from previous ventures with Phillip how he felt about alcohol when he was working. They settled back on the cockpit cushions to wait.

PHILLIP SAW from a lighted digital clock on the bulkhead in the captain's cabin that it was 3:25 a.m. Everything had gone according to plan, so far. The two crewmen had duct tape over their mouths and their eyes before they were awake, and they were secured in the forecastle for now.

Sharktooth had gone below in search of the engineer. The noise of a generator was audible throughout the ship, conveniently masking the various little scraping and bumping sounds that Sharktooth and Phillip had made as they felt their way around in the dark.

The captain was snoring, loudly. Phillip decided to wake him up. He was sure he could keep him entertained until Sharktooth and the engineer joined them. He reached out and shook the man, none too gently. The captain sat up quickly, the reflex action a result of years at sea, no doubt. He was immediately awake.

"*Qué pasa?*" he asked, turning on the cabin lights, momentarily dazzling Phillip. "*Quién es?*" he asked, looking at Phillip with his one eye.

"You speak English?" Phillip asked, shoving his flashlight into the man's solar plexus as he tried to stand. The captain doubled over and sat down hard on the edge of his berth, gasping for air. Phillip stood over him, waiting until he recovered.

"I asked you a question, Julio," he said in a conversational tone. "It is better for you if you answer me."

"*Sí*, okay. Yes," the man said, still sitting, trying to catch his breath.

The cabin light flickered and went out, and the generator stopped. The captain seized the chance to deliver a head butt to Phillip's chin, knocking him down and stunning him for a moment.

Phillip shook his head, trying to clear his vision as he got to his feet. Just as he stood up, the captain turned from the drawer by his berth, a rusty revolver in his hand, pointed at Phillip.

"Now I will ask the questions," Julio said, then yelled in pain as he grabbed his right wrist. Phillip's foot had moved so fast that Julio never saw the kick that broke his arm. Phillip picked up the gun from the cabin sole.

"You're going to need this later, Julio. I'll just keep it for you," Phillip said, as the generator and the lights came back on.

He put the pistol into a small waist pack and pulled out two zip ties.

"I'm going to put these on you now. You can make it easy, or not. Your choice."

The captain glared at him for a few seconds, fury in his one eye. Then he looked down and extended his arms toward Phillip, wrists together.

He winced as Phillip tightened the tie around his right wrist, already swelling from the damage wrought by Phillip's kick. Phillip had just shoved him back to a sitting position on the berth behind him when Sharktooth came in.

"Irie," Sharktooth said, an evil grin displaying his collection of gold teeth.

"Where's the engineer?" Phillip asked.

"He have a accident. He fall in the 'lectricicals, stop the generator. Stop he, too. He try to run away. 'Lectricicals very dangerous. You need one more engineer, Julio," Sharktooth said, pulling the gleaming filet knife from his waistband. "Julio look hot, Phillip. Okay I he'p he take he shirt off? Cool he down some?"

Phillip nodded, and Sharktooth made a graceful, waving motion around the seated man with the hand that held the knife. Julio's shirt fell away in three pieces as he screamed, in fear or pain. Phillip wasn't sure which.

"Uh-oh, I cut he, Phillip. Nassabad, though. Jus' a wee bit. Need to get practice again," Sharktooth said, running a banana-sized index finger along the thin red line on top of Julio's shoulder as a few drops of blood oozed out.

"Not so bad is right, Sharktooth. It's not your fault. I saw him move. I don't think you would have cut him if he had been still. You think if I stand him up, you can take his pants off without cutting him?"

"Don' know. I try."

Sharktooth turned on the evil grin, licking his filet knife as he gave a bone-chilling laugh. The cabin lights gleamed on his bald head as his dreadlocks shook with his demented laughter. Phillip was a little worried that he had truly gone around the bend.

Phillip jerked the captain to his feet, turning him to face Sharktooth.

"What do you want?" the captain asked. "I have the drugs. I show you. Give them to you. Maybe you can get away before my bosses catch you. You could be rich, maybe."

"That's the way, Julio. Sharktooth can practice another time, if you'd rather talk to me."

"Yes, yes. What you want to know?"

Julio told Sharktooth and Phillip all about the operation at Baliceaux, including the names that he knew, the routines of the establishment, and the number of guards and their normal patrolling arrangements.

As Phillip and J.-P. had suspected, the people on the island felt secure. Their competitors didn't know of their existence, and the local authorities were their allies.

Before Phillip and Sharktooth left, Sharktooth made another showy sweep with the filet knife, and the zip ties fell away from Julio's wrists. Sharktooth handed Julio his rusty little revolver, and Julio, apparently overcome with remorse for his evil ways, or perhaps by Sharktooth's superior strength, put the muzzle in his mouth.

With only a little help from Sharktooth, he was able to pull the trigger, even with his swollen wrist. There was a loud snap, as the primer in the corroded bullet casing failed to ignite the powder, and Julio had to try a second time.

Sharktooth bowed his head and made the sign of the cross over Julio's remains, while Phillip gathered up everything that they had brought aboard. They went back to the forecastle, gave the two crewmen each a gentle tap on their heads to put them back to sleep, and took off the duct tape and the zip ties.

No longer worried about stealth, they cranked the outboard and went back to *Kayak Spirit*. Phillip was hoping for a nap before Sharktooth got involved in preparing his next meal.

27

Phillip had enjoyed a brief nap, and while Sharktooth was cooking breakfast, Phillip took the dinghy to the yacht club. He was the first in line at the Customs and Immigration office, and he quickly secured his outbound clearance for Union Island in St. Vincent and the Grenadines.

He was back aboard *Kayak Spirit* by 8:10, and he and Sharktooth had stowed the dinghy and gotten underway by 8:30. After an early morning check-in with J.-P., they had decided to sail to Mustique today.

Union Island was the first port of entry for St. Vincent and the Grenadines on their way north, and it was convenient for a quick stop. It would be a push to get to Union today before the customs and immigration offices closed, but they had a fair wind, about 20 knots from the southeast, and full diesel tanks. They would make it, even if they had to keep the diesel running the whole way.

Once they cleared in at Union Island, Mustique was only another 20 miles. They should be there by late evening, and they planned to pick up one of the moorings in Britannia Bay. The moorings were expensive, priced to keep the riffraff out, but the people in the big houses liked to have a few visiting yachts in the harbor to enhance their view.

It was only three miles from Britannia Bay to Landing Bay on Baliceaux, and *Kayak Spirit* would be hidden in plain view among the other visiting vessels in Britannia Bay. They would take the dinghy for the short run to Baliceaux in the early hours of tomorrow morning.

They were gambling that there would be no delivery in progress at Baliceaux, but Phillip reasoned that it would be easy enough to abort and come back later if they found Landing Bay occupied. If things went smoothly, they would be back on *Kayak Spirit* with Dani before sunrise. They would leave for Bequia promptly.

Phillip planned to stop in Bequia long enough to clear out, but they would leave immediately. He wanted to be out of St. Vincent's waters before anyone discovered what had happened on Baliceaux.

He would not mention Dani on the clearance documents, which was illegal, but he didn't have a passport for her, so he had no other option but to conceal her presence. Their next stop would be Martinique, which was 90 miles away.

It was a long haul, but the French islands were notoriously lax about clearance for yachts. The French knew what made a destination attractive to tourist trade, and it didn't involve lots of official paperwork.

Besides, Dani had dual French and U.S. citizenship, and Sandrine ran the customs office in Marin, where he would clear in. Sharktooth would fly home from Martinique, and Dani could recuperate from her ordeal at Phillip's place.

That was their plan, except for the details of freeing Dani. They had learned from Julio that there were no other captives being held on Baliceaux now. He had explained that Dani was in a cell that was fitted out as a 2-bed infirmary, and she was under the care of a well-qualified medic named Rosa, with two military-trained nurses to assist.

The three women were there because, as Julio put it, "Sometime, the women we bring, they are not so well, and Rosa, she take care of them, so they sell better, for more money."

The holding area for the women was a motel-like structure covered with camouflage netting to prevent notice from the aircraft that were frequently in the area. From the little harbor, Landing Bay, it was about 300 yards up the hillside, in a northerly direction.

There was a path up the hillside, but neither the structure nor the path could be seen from the harbor. There were also three men who served as security guards and stevedores. They lived in a rough shack right on the shore of the harbor.

It had been a fisherman's camp, at some point. Merchandise was stored on pallets under camouflage tarps in the woods, immediately behind the guards' shack. The three men were normally armed.

Julio didn't think that the three women were armed but he didn't know. He said that they had all been soldiers — Rosa, the boss, in Cuba and Angola, and the other two in Venezuela. Phillip knew better than to underestimate them.

He and Sharktooth would assume everybody but Dani was dangerous. Julio's final contribution was that "*El Jefe*," the big boss, called Big Jim, usually came to the island only when a shipment was expected. He lived nearby on Mustique, but Julio didn't know his real name.

As they sailed from Grenada to Union Island, Sharktooth and Phillip took turns, one sailing, the other resting. They had only slept a few hours last night before their visit to *Erzulie Freda*, and they had a couple of hard days ahead of them.

Veteran campaigners, they took rest where they could. They both knew that sleep and food always improved the odds of success.

They anchored behind the reef in Clifton Harbor on Union Island at about four o'clock, and Phillip waved down a local boat and caught a ride ashore to save the time of assembling his dinghy. He gave the fisherman $10 E.C. and two cold beers to drop him at the main freight dock, just across the street from Customs.

He cleared customs with 15 minutes to spare before the office closed, and took a taxi to the airport to the immigration office there. The officer was idle, as there were no flights for a couple of hours, and Phillip was finished quickly.

He went back outside to look for a taxi, and found the driver who brought him, flirting with the ladies in the tourist office. Phillip was back on *Kayak Spirit* and they were under way for Mustique by five o'clock.

Phillip figured that they would arrive in Mustique and pick up a mooring or, if all the moorings were taken, they would anchor. It would be too late for anyone to collect the fee.

If their business went smoothly, they might be gone before the harbormaster showed up the next morning, in which case there would be no record of their visit. He was hoping that it would work out that way.

He and Sharktooth were both well rested and awake on this leg of their journey. They used the time to refine their plans for their raid on Baliceaux.

They both favored the window of time between three and four in the morning. Even most night owls had gone to sleep by then, and any sentries who were awake were likely to be groggy from boredom.

From what Julio told them, there would be no guard on duty, but they were both still alive because they were cautious. After a look at the chart showing the island and the reefs around the southern tip, they decided to land the dinghy in the large cove to the north of Landing Bay.

They would kill the outboard and paddle the last half mile of their three-mile trip to avoid making noise that might announce their approach. Landing in the northern cove would put a ridgeline between them and the guards' camp in the harbor.

They would ready the dinghy for a hasty departure, just in case, and swim or wade across the reef on the point between their landing spot and Landing Bay. Once around the point, they would go ashore and work their way through the brush to approach the guards' camp from the rear.

They would eliminate the three guards, silently if possible, with silenced weapons otherwise, and go up to the house. They planned to lock Rosa and her two aides in one of the unoccupied cells, find Dani, and leave as quietly as they came.

PHILLIP AND SHARKTOOTH were hip-deep in the warm, calm water. They had tied the dinghy to a large piece of driftwood along the steep stretch of shoreline at their chosen spot. Phillip was relieved that they didn't have to beach the dinghy; that would have slowed their departure.

He didn't expect that they would be in a hurry, but it was best to avoid potential complications. You never knew what could go wrong.

They were able to wade over the coral reef that came out from the north point of Landing Bay, which eliminated another of Phillip's worries. They might have to carry Dani back to the dinghy, and it would be better if they didn't have to swim with her in tow.

As they rounded the point, they could see into Landing Bay. The moon was near full, and the silvery light rendered the landscape in eerie tones, not quite black and white, but colors weren't distinguishable, either.

There was less vegetation than they had expected, so they moved from rock to rock, making the most of the little cover that they found. They were working their way along the shoreline of Landing Bay, about 50 yards uphill from the water.

Phillip was in the lead, and Sharktooth was about 10 paces behind him, far enough so that if someone spotted Phillip, they would most likely mistake him for a lone intruder. They carried silenced .40 caliber pistols, but both preferred edged weapons for this sort of work.

It was a matter of pride with Phillip. If he had to shoot someone, he counted it as a failure of planning or execution, and he didn't like failure of any kind.

Phillip stopped, dropping to a crouch, and looked around, listening intently as his eyes scanned the moonlit terrain. He could barely make out Sharktooth, but saw that he, too, was melting into the rocky hillside, motionless.

Satisfied that they were unobserved, Phillip took careful note of his immediate surroundings. He had stopped because the character of the terrain underfoot had changed abruptly. He had come upon a well-worn path, perpendicular to his direction of travel.

That would be the path from the camp at Landing Bay up to the compound where Dani was being held. He motioned Sharktooth forward and pointed out the path. Sharktooth nodded.

They turned to their right and started down the hill toward the camp, Phillip a few yards to the right of the path, Sharktooth a few yards to the left. Within a few paces, they came upon the goods stored on pallets — low, bulky shapes in the moonlight.

They went around opposite sides of the pallets, and as soon as they could see one another again, they spotted the back wall of the guard shack. They maintained their separation from each other and moved forward, planning to round the sides of the shack and converge on the entrance.

As Phillip approached the back corner, he smelled stale cooking odors, and he could hear snoring. It didn't take much of an ear to realize that there were at least two participants in the nocturnal concert.

Phillip concentrated on the rhythms, and then began to separate the higher and lower pitched sounds. Three. All of them were asleep.

Phillip reached the front corner and peered around it, crouching and keeping his body pressed to the wall. He made out Sharktooth doing the same from the other side. Sharktooth grinned at him, moonlight glinting on gold teeth.

Phillip held up three fingers on his right hand and then folded his hands together, putting them against the side of his face as he tipped his head to the side. Sharktooth nodded.

Phillip stood and stepped around the corner, Sharktooth mirroring his movements until they came together at the doorway in the front wall of the shack. With the coordination that came from having done this sort of thing together before, Phillip stepped in and to the left as Sharktooth stepped in and to the right.

Two members of the chorus were silenced abruptly as knives entered their kidneys, strong hands covering their mouths and pinning them in place briefly. The men died almost soundlessly, and Phillip was surprised to turn and find the third man awake and charging him.

Light sleeper, he thought, as he pivoted at the hip and slammed the sole of his right foot into the man's sternum, lifting him clear of the floor. Before Phillip recovered from his kick, he saw a huge brown arm snake around the man's neck from the back.

Sharktooth put his other hand on the crown of the man's head. There was a muffled snap, and he laid the man back in his bed.

Phillip and Sharktooth held their silence. They went back to the trail, retracing their steps, and worked their way quietly up the hill, each a few yards off the path. There was still the possibility that Big Jim was on the island, or that one of the women was awake.

They reached the little building without any further excitement. It looked like a seedy motel with 10 rooms, each having a door onto the long, roofed front porch.

They started at opposite ends, knowing that Rosa and her helpers had an apartment made by combining the two rooms in the center. Sharktooth worked from the left end; Phillip from the right, converging on Rosa's quarters.

There was an unlocked padlock hanging on each door they passed. Sharktooth opened the unlocked doors as he went, finding each room empty. Phillip did the same, until he reached the door next to the two in the center.

He looked over and saw Sharktooth watching him, waiting for him to approach the two remaining doors. Phillip pointed at the lock on the door where he stood.

Sharktooth nodded, and they entered the two unlocked center doors at the same time. They found a single large room, dimly lighted by a kerosene lantern turned down to a minimal flame. There was a kitchen along one side wall and three occupied beds along the other one.

The two men moved simultaneously, advancing on the beds at each end. The two women in the end beds were duct-taped and zip-tied to their beds with almost no sound.

Phillip looked up as he finished, right into the gaping muzzle of a .45 Colt. He barely had time to process what he was seeing when the hand holding the pistol opened, dropping it, as the woman gasped in shock.

Phillip caught the pistol instinctively and stepped aside as she collapsed. Sharktooth pulled the filet knife from her right kidney and wiped it on her nightgown.

"Keys," Phillip said. It was the first word either had uttered since leaving *Kayak Spirit*. Sharktooth shook his head.

"No need," Sharktooth said, walking outside. He took the

padlock on the locked door in his big right hand and rolled it to the side, almost effortlessly.

There was a tearing sound as the wooden doorjamb gave way, and they went into the room, using flashlights for the first time. Dani was unconscious, an IV bag hanging beside her hospital bed.

"Looks like we carry her." Phillip disconnected the tube from her arm.

"No problem, mon," Sharktooth said.

"Phillip?" Dani asked, sitting up and opening her eyes.

Phillip jumped, startled. Sharktooth would have looked pale, if he knew how.

"Dani, we thought you were in a coma," Phillip said.

"I was, I guess, but I've been awake for a couple of days. I've just faked being semi-conscious, trying to figure out what was going on. I could tell something was strange, from what I was hearing. I knew this was no hospital. Where am I?"

"Baliceaux, but that's a long story. I'll tell you what I know later. Right now, we need to get out of here. Can you walk?"

"Sure. I mean, I think so. I haven't tried," she said, getting unsteadily to her feet.

28

Liz was in *Sea Serpent's* head putting on her makeup. She and Mike had enjoyed a glorious sail from Marie Galante to Les Saintes yesterday afternoon, arriving ahead of the daily crowd of bareboat charters. Getting in early, they had their choice of anchorages. They settled on the little bight on the south side of Îlet à Cabrít, where they dropped the anchor 50 yards from the beach.

Liz had jumped in the gin-clear water to swim ashore with a stern line. Once she tied it to a bush growing among the rocks along shore, Mike winched it in, pointing the bow out into the slight swell that wrapped around the little island.

With the swell on the bow instead of the beam, *Sea Serpent* was as steady as if she were sitting on shore, and they could sit in the cockpit and watch the fish on the live coral reef a few feet below them. They had dined in the cockpit, making a meal of *baguette*, *pâté*, cheese, and olives that they brought from Marie Galante. Washing it all down with a crisp, white French table wine, they had watched the stars until the wine was finished. They had gone to bed early, waking with the sun this morning.

Bourg des Saintes, the big town, was a short dinghy ride

across the harbor. Liz wanted to do some shopping, having read about several well-known local artists who sold from small galleries in the town.

She was about to put her things away in the locker that Mike referred to as the "guest" locker when she inadvertently opened the one next to it. As she pushed the door closed, she glimpsed an expensive designer handbag. Liz wondered about that; it didn't fit in with what Mike had told her.

The topic of other women hadn't entered into their conversation, except for a passing reference to his ex-wife. He had been single for years, so she didn't think that the bag could have been his wife's. Liz wasn't a nosy person, and it was none of her business, anyway, so she put it out of her mind. As she stowed her makeup bag and retrieved her own purse, she heard Mike's voice from the cockpit.

"What's that, Mike? I'll be right up," she called, her voice soft. She didn't want to disturb their neighbors. There were other boats anchored close by, and it was early. Mike didn't answer; she thought that maybe he was conversing with someone on another boat.

Slinging her bag over her shoulder and closing her locker, she walked barefooted to the companionway. Her sandals were in the cockpit. Most people didn't wear shoes below deck, especially on yachts with such finely varnished cabin soles.

As she climbed the ladder, she could hear Mike quite clearly. He was talking with two people, she thought, Michelle and Dani. They must be from one of the charter boats nearby. Maybe they were out for an early morning swim. As she came into the cockpit, he turned to her, a faraway look on his face.

"I'm ready to go when you are, Mike," she said.

He looked at her blankly, for just a couple of beats longer than she thought normal.

"Mike?" she said, frowning.

He jerked in his seat, startled. "Oh! Good morning. Must have spaced out. Sorry." He smiled sheepishly.

She looked over the side, peering around.

"What's wrong, Liz?"

"Nothing. I thought I heard swimmers. That's all," she said, deciding not to mention hearing him talking. She sensed that he was already a little uncomfortable that she had caught him daydreaming.

"Oh. I didn't see anybody," he said. "Ready to do the town?"

"Let's go. First, we'll hit the galleries and then pick up a couple of baguettes somewhere. Maybe we can get back here for lunch before the hot part of the day." She picked up her sandals and pulled the dinghy alongside as Mike closed and locked the boat.

PHILLIP AND SHARKTOOTH brought *Kayak Spirit* into Admiralty Bay and anchored under sail. They had managed to get away from Mustique before dawn, covering the twelve miles to Bequia in about two hours. By the time they were anchored, it was late enough for Phillip to take the dinghy ashore and clear out for Martinique.

Since the entire trip was in protected waters, they had towed the dinghy. That made for a quick trip ashore. Phillip was back within 30 minutes. He and Sharktooth took the outboard off and stowed it on Kayak Spirit's stern rail. Hoisting the dinghy, they swung it aboard, since they were going to push all the way to Martinique nonstop. Phillip didn't want to be caught in a squall in open water with the dinghy trailing astern.

As they made sail again, Dani came up into the cockpit and sat down, taking the tiller. Phillip and Sharktooth trimmed the sails as she held them on a broad reach.

"Sure you feel up to that?" Phillip asked.

Dani had been too unsteady on her feet to walk to the dinghy when they left Baliceaux. Once aboard *Kayak Spirit*, she stretched out on the settee and fell asleep.

When they were close enough to Bequia to have cellphone service, she had still been sleeping soundly. Phillip had called J.-P. to report that Dani was safe aboard *Kayak Spirit*, and that they would call him again when she woke up. J.-P. thanked him profusely and told him that he had arranged to have a replacement passport for Dani sent overnight to French Customs in Martinique, to Sandrine's attention. It should arrive tomorrow morning.

"I'm okay," Dani said. "I had a bowl of cereal before I came up, while you were hoisting the dinghy. Washing my face did wonders, too. Besides, I've had plenty of rest, lately. We were in Bequia?"

"Just checked out. Next stop, Marin. Sharktooth's flying home from there, and you can recuperate at my house."

She looked at him for several seconds, frowning, and shook her head. "I'll recuperate while we chase that son of a bitch on *Sea Serpent*. I have a score to settle with him. How long have I been out, anyway?"

"A little over a week, we think," he said, happy to see that she was indeed almost back to her normal, pugnacious self. "You need to call your father, before we lose cellphone service again. Phone's in the drawer under the chart table. I talked with him a little while ago and let him know you were with us, and sleeping off your ordeal." Phillip took the tiller from her, falling off to a west by northwesterly course as Sharktooth trimmed the sails again.

Dani went below to make her call, and Sharktooth looked at Phillip. "She some vex, that gal. I not wish to be that Mike Reilly." He displayed the gold teeth.

"Me either, Sharktooth."

"I stay, if you need me."

"I know you would. I'm not sure what's next, though. I think we want to get her checked out by a doctor before we make too many plans. You might as well go home. I'll call you."

"Okay, Phillip, but if they gonna be a ruckus, I don' want to miss it, mon."

"Don't worry. We wouldn't let that happen."

Dani returned to the cockpit and sat back on the leeward seat next to Sharktooth.

"It was all I could do to keep him from getting on a plane," she said. "The only way I could stop him was by telling him we might not be going to Martinique. Reilly's headed north; he spends the winter working in the Virgins. I'd like to catch him before he gets that close to civilization."

"What does your father think about that?" Phillip asked.

Dani shrugged. "I don't know. I told him, but he was still yelling. I hung up; you can't have a conversation with him when he's like that."

"I'm surprised he hasn't already called back," Phillip said.

"I turned off the phone. He'll figure we've lost service, and that'll give him time to cool off. I'll call him back later."

Sharktooth was laughing quietly, shaking his head. "She jus' like the ol' man, Phillip. Jus' like he."

"Since you're up here, you might as well tell us what you remember," Phillip said. "All we know is that you left *Rambling Gal* unexpectedly in Mayreau."

"Yeah, that guy was a jerk. He was bad enough the first time I was aboard, on the trip out from the U.K. When we started this season, he made it plain that he wanted some personal attention, besides my official duties, which already covered everything *but* sleeping with him.

"He got insistent while his wife and the kids were touring the turtle sanctuary in Bequia. I should have bailed out then, but I didn't. Anyhow, while he and his wife were ashore in Mayreau, I scouted the boats in the anchorage.

"Reilly was there, on this gorgeous old Concordia yawl. He's a single hander, in a hurry to get north and get to work. I have a soft spot for old wooden boats, so I joined him. I expected to have to fight off his advances, but that's nothing new. Besides, he wanted to sail straight through, so I figured we wouldn't be seeing much of one another anyway. He was a fruitcake.

"We went to the Tobago Cays right after I came aboard, so that guy from *Rambling Gal* didn't get a chance to make trouble in Mayreau. We met another couple right when we got there. They came aboard for drinks. Everything was fine until they left.

"While I was putting away the snacks and stuff in the galley, he stayed up in the cockpit to finish his drink. He started talking to himself. Actually, he was talking to a bunch of different people, but nobody was there. I think they were all women, too.

"That was pretty creepy, you know? I finished in the galley and took a shower while he was still jabbering away. When I came out, he was still in the cockpit, but quiet, so I went to sleep on the settee berth in the main cabin. I guess he came below and went up forward sometime during the night. When I woke up, he was asleep in the V-berth.

"I made a pot of coffee, and he woke up. He seemed normal, then. We made sail, and I asked him about customs. He said he'd cleared from St. George's to Rodney Bay. I pointed out that I wasn't on any of the documents. He looked worried, so I suggested we make a stop in Martinique or Guadeloupe.

"Either place, they don't usually ask for the clearance from your last port, so he could add me to the crew list there, and nobody would know the difference by the time we hit the Virgins. He thought that was a good idea.

"He said since he was already sailing, he'd take the first watch. I went below, set an alarm, and went to sleep. Four hours later — must have been around one o'clock in the afternoon, I guess — I put on my life vest and went up on deck to relieve him. He looked at me like I was a Martian or something.

"He was completely spooked. He shoved me away, and before

I could get my feet under myself, he swung at me with a winch handle. I tried to duck, but I was still down. I guess he got me with the winch handle on his second try. That's all I remember, until I started coming around at that place where you found me."

"I'm impressed," Phillip said.

"Why, Phillip? I should have been able to take him."

"No, Dani, not that. I'm impressed that your recollection is so coherent."

"Oh. Well, I had a couple of days in bed with almost no interruptions between the time I came out of my coma and the time you showed up. I had nothing to do except try to figure out how I got there. I have no idea what happened after he attacked me."

"Well, here's what we learned," Phillip began, and he brought her up to speed.

Sharktooth went below and came back with the makeup kit he'd found on *Sea Serpent*. Dani was pleased to get the watch back, but she was puzzled about the bag and the rest of the jewelry.

"I put the watch on a ledge over the settee berth before I went to sleep. I've never seen the other things. I don't wear stuff like that. Think it's souvenirs he's collected?"

"Who knows?" Phillip asked.

Dani, Sharktooth, and Phillip each stood watches through the day. Phillip wouldn't let Dani stay on watch for more than two hours at a stretch, but her condition improved steadily through the day. By mid-day, Phillip wouldn't have known there was anything wrong with her, except for the shaved area with the stitches above her left ear.

They got into Marin about one o'clock the next morning and eased *Kayak Spirit* into her slip at the marina. Too tired to get in Phillip's car and drive the few miles to his house, they spent the rest of the night aboard.

29

As Dani had predicted, J.-P. had cooled off after his first conversation with her. Once he was over the shock, he was amused. She was his daughter. No question about that; her temper alone was sufficient proof.

He agreed that Mike Reilly should be brought to justice, but he had a little more patience than Dani, and now that he thought about it, a little less of a need for personal, hands-on vengeance. He could understand her desire to have Reilly at her mercy, though.

He had called Mario to tell him the good news and caught him at breakfast with his cronies, again. After J.-P.'s summary, Mario told him that Paul Russo had taken a personal interest in Reilly. He had passed his phone to Paul at J.-P.'s request.

"Thank you for all of the work you did. I'm forever in your debt," J.-P. said to Paul.

"I'm relieved to hear that your daughter is well, Mr. Berger," Paul said. "I think that Reilly should be arrested and brought to trial. With her testimony, I think we could put him away for a while — maybe for life. I don't think Dani's his first victim, and if somebody doesn't stop him, she won't be his last. That's for sure."

"Please, Paul, call me J.-P. I am just another old warrior like Mario. He has told me about your suspicions of this Mike Reilly. Do you think that Reilly killed his wife?"

"Well, I do, and so does the detective who investigated her disappearance, but there's no evidence to tie him to it, unfortunately. There's no doubt that he tried to kill Dani, from what I overheard of your conversation with Mario."

"No, I do not think there is doubt. I believe he tried to kill her. You do not know my daughter, but she's a hot-tempered girl. She's going after Reilly, personally. I understand that. She has inherited this from me, I think.

"However, I do not want her to get herself in trouble with the authorities over a vendetta. I would prefer that this Reilly is arrested. My daughter can have her vengeance through the courts.

"She thinks I am just being an old man, and perhaps I am. The problem is, I worry that Dani may kill this Reilly before the authorities are able to arrest him. Then she may be the one in trouble."

"I think I know how to have him arrested," Paul said. "*Sea Serpent* is U.S.-flagged. That makes her and anybody on board subject to the jurisdiction of the U.S. federal courts, and a federal officer can board her and arrest Reilly for crimes committed on board, anywhere in the world — even down in the islands."

"Are you a lawyer besides being a policeman, Paul? You sound like Mario's son."

"No, just an old, retired policeman, but I've done this before. You can't work homicides in South Florida for as long as I did without running across this sort of problem. Every know-it-all crook down here thinks he can do anything he wants as long as he does it on a boat outside the 12-mile limit."

"So how would this work?" J.-P. asked.

"Well, here's what I think we should do. We'll get Mario's son to find a federal judge who'll sign an arrest warrant. That shouldn't be a big deal. I'm already a special deputy U.S. Marshall, from when I used to do this kind of thing.

"I'll fly to Martinique with the warrant tonight and go with your daughter. That way, whatever happens, there won't be any trouble with the local authorities."

"I see, Paul. I am grateful for your offer, and I accept. I will never be able to repay you, but anything you ever want that is in my power is yours. That is my only condition."

"All right. Just so there's no misunderstanding, you tell your daughter that my goal is to bring this scumbag back and lock him up until the court decides what to do with him. He might decide to resist arrest. I understand that. If he doesn't come willingly, anything could happen. We might have to kill him, but we're setting out to arrest him, not to lynch him, okay?"

"I understand. I will explain this to her. Thank you again," J.-P. said.

"I'M HOME FROM THE SEA," Phillip said, when Sandrine answered his early morning call.

Her voice was husky with sleep. "You are at the villa, Phillip?"

"No, we're on the boat, at the marina."

"Who besides you?" she asked.

"Sharktooth and Dani. Why don't you come down to the restaurant on the dock and we'll all have breakfast before you go to work?"

"Yes, Phillip. Okay. I have try all yesterday to call you, but I go to the voice mail. I have some news."

"What news, Sandrine?"

"It is keeping. I tell you at the restaurant, soon, yes?"

"Okay," he said, disconnecting.

Dani took the phone from his hand.

"I'll go first thing when the place across the street opens and get a new phone. I lost mine... Oh, but you know that."

She scrolled through the directory to find her father's number and called him.

"Hello, Papa," she said.

There was a pause of a few seconds as she listened to J.-P.

"Yes, we're in Marin," she said.

She listened again.

"Okay. He is here? Paul Russo?" Another pause, then, "You want to speak to Phillip?" Pause. "Okay, I'll tell him. He can call if he has a problem with it. Love you, too, Papa."

She disconnected the call and turned to Phillip.

"There is a man here, a friend of Mario's, named Paul Russo, from Miami. He's a U.S. Marshal, and he has a warrant to arrest Michael Reilly. He'll go with us to look for *Sea Serpent*, so that we're covered with the local authorities if we have any trouble. My father says '...do not worry,' he is one of us. He'll be calling on your cellphone. You know him?"

"We've spoken a few times," Phillip said, and he went on to explain Paul's involvement.

"Good morning, Sandrine," Phillip said, holding her chair as she sat down at their table. "You know Sharktooth, and this is Dani Berger."

"Good morning, everyone," Sandrine said, picking up her napkin. "Dani, I am so happy that you are well. I have heard all about you from Phillip."

"Thank you," Dani said. "Phillip has told me how much you helped. Thank you for that, especially."

Sandrine smiled and nodded.

"Okay. What's your news?" Phillip asked.

"Yes. I have two news. First, the trap. The trap has catch the

Sea Serpent. She has clear in at Marie Galante, some days ago, at the tourism office and they are not fax the form, just as we thought. I have call the police there, and he say that the *Sea Serpent* is not there now.

"Also, it is small town, everyone watches. A girl leaves on the *Sea Serpent* with Mike Reilly. She has been staying there at a hotel. She is Liesbet Chirac, on holiday from Belgium.

"The police, he also tell me that Mike Reilly is cut badly on both arms, and goes to the clinic there, to be stitched. Mike Reilly tells the nurse it is from the fishing, but she does not believe him. She sees many injuries from the knife fights when she work in Pointe-à-Pitre, she say. She say these cuts is from the knife fight."

"What about Michelle Devereaux?" Phillip asked.

"That is my second news. She is not on the form from the *Sea Serpent* coming to Guadeloupe, so, where is she? We don't know, but that is not really the second news. Really, the second news is the police here find her missing boyfriend in Marin.

"He is dead some days, and the other people in the building are smelling him. They call the police, who discover him. He is cut many times, and has died from bleeding. The police are want to ask questions to Michelle Devereaux. I have told them what you have told me about her, but nobody finds her, anywhere."

Sharktooth, having put away enough food to hold him for a few hours, excused himself to go to the airport. "But Phillip, don' forget, if there is a fight, I mus' not be lef' out. You promise me this."

Phillip grinned. "I promise."

30

"Phillip Davis? This is Paul Russo. I hope you were expecting this call," Phillip heard, as he answered his cellphone. He was holding the front door open for Dani. "Yes. Mario told me you'd be calling. Bear with me a minute, please. Dani and I just walked in the door."

"No problem," Paul said.

Phillip held the phone as he and Dani opened the windows on the ground floor, letting the cool breeze blow through. They opened the doors onto the veranda, and Phillip motioned Dani to a lounge chair, taking another for himself.

"Sorry, Paul. Thanks for waiting. The place is like an oven. It's been closed up tight for a few days. J.-P. told us that you'd be in Martinique this morning."

"Yes. I got in late last night. I'm in a funky little resort hotel — can't figure out if it's in Anse Mitan or Trois-Îlets. There seems to be some confusion."

"If you look out over the water, do you see anchored yachts in front of you and a ferry dock to your left?" Phillip asked.

"Yes, that's right," Paul said.

"Okay. I know where you are. Why don't you go ahead and check out, and I'll come pick you up as soon as I get Dani settled. I'll be coming down the street that dead ends into the dock, driving a yellow Jeep Wrangler with no top. If I don't spot you right off, I'll park and call you. It can get crowded there, this time of day."

"Fine. See you soon," Paul said.

Phillip put the phone down and turned to Dani. "Sandrine has a closet full of clothes in the guest room. She said you were welcome to take what you need. There's all kinds of girl stuff in the bathroom, too."

"Yes, she told me. I'll make myself at home. You go get Paul, so we can get moving," Dani said, standing up and gesturing for him to go.

"What about getting you to a doctor?"

"I'm fine, Phillip. I've had enough concussions to know what's what."

"But your stitches..." he said.

"I'll check them before I shower. It should be about time for them to come out, I think."

"Well, we can take you to a walk-in clinic. There's one at the hospital not too far from the marina."

"Nonsense. I'm sure Sandrine must have nail scissors here. If the cut's closed, I'll take them out. I've had plenty of practice. Now, go." She made shooing motions at him again.

Knowing when he was beaten, Phillip complied without further protests.

PHILLIP RETURNED with Paul about an hour later. They found Dani in the kitchen, and they could smell fresh coffee. Phillip made the introductions, and they moved out onto the shaded veranda to enjoy the cool breeze while they plotted their next move.

"First, have you eaten breakfast, Paul, or can I get you something?" Phillip asked.

"I've eaten. Coffee's fine for now, thanks." Paul set his mug on the glass-topped table. "So, where's Reilly, these days?"

"The last fix we have on him, he was in Guadeloupe. He's got a new girl on board; picked her up there, in Marie Galante. When he left Dominica, he had a girl from here on board, named Michelle Devereaux; at least, she was with him when he checked in at Portsmouth, and we assume she left with him." Phillip explained about the two-week in/out clearance procedure in Dominica. "She's not on the paperwork he filled out to check into Guadeloupe." He went on to tell Paul what Sandrine had learned about Michelle's old boyfriend, and about Reilly's injuries.

"So, you figure Reilly and this Devereaux woman quarreled and she cut him, or something else?"

"I don't know, Paul. Did Mario or J.-P. tell you about the missing women down island?"

"No. What missing women?"

Phillip filled Paul in on the women who had disappeared after telling their acquaintances that they were leaving on *Sea Serpent*.

"There's a pattern, all right. Any firm evidence as to what happened to any of them?" Paul asked.

"No. It's just supposition that he was involved," Phillip said.

"Given what he did to Dani, I think it's a little more than supposition," Paul said. "Do you think he deliberately picks women who don't have any close ties?"

"It looks that way, except for me," Dani said.

"Yeah, but you were a deviation from his pattern, and look what happened," Paul said. "He called a lot of attention to himself when he got mixed up with you. We've got Andrea, Agnes, Sylvia, you, maybe Michelle. There are probably more that we don't know about. I think he's deliberately picking women with no attachments. He may have mistaken you for one. Could be conscious on his part, or it could be some unconscious result of his own background.

"He has a lot of the traits of a serial predator. I think if we could get into the sealed records from his time in foster care, we'd discover that he has all of them, but that's just an old cop's hunch. We've got enough without the juvenile records."

"Back to Michelle," Phillip said. "If she carved up her boyfriend, seems to me that she probably cut Reilly before they parted company."

"Yes," Paul said, and Dani nodded in agreement.

"Wonder where she is?" Dani asked.

"I don't know," Paul said, "but we should keep focused on Reilly. Sounds like there are plenty of people looking for her. If the police find her, she might be able to tell us something, but until then, I think we just treat her as another puzzle piece that fits the pattern. We have enough on Reilly to lock him up for good with your testimony, Dani. The rest of it can be sorted out once we've got him."

"Let's stock *Kayak Spirit* and go to the Saintes. We're not going to find him by sitting here," Dani said.

"Okay, but what about your stitches?" Phillip asked.

Dani pulled her hair away from the cut and turned her head toward Phillip. "All healed, mother," she said. "I took 'em out while you were gone."

LIZ HAD NEVER SEEN as many shoe stores in her life, at least not all in the same place. "Not even in Paris," she said to Mike. "Why only shoes?"

"No idea." Mike shrugged.

He was getting tired of following her around, as she tried on one pair of shoes after another without buying any. They were shopping in Pointe-à-Pitre, having sailed up from Les Saintes the day before.

Liz had told Mike that she was craving a bit of city life. Although Pointe-à-Pitre was hardly competition for Paris, by Caribbean standards it was a thriving metropolis.

Liz couldn't get over the fact that there were several city blocks packed with shoe stores, one right next door to the next. It made things convenient for shopping, but she did wonder how it came to be.

"Okay. Enough," she said, to Mike's relief. "Let's find a café and have a cold beer before we go back to the market."

They had left their dinghy tied to the seawall near the old city market, redolent with the aromas of spices, fresh fruits, and produce. They had been wandering the city's narrow streets for a couple of hours before she spotted all the shoe stores.

Mike paused at the next sidewalk café and pulled out a chair for her. He went inside to the counter and bought two icy cans of beer, asking for glasses as well. When he had poured a glass for each of them, he looked up at Liz and asked, "So, how's your craving for city life, now?"

"I've had enough. It's overwhelming, after so long on the little islands, with so few people. I'm ready to go back."

Mike looked at his wristwatch. It was one o'clock. "If you want, we could make it to Îlet du Gosier before sunset. You could fix sandwiches while I get us out of the river. The island's about two miles to the east from the mouth. Probably won't be crowded during the workweek.

"We could spend the day there tomorrow, get in a little beach time. Then, the next day, we could head back to the Saintes, just to stage ourselves for an easy run up to Deshaies the following day. If we feel like it, we could spend a day or two enjoying Deshaies. There are some good hikes there. Or, we could just go on to Antigua. Antigua is worth some time, too, especially since you haven't been there."

"You're the captain."

Liz smiled. She hadn't heard Mike talking to himself in the last day or two. He was being completely charming, and she had almost forgotten her uneasiness of a few days ago.

This cruise was turning out to be something that she was sure she would remember fondly in years to come. This was a beautiful part of the world, and a boat like *Sea Serpent* was the perfect vehicle for exploring it.

The history of the European settlement of the islands centered on the sea, so arriving in each new place under sail was like a trip back to the early colonial era. She was once again glad that she had struck up an acquaintance with this somewhat odd man.

Liz was a bit worried that he seemed excessively attached to her, though. She liked him well enough, but she wasn't looking for an extended relationship, and she was beginning to sense that he was.

She needed to find a way to part gracefully at some point. She hoped that it would work out so that she could enjoy island hopping the rest of the way to the Virgin Islands with him, but she was steeling herself to leave sooner if he started acting strangely again.

"Let's go, then. You finished with your beer?"

"Yes," she said, as he got to his feet and came around the table to help her up.

DANI AND PAUL had inventoried the galley stores on *Kayak Spirit* and gone grocery shopping. Sharktooth had put a serious dent in the stock that Phillip had laid in a few days ago. While they did the shopping, Phillip went to visit Sandrine at the customs office to say goodbye and clear out for Guadeloupe.

When he walked in, she presented him with a DHL envelope, addressed to her, care of the *Douane* in Marin. He lifted the torn flap, and took out a fresh new French passport.

"It came this morning, from Paris. How does J.-P. do these things, Phillip?"

Phillip shrugged and finished filling out the clearance documents, adding Dani's new information to the crew list. Sandrine stamped the form and gave him a brief, tantalizing kiss.

"You will be safe, please, and hurry home to me?"

He nodded, gave her a hug, and went back to the boat. He got back there before Dani and Paul, and he was busying himself with the minor repairs that were part of sailing a vintage vessel. He had just stopped for a glass of water when Sharktooth called.

"Good afternoon, Phillip," Sharktooth said.

"Hello, Sharktooth. How was the flight?"

"Flight good, Phillip, thank you."

"What's on your mind?" Phillip wiped the sweat from his brow with his forearm.

"One of the guides take some people to Toucari Bay this morning to snorkel the reef, an' they find a dead lady. He call on the radio, and I take the p'lice 'round to pick she up just now. Was the lady from *Sea Serpent*, Michelle. She been in the water a while, but I see the tattoo."

"I don't know about a tattoo, Sharktooth."

"You get old, Phillip. Don't see the pretty girl any more. She got butterfly, down low on the belly. Only see if she in bikini, or not in clothes."

"I'll trust you on that, Sharktooth. Do they know the police in Martinique are looking for her?"

"They know now. I tell them."

"Any idea how she died?"

"Look like she neck bust to me. P'lice, he t'ink so, too. They take she to Rouseau for the coroner. I call when I hear more, Phillip."

"Okay, Sharktooth. Thanks."

"Blessings, Phillip."

Dani and Paul had come back while Phillip was finishing his call, so he filled them in while they stowed the groceries. Within thirty minutes, they were underway.

As they maneuvered away from the dock, Phillip learned that Paul was an experienced weekend sailor with some offshore races under his belt. The three of them had a quick discussion as they motored out of the channel.

They decided to go all the way to Les Saintes. It was about a hundred miles, so they would get there mid-morning tomorrow. It was an easy overnight trip with three experienced hands. They should arrive in time to clear in with customs and scout the anchorages around Les Saintes for their quarry.

If they came up empty-handed, Dani and Phillip agreed that they would move on up the west coast of Guadeloupe to Deshaies. They reasoned that although there were many places in Guadeloupe for *Sea Serpent* to spend time, she would almost certainly call at Deshaies before leaving for Antigua. Paul, new to the islands, bowed to their experience.

Deshaies was a likely choke point for vessels bound for Antigua from Guadeloupe. And Reilly had told Dani that he always stopped there and in Jolly Harbour, Antigua, on his way north.

Once they were under sail in open water, Paul took the first watch. Phillip and Dani went below. Phillip stretched out to rest, as he had the next watch, and Dani reheated a pot of Sharktooth's curried chicken for their dinner. She would rest while Phillip was on watch. Her watch would then take them to the north end of Dominica before dawn, when Paul would take over again.

DANI POURED herself a mug of coffee from the thermos she prepared before she relieved Phillip. She was one hour into her early morning watch, sailing north along the west coast of Dominica. She saw only a few lights along the shoreline, a few miles to the east.

These were Sharktooth's home waters; she smiled at the thought of the big man. He wanted in on the action when they found Reilly, but she was in a hurry. Sharktooth might miss out on that, but there would be other chances for him.

Reilly was only the first of her targets. She meant to have her revenge on this Big Jim character, whoever he was. Not wanting to worry Phillip or her father, she kept that to herself for now.

She didn't think it was fair that Phillip and Sharktooth got to have all the fun. They took care of the people who worked in Baliceaux, but she missed out on that. Now she wanted to ensure that Big Jim's operation wouldn't be rebuilt.

The best way to kill a snake was to cut off its head. Her father taught her that long ago. Big Jim might not be the head of the snake, but he was the next in line.

The bastard thought he could treat her like his property, and then sell her off. That infuriated her. She intended to straighten him out on that before she killed him. Besides, she wanted to know who else he worked with.

There wasn't room in the islands for people like him. She was going to make her home here, and she wasn't going to share the neighborhood with people who thought they could push her around.

She didn't want to tip her hand yet, but before they were through with Reilly, she would find out more about Big Jim. Reilly didn't appear to be connected to Baliceaux, from what Phillip and Paul said.

Reilly was just an appetizer, as far as Dani was concerned. Her main course would be Big Jim and whoever employed him.

Finishing the coffee, she leaned back against the cockpit coaming and put her bare foot on the tiller. It was too nice a night to spend her time plotting mayhem; there would be time for that later. For now, she was alive and sailing; she would make the most of it.

31

After a quiet night at Îlet du Gosier, Liz and Mike agreed that they didn't need another idle day of beachcombing. They had an ideal breeze to lay Les Saintes on one tack now, although it was forecast to clock throughout the day. If that happened, the anchorage at Îlet du Gosier would probably get a bit choppy, so after a leisurely breakfast in the cockpit, they made ready to leave.

Mike hoisted the outboard from the dinghy, stowed it on the stern rail, and attached the towing bridle to the dinghy. Liz squared away the galley. They would be hard on the wind, and the water was often rough in the channel on the north side of Les Saintes. They had a short trip ahead; it was only a little over 20 miles, but if the wind clocked, they would have to beat. Depending on the sea state, it could be a relatively slow trip.

They expected to arrive in Les Saintes late in the afternoon. They might be too late to have their choice of anchorage, but they were planning to leave for Deshaies early tomorrow anyway. They would take what was available for one night. It would be more comfortable than bouncing at Îlet du Gosier in a southerly wind, and if the wind held, they would have a good sail to Deshaies in the morning.

Liz took her time putting things away below decks, listening as Mike raised the anchor and hoisted the sails. Normally, she would have helped him, but he had seemed distant this morning, and a bit grouchy, as well. He had called her Dani, once, and when he saw her reaction, he quickly stammered an apology, but he called her Michie when he apologized.

It wasn't lost on Liz that those were the names she had heard when she thought he had been talking to swimmers at Îlet à Cabrít the other day. That reminded her of the unexplained purse. She wasn't nosy, but she was curious, especially since he kept slipping up with those two names.

She listened carefully again, to be sure he was still occupied. Over the sound of the idling diesel, she could hear him working on the foredeck. He was taking the jib out of its bag, laying it out so it would be ready to hoist when he got the anchor up. She heard the anchor windlass, clanking as the chain came aboard. He would be busy for a few minutes. She had plenty of time for a quick look at that handbag.

She opened the locker next to hers, took the bag out, closed the locker, and stepped into the head compartment, latching the door. Liz set the bag on the countertop and opened the clasp. In the bag, she found a French passport and a wallet.

She flipped the passport open and began to tremble as she saw the name. Michelle Anne Devereaux. Her hands shook as she looked at the passport picture. She didn't recognize the girl, but this had to be Mike's Michie, this beautiful young girl from Martinique.

Liz put the passport back and opened the wallet. There was a bit of money, euros and Eastern Caribbean dollars. She didn't count it. There was a bankcard from BNP, also with Michelle's name on it.

There was nothing else in the purse, except for the normal

things: lipstick, nail file, tissues, a comb, and a hairbrush. She closed the purse and listened again, still hearing the rumble of the anchor chain. She was amazed that no more time had passed. It only took a couple of minutes to retrieve the anchor. It seemed like longer since she had opened that purse.

Liz put the purse back in the locker where she had found it. Running her hands through her hair in agitation, she made her way back to the galley. She busied herself, bustling around in the lockers, to give herself time to think.

She couldn't come up with an explanation for that purse, at least not one that didn't make Mike look a bit suspicious. She recalled the personal history that he had related during their acquaintance.

He told her that he hadn't dated or had any women friends, even, since his wife had left him. That was years ago. That by itself seemed strange to her; he was handsome enough, and pleasant company, if a bit odd at times.

Had he found the purse somewhere? If so, why had he not turned it in to the police wherever he found it? Had he stolen it? He didn't seem the type to be a petty thief. She couldn't imagine that this Michelle Devereaux had been on board the boat and left without her purse. That was not something a woman would do.

Liz stopped herself; she was making excuses. Clearly, Mike must know Michelle, or must have known her at some point, because he had called her Michie this morning. Unless he was accustomed to using that name frequently, why would he have used it by mistake?

The way he said the name, it was one that he was accustomed to saying. As the implications of that registered with her, she wondered who Dani might be. If Mike knew Michelle well enough to use her name by accident, he must know this Dani equally well.

What a puzzle this man was turning out to be. For the most part, he was a perfect host. Occasionally, he seemed to drift into some sort of detached state, but only when he was alone. When she had heard him talking to himself, he seemed to be carrying on a conversation.

Now she realized that she had overheard him talking to both Michelle and Dani, usually one or the other, but sometimes both in one conversation. The times when Liz had approached him after hearing him talking to himself were the times that she had noticed that he was spaced out.

A few of those times, earlier today being one, he had seemed surprised to see her. Those were also the times that he seemed most likely to call her by the wrong name.

She wasn't alarmed by this, but it worried her a little. The other thing that troubled her about Mike was that he wanted her to stay aboard indefinitely. While she found him pleasant enough company most of the time, she wasn't interested in a long-term relationship with him.

For that matter, Liz wasn't interested in any kind of relationship with him beyond their shared passion for sailing. When she first met him, she had been looking for a little diversion, and he had seemed attractive enough.

He was on a yacht, so Liz had assumed that he would be moving on at some point, as she would herself. In her view, he had been a candidate for something longer than a one-night stand, but nothing with a future.

Oddly, in Liz's experience, he had seemed interested in her only as a fellow sailor. Romance had never entered the picture. Liz might have found that frustrating, since a brief affair had been her original goal, but the love of sailing together had turned out to be quite satisfactory.

She was getting the feeling, though, that it might be as difficult to end their sailing relationship as it sometimes was to end a romance when one partner was ready and the other wasn't. Liz already had her guard up on that account, and his increasingly frequent bouts of strange behavior made her glad that they had not progressed beyond sailing together.

Lost in her thoughts, Liz hadn't noticed until just now that the diesel was quiet. Mike had the sails up. Accustomed to single handing *Sea Serpent*, Mike didn't need her help to get under way.

Alarmed, Liz wondered how long she had been fumbling in the lockers. She decided to go up on deck and enjoy the sail. Whoever Dani and Michelle were to Mike, she didn't intend to let them spoil her pleasure.

"What's wrong, Dani?" he asked, when she came into the cockpit.

"Who is Dani, Mike?" she asked, deciding to bring this strange behavior into the open. Maybe if she called him on it, he would pay more attention.

"What?" he asked. "What did you just ask me?"

There was no hostility in his look, but she saw intense concentration on his face.

"You called me Dani again. I just wondered who Dani is, that's all."

"I called you Dani?"

"Yes, a couple of times this morning."

He shook his head, perplexed. "Sorry. Can't think of why I'd do that."

"Well, do I remind you of someone named Dani? Someone you used to know?"

"No. I don't know anybody named Dani," he said, avoiding her gaze.

"Was Michelle your wife's name?" she asked, thinking that if she had come this far, she might as well keep going.

"No," he said, holding eye contact with her this time. "Andrea."

"So Andrea was your wife. Did you maybe have a girlfriend named Michelle, sometime?"

"No," he said, looking away again. "Why? Did I call you Michelle, too?" He was looking her in the eye again.

"Yes, earlier this morning. Sorry, Mike. I don't mean to pry, but it just makes me feel a little uncomfortable. You call me by both those names, but you don't remember mine."

"I'm sorry, Liz. I can't explain it. Maybe some book I read recently, or a movie or something. My memory's been playing tricks on me, lately. Please don't be put off. I'll concentrate on doing better with the name thing. We've been getting along so well, I don't want to chase you away over something dumb like that. I'm looking forward to sailing together for a long time. You know, we don't have to stop in the Virgins. We could keep going. Head south down to Grenada next summer for the hurricane season, or maybe to Colombia. I hear it's really nice there."

"We'll see, Mike, okay? I do want to get to Antigua to catch up with my friend Suzanne. I haven't seen her since university. I want to spend some time with her, maybe even work in her art gallery for a while. I might take up painting again."

"Sure," he said. "You told me that. Don't worry. I'm not in a hurry. We can stay in Antigua as long as you want. In fact, I can work there. I've done it before. Just have to keep it quiet, because I don't have a work permit, but with all the big, crewed charter yachts there, there's plenty of business for me. We could stay there the whole winter if you want."

Frustrated now, she stood up. "I'd better go make a few sandwiches for us before it gets too rough to work in the galley. We'll get hungry before we get to Les Saintes."

Liz went below and started rummaging in the lockers again, taking her time. Mike was starting to annoy her with his assumptions about a longer-term relationship. Maybe she should just move in with Suzanne when they got to Antigua and hope Mike got tired of waiting for her.

While she made the sandwiches, she listened to Mike murmuring, consoling somebody, it sounded like. He's probably talking it over with Dani, she thought. Or maybe Michelle. Guess he's explaining that they may have to stay in Antigua longer than they'd planned.

Paul and Dani were both on deck and alert as Phillip steered *Kayak Spirit* through the Passe du Sud, into the protection of Les Saintes. They examined the boats in the anchorage at Pain de Sucre, to their starboard side on the way in.

Phillip pulled the tiller to the port, bringing *Kayak Spirit* up on the wind a bit, as Dani and Paul trimmed the sails. Phillip had the diesel idling, just in case the wind was erratic around the islands, but so far, they were doing nicely under sail. He held the boat close hauled on the starboard tack until they could get a good look at the boats anchored at Îlet à Cabrít.

As they passed the outermost boat, the breeze died. Phillip used *Kayak Spirit's* momentum to come about, and a gentle puff filled the sails on the port tack. *Sea Serpent* wasn't in this anchorage, either.

They sailed on to the east, into the anchorage off Bourg de Saintes, and came about onto the starboard tack, making their way through the anchored boats and out through the Passe de la Baleine. Phillip shut the diesel down without ever having put it in gear.

Sea Serpent wasn't in Les Saintes. It was noon, and they were 30 miles from Deshaies. They would be there before sunset. They could check the harbor there in the morning and clear into Guadeloupe. Then they could decide what they should do next.

32

PHILLIP WOKE UP AND LOOKED AT HIS WATCH, SURPRISED TO SEE that it was 7 o'clock already. He sat up in his berth and peered out the porthole to see the sun just peeking over the mountains behind the town of Deshaies. He had forgotten how the close-in part of the anchorage here was shaded from the morning sun. It was well past sunrise, but the gray, dawn light that normally served to awaken him came later in this spot.

Just as well, he thought. They were all tired from the last two days; they needed a solid night of sleep. He went back to the galley to put on a pot of coffee. By the time it had brewed and he had taken a cup up into the cockpit, Dani and Paul were stirring. Dani appeared in the cockpit first, mug in hand. Paul was less than a minute behind her.

"Great way to wake up," Paul said. "Nothing like the smell of fresh-perked coffee and salt air to get the juices flowing."

Dani was on the foredeck with binoculars, scanning the anchorage, before Paul and Phillip had finished their first cups of coffee.

"No sign of *Sea Serpent*," she said. "They're either south of us somewhere, or they've gone on to Antigua. I think we should push on, guys."

They had hugged the west coast of Guadeloupe yesterday afternoon, checking the common anchorages along the way. At Sandrine's last report, *Sea Serpent* had not cleared out with customs, so Reilly was probably still somewhere along the south coast of Guadeloupe.

Phillip and Dani had decided that there were too many places down there, and too many other boats, to make it worthwhile to look for him there. They knew he would eventually head north, either to Deshaies, or maybe all the way to Antigua.

"I can't stand to just sit here," Dani said. "Let's go on to Antigua."

"If you can wait a few more minutes, I'll call my friend in Antigua and find out if they've cleared in," Phillip said.

"Okay, but why not just go?" Dani asked.

"Because you know how picky they are in Antigua, Dani. Our clearance from Martinique showed us stopping in Guadeloupe. Unless we discover that there's a reason to hurry, we can go ashore here, clear in and out at the Internet café and eat breakfast. It's less than 50 miles to Antigua. If Reilly's not already there, we can leave late this morning and get in this evening, and we'll still beat him there," Phillip said. "That way we'll have fewer questions to answer in Jolly Harbour when we clear in. Besides, we old folks need to conserve our energy. We'll need it when we catch him."

"Yeah, that makes sense," Dani said. "I just want to get my hands on him, just for about 30 seconds." She went below, refilled her cup, and passed the coffee pot up. Once everyone had another round in their cups, she brought Phillip's cellphone up and joined them in the cockpit. By ten minutes after eight, they knew that *Sea Serpent* had not checked into Antigua.

They launched the dinghy and motored into Deshaies's small boat harbor, where the local fishing boats were berthed. They tied the dinghy to the concrete wall where the Deshaies River flowed into the harbor and walked into town along the main street.

They were the first customers at the Internet café, where they secured their clearance documents. Phillip chatted with the man behind the counter a bit, remarking that the formalities were much easier since the café had become an agency for customs.

"Used to have to walk all the way up the hill, most of the way out of town," Phillip said, explaining to Paul. "Strange place for a customs office, I always thought."

"Yeah, and then half the time, they had a sign in the window, saying that they were closed, and no indication of when they might open again," Dani said.

"There. All finished," the man behind the counter said, handing the stamped papers to Phillip. "Enjoy your breakfast, and bon voyage to Antigua."

As Phillip put the documents back in his waterproof folder, Dani caught a glimpse of the snapshot of her with Reilly.

"Wait," she said, reaching for the picture. She showed it to the shopkeeper.

"Have you seen him?" she asked, holding the print.

He took the picture from her and put on a pair of reading glasses, studying it.

"No," he said, shaking his head. "Sorry, but I have not seen this man."

He handed the picture back to Dani.

They had a quick breakfast at the café on the corner and went back to *Kayak Spirit* to dismantle the dinghy and bring it aboard. By 9:30, they were out of the harbor, on the way to Antigua.

It was a beautiful, clear morning with a solid 20-knot breeze, just a little south of east. Their course to the southwestern corner of Antigua was five degrees magnetic, and they were on a perfect beam reach, making a little over seven knots.

Everybody was in the cockpit, enjoying the sail. This would be a day trip; they wouldn't need to stand watches.

"If we keep this up, we'll get to Jolly Harbour and have the hook down before sunset," Phillip said, a grin on his face, his bare foot resting lightly on the tiller.

The tiller felt almost alive as *Kayak Spirit* surged over the big, smooth, evenly spaced swells.

"Look, Paul. That's Montserrat over there, 20 miles or so. Looks like the volcano is acting up a bit," Dani said, pointing to the northwest, where a plume of ash trailed out across the sky, borne by the upper level winds.

Paul studied the direction of the upper level winds for a minute. "Looks like the wind up there is out of the northeast. Does that mean we're going to see the wind back?" he asked.

"Maybe, but probably not right away. The trades back over the fall months. They're south of east in the summer and north of east in the winter, so the wind will surely back over the next few weeks," Phillip said. "We'll probably keep what we have for a day or two, though. Not to worry. We won't have to beat to Antigua today."

Sea Serpent was having a nice sail as well, some sixty miles to the south. Mike and Liz had arrived in the Saintes at about 3:30 yesterday afternoon and had gone ashore to clear out. They found a mooring available off Bourg de Saintes.

They made a quick trip to the town hall where the one policeman had explained that he could only handle inbound clearances by faxing the forms to Pointe-à-Pitre. To clear out, they must go to Pointe-à-Pitre, or Deshaies. He spoke no English, so Liz had translated for Mike.

"That's okay," Mike said, when he grasped the problem. "We wanted to go there anyway."

He had slept in the cockpit last night, enjoying the stars overhead until he fell asleep on the cushions. Liz had stayed up late reading and was still asleep this morning. Awakened by the sound of Mike fixing coffee, she commented that she hadn't slept well, so he encouraged her to sleep in.

Mike enjoyed the solitude while the wind-vane steered *Sea Serpent* across the channel into the lee of the big island of Guadeloupe. He had an easy sail up the west coast of Guadeloupe until he lost the wind north of Basse Terre.

Mike stowed the sails and started the diesel, engaging the autopilot for the rest of the run up the coast to Deshaies. He figured the diesel would wake Liz, but at least she got some extra sleep.

Wouldn't want her to sleep through all of such a beautiful day, anyway. If she doesn't wake up, I'll go right on to Antigua. Get there about dawn. By the time I get to the customs dock at Jolly Harbour, they should be open. I'll check in and go back out to the anchorage. Sleep for a while.

He yawned and stretched.

Then I can go get some of that fried chicken at the grocery store. Best damn fried chicken in the islands.

Liz woke up to the droning of the diesel. It took her a minute to orient herself. She felt the motion of the boat and remembered talking to Mike this morning and then crawling back in her berth. She had been wound up last night, and she had read until the wee hours of the morning.

She knew when she did it that she would regret it this morning, but reading was better than lying there wishing she could sleep, her mind churning. At least the book had held her attention so that she didn't worry about how to part ways with Mike without a scene.

She got up and made two cups of instant coffee, taking them up into the cockpit. She handed one to Mike and sat down across from him.

"Good morning again," she said with a wry smile.

"Good afternoon, Liz." He was careful to get her name right, proud of himself.

"What time is it?" she asked.

"A little after one o'clock. Deshaies is just around that point up ahead. We'll be anchored and ashore in less than an hour."

"I can't believe I slept so long."

"It's fine. Guess you needed it."

"Yes, but I hate it when I do this. Now I won't sleep tonight, either."

They finished their coffee in companionable silence and stowed the sails, getting ready to go ashore. As Mike had predicted, they were in the Internet café by two o'clock.

Mike was at the counter, dealing with clearing out of Guadeloupe, and Liz was looking at the local crafts on display. As she joined him at the counter, the man was explaining that if *Sea Serpent* left within 24 hours, no further paperwork would be necessary. Customs in Antigua would accept the stamped document he had just given Mike as his outbound clearance.

"Oh, by the way, did Dani find you?" the man asked Mike.

"What?" Mike asked.

"Dani. A French girl. She was in here visiting with two Americans who were clearing for Antigua this morning, but I don't think she was sailing with them.

"She was French, you know. I can tell. Probably she met them on the sidewalk, and told them where to check in, so I think that she is maybe in one of the hotels.

"She had a picture of you together with her. She showed it to me and asked if I had seen you. I told her I had not, of course, and they left to have breakfast together before the Americans sailed to Antigua. Perhaps she's still around town. Pretty girl."

Liz pretended not to hear that exchange, but she could see that Mike was shaken.

"Let's get on back to *Sea Serpent*," he said, frowning.

Liz figured he was worried that he would run into this Dani if they lingered ashore. She wondered why the prospect seemed to worry him, but she was well rested and eager to get to Antigua. When they got back to the boat, Liz suggested an overnight trip.

"I know you must be tired, Mike, but I'm feeling great. We've got a nice southeast wind, and the sea is quiet. I think we should go. I'll take us out; I'm good until midnight or so. You can sleep, and when you get up, we'll trade off."

"That's a great idea, and you'll get to see your friend sooner, too," he said. "Let's go."

As PHILLIP HAD PREDICTED, they dropped their anchor just south of the approach channel to Jolly Harbour about thirty minutes before sunset. With the three of them working, it only took a few minutes to bag the headsails and cover the main. Once *Kayak Spirit* was shipshape, there was time to enjoy a round of cold beers from the ice chest as they watched the last of the color fade from the western sky.

"Boy, the sunset through the ash plume from Montserrat is really something," Paul said. "That's worth the trip, right there."

Phillip and Dani smiled at one another.

"You guys are lucky to live where you see stuff like that every day," Paul said. "Miami's nice, but there's something special about a sunset over the water, you know?"

"There sure is," Phillip said. "You're going to talk yourself into moving down here, if you're not careful, Paul."

"I suppose I could," Paul said, with a faraway look on his face.

"Can I get you guys another beer while I rustle up dinner?" Phillip asked, going below.

"Sure," Paul said.

"Need a hand?" Dani asked. "What are you fixing?"

"Steaks and garlic toast on the grill. You can toss us a salad, if you would. Stuff's all cut up, in the fridge. Just let me get the steaks out and get the bread ready, and the galley's all yours, Dani."

Pleasantly tired from the day's magical sail, their hunger sated, they were all asleep by 8:30.

DAMN, it's pretty out here. Look at all those stars.

Mike was about halfway across the channel between Guadeloupe and Antigua. It was 1 a.m., and the wind had dropped to a zephyr. There was enough breeze to keep the sails full, but his speed had dropped to a little over one knot. Liz had been gone for about an hour.

Never gonna get there at this rate.

Mike started the diesel, and engaged the electronic autopilot, disconnecting the wind vane. He set the autopilot to steer to a preprogrammed GPS waypoint on the southwest tip of Antigua and trimmed the sails in enough to keep them quiet.

Too bad about the wind. Guess it can't be perfect every day.

He was exhausted, and the droning of the diesel made him even sleepier. He began to nod off. His head jerked up as he woke momentarily. He blinked a few times and looked around.

All alone. No boat traffic to worry about. Set the guard band on the radar. In a minute. I'll get it later.

He yawned; his head dropped to his chest again. He rolled onto his side and settled into a comfortable slumber, dead to the world.

33

PHILLIP BROUGHT *KAYAK SPIRIT* ALONGSIDE THE CUSTOMS DOCK IN Jolly Harbour. He was coasting at a speed of less than a knot, barely making steerageway. Dani and Paul both stepped over the narrow gap onto the dock, each with a line in hand.

Dani had the bow line; Paul had the stern line. They both snubbed the lines on the cleats along the edge of the dock, bringing *Kayak Spirit* to a gentle halt as her stern drew even with the end of the dock. Dani tied off the bow and walked a few steps back along the side of the boat, reaching over to pick up the midship spring lines. She handed one to Paul, and she took the other one forward.

By the time they had fenders rigged to keep *Kayak Spirit* off the dock, Phillip was up at the office doing the paperwork. He was the first arrival of the day, so there was no waiting. They were back out in the anchorage in a few minutes, assembling the dinghy. They had decided on breakfast ashore at a favorite restaurant on the marina grounds.

As they walked into the restaurant, Phillip heard someone call his name. He spotted the Morrises, menus in hand. He walked over, followed by Paul. Dani had gone to the ladies' room.

"You have a good memory," Phillip said, shaking hands with the man.

"Jim Morris, Phillip. You came by our boat out in the anchorage a week or two ago, remember?"

"Of course, I remember you, Jim, but I was looking for you by name last week. I'm surprised you remember me, though."

"It's a holdover from my days in sales," Jim said. "Join us. Joann and I just sat down."

"Okay," Phillip said, introducing Paul as they pulled up chairs. "I'm going to drag another chair over. Someone else will be..."

"Dani!" Joann said, interrupting Phillip, calling out to be heard over the din of conversation in the crowded little place. "Sorry, Phillip. I just saw her looking for you guys. Guess you found her, huh?"

"Yes," Phillip said, getting a chair for Dani.

"I guess you decided not to join Mike on *Sea Serpent*, Dani," Joann said. "Lucky for you, too."

"You don't know the half of it," Dani said. "It's a long story, but why do you say it's lucky for me?"

"You didn't hear?" Joann asked. "It was on the cruisers' VHF net this morning."

"No," Dani said. "What happened?"

"*Sea Serpent* hit Cade's Reef, down on the southwest corner of the island, sometime last night. Two fishermen found the wreckage about dawn this morning. Not much left. The Antigua Coast Guard figures he was cooking along with the autopilot set. Probably fell asleep. They didn't find any survivors. They said he had cleared out from Guadeloupe yesterday, late in the afternoon. He must have sailed all night. The life raft was still on board, and you know how that current rips through there. They figure it was running three or four knots in the early morning, so anybody that was aboard would be far out at sea by now."

"What a shame," Paul said.

"Yes, a shame. That old Concordia yawl was a beauty," Dani said, her blue eyes cold as ice. "Sad to lose her."

The Morrises looked at her strangely. They were so focused on her that they didn't see Phillip and Paul share a smile and a wink as the waitress came to take their orders.

LIZ SHIFTED IN HER SLEEP; she couldn't find a comfortable position. She felt clammy, although the surface upon which she slept was soft and warm. Her cheek rested on the back of her hand, and her skin felt gritty.

Giving up on sleep, she forced her eyes open, blinking. She was face down on a sandy stretch of beach, and the sun was well up in the sky. Her head ached. As she rolled herself to a sitting position, the memories came flooding back.

She had been asleep on the starboard settee in *Sea Serpent's* main cabin when she'd been thrown to the cabin sole. Her forehead had struck a sharp corner, and her vision had blurred. *Sea Serpent's* motion was erratic — rising, rolling, and then crashing down with a jolt.

Confused, Liz lay there on the cabin sole for some time; she couldn't guess how long. When she felt seawater rising around her, she realized the boat was sinking. She scrambled to her feet in alarm, only to fall to her hands and knees when the boat crashed to a sudden stop a second or two after she'd gotten her feet under her.

We're aground and taking on water. Timing her movements to the boat's as best she could, she managed to stand up and get a grip on the handrails that were positioned along the cabin overhead. She worked her way to the companionway and climbed into the cockpit.

Mike wasn't there. She called him, but there was no answer.

In the distance, she could see a few lights off to the right along what had to be the south coast of Antigua.

Liz had laid their course to take them up Antigua's west coast to Jolly Harbour. There was a big reef close along the island's southwest corner — Cade's Reef, she remembered. They'd struck it.

Better oriented, she looked to the north and was able to pick out the shoreline a few hundred yards away. It was in shadow, but every so often, she glimpsed the white foam of a small wave breaking on a tiny stretch of beach.

She could swim that if she had to, but they'd been towing the inflatable dinghy. Feeling around the stern, she found the tow line and pulled it in hand over hand. There was little resistance; the dinghy was gone. She reached the end of the line and saw that it had been cut cleanly.

Every man for himself. Bastard took the dinghy and left me. Guess I don't need to worry about Mike now.

She opened the cockpit locker and found the inflatable life vest she'd been wearing when she was on watch. She put it on and pulled the lanyard to inflate it.

Walking along the port side deck to the point where it was submerged, she gripped the toe rail and eased herself into the water. A vicious current swept her legs out from under her, almost wrenching her arms from their sockets.

She let her body float to the surface, aligning herself with the current's axis. That reduced the strain on her muscles, but she dared not let go. She held on, thinking.

The current ran parallel to the shoreline, and she estimated that it was three or four knots. Swimming across that to shore was out of the question. She'd be swept clear of the island before she reached land.

The current would probably lose some of its strength once in open water, and she could ride it to the west, but as best she could recall from her quick look at the charts, it was forty miles or so to Nevis, the next island to the west. That was a long way to swim, even with the life vest.

There wasn't much tidal range here — maybe a half a meter. She didn't know the stage of the tide, but given the current's strength, it must be close to turning.

The prevailing current across the islands flowed from east to west at about a knot at most, and there wasn't much wind, so most of the current had to be tidal. If she waited for slack water, she could swim the few hundred yards to the beach. She rolled herself back onto the deck, which was only inches above the sea surface, and settled in to wait.

As she predicted, the current began to diminish, and after about an hour, she started swimming. It wasn't easy; she was still angling across a current that was moving almost as fast as she could swim. But she was fit and determined to survive.

She remembered crawling out of the water onto the beach and collapsing. Now, here she was. She needed to find her way to civilization and call her friend Suzanne, but that wasn't much of a challenge, given what she'd just been through.

***

PAUL AND DANI were waiting in the Italian restaurant at Jolly Harbour's marina that evening when Phillip came in. He'd been to meet an old friend who was a senior member of the country's coast guard.

They had moved *Kayak Spirit* to a slip in English Harbour earlier in the day, so that Paul could tour the Nelson's Dockyard National Park. When Phillip had told Dani and Paul about his meeting in Jolly Harbour this afternoon, Paul had suggested they share Phillip's taxi and stay to have dinner at this little Italian place he'd read about.

"Thanks for waiting," Phillip said. "Did you order yet?"

"No," Dani said. "We've been enjoying the wine, talking about

Mario and Papa. You're even a little bit early; we weren't expecting you yet. Any news?"

"Yes, a bit. The woman who was with Reilly survived. She made it ashore from the reef and crashed on the beach. Had a little concussion. She — "

"That asshole hit her?" Dani asked.

"No, she was asleep when they hit the reef. She fell off the settee berth and hit her head. Came to when the water rose over the cabin sole. Reilly was gone.

"She saw where she was; recognized the reef from the chart. She'd laid the course from Deshaies, so she remembered it. They were just a few hours behind us, apparently. Anyhow, they'd been towing an inflatable. When she couldn't find Reilly, she pulled the towing bridle in and discovered it ended in a clean cut. He must have taken off in the dinghy."

"So he got ashore, then?" Paul asked.

"They don't think so. The outboard for the dinghy was still on *Sea Serpent's* stern rail, and the oars were in a cockpit locker. So he's adrift in the dinghy, they figure."

"What happened to the woman, then?" Dani asked.

"Smart lady, apparently. She could see the shoreline on the other side of the reef, but the current was running too fast for her to swim ashore. She figured the wreckage wasn't going anywhere in a hurry, so she waited until slack water. Swam ashore and crashed on a tiny little strip of beach. She woke up after several hours and worked her way through the undergrowth until she found a road. She flagged down a car and called a friend of hers who lives here. The friend runs an art gallery over near English Harbour. Her friend picked the woman up and took her home. They called the coast guard after the woman got her wits about her. She was pretty rattled, from what my contact said. Liesbet Chirac is her name, by the way. She's Belgian, the same woman Sandrine told us Reilly picked up in Marie Galante. And that's about the end of the story."

"So Mike Reilly got away?" Dani asked.

"They're broadcasting on channel 16 every 15 minutes — a notice to vessels in the area to watch for him," Phillip said, "but that's like looking for a needle in a haystack. He'd been adrift in a dinghy without propulsion for 10 or 15 hours, by the time they started. With the current and a 20-knot wind, he's probably 50 miles from here, if he's lucky. Dead if he's not. Chirac said the dinghy leaked air badly; they had to pump it up every few hours, and the pump was in the locker on *Sea Serpent* with the oars. Reilly's swimming by now. Or drowned."

"So they're not searching?" Paul asked.

"Nobody knows where to start," Phillip said. "Somebody may spot him. All the customs and immigration offices have bulletins with a passport picture, but my friend with the coast guard figures he's a goner."

"Damn," Dani said.

"What?" Paul asked. "He got what he deserved."

"No, he didn't. What he deserved was about 30 minutes alone with me. Drowning's too good for him."

Paul frowned, shaking his head and looking at Phillip.

"Well, since you can't settle your score with Reilly, what's next for you, Dani?" Phillip asked.

Dani shrugged. "I don't know. I'll find another crew berth, but I'm not in a hurry, now."

"You need something else to do, Dani," Phillip said. "I get that you don't want to go back to work in investment banking, but you need something to sink your teeth into, some kind of business of your own, maybe."

"Well, I wanted to work with Papa, but you know that story. No way, as far as he's concerned."

"Yes, and I hate to sound like your big brother again, but he's right."

"You were partners with him," Dani said. "Why not me?"

"Because that business isn't what it used to be," Phillip said.

"That's why I got out. The world's a different place than it was when he and Mario and Sharktooth started out. You know that."

"I'm not going back to any job in the financial services industry, Phillip. And that's all I know, besides what I learned about black ops hanging out with you and Sharktooth."

"You're a hell of a sailor," Phillip said. "Never saw a better one. But I think you're the kind of person who can't work for somebody else. Find yourself a yachting-related business opportunity and give it a shot for a while. You might like it."

"Maybe," she said. "Right now, I just want a nice dinner and then a hot shower ashore, with unlimited fresh water and plenty of elbow room. And vengeance, but that'll keep."

"Vengeance?" Paul asked. "But there's nobody left. Sounds like Reilly's toast."

"And nobody was left alive on Baliceaux," Phillip said.

"You said those people worked for somebody called Big Jim. I'll settle for his head on a platter. That's a start on vengeance, anyway. Let's eat."

The End

MAILING LIST

Thank you for reading *Bluewater Killer*.

Sign up for my mailing list at http://eepurl.com/bKujyv for notice of new releases and special sales or giveaways. I'll email a link to you for a free download of my short story, **The Lost Tourist Franchise**, when you sign up. I promise not to use the list for anything else; I dislike spam as much as you do.

A NOTE TO THE READER

THANK YOU AGAIN FOR READING **BLUEWATER KILLER**, THE FIRST book in the **Bluewater Thriller** series. I hope you enjoyed it. If so, please leave a brief review on Amazon.

Reviews are of great benefit to independent authors like me; they help me more than you can imagine. They are a primary means to help new readers find my work. A few words from you can help others find the pleasure that I hope you found in this book, as well as keeping my spirits up as I work on the next one.

I ALSO WRITE two other sailing-thrillers series set in the Caribbean. If you enjoyed this book, you'll like the Connie Barrera Thrillers and the J.R. Finn Sailing Mystery series.

The **Connie Barrera Thrillers** are a spin-off from the **Bluewater Thrillers.** Before Connie went to sea, she was a first-rate con artist. Paul Russo signed on as her first mate and chef, but he ended up as her husband. Connie and Paul run a charter sailing yacht named *Diamantista*. They're often drawn into problems unrelated to sailing, usually those brought aboard by their customers.

The **Bluewater Thrillers** and the **Connie Barrera Thrillers** share many of the same characters. Phillip Davis and his wife Sandrine, Sharktooth, and Marie LaCroix often appear in both series, as do Connie, Paul, Dani, and Liz. Here's a link to the web page that lists those novels in order of publication: http://www.clrdougherty.com/p/bluewater-thrillers-and-connie-barrera.html.

My newest series, the **J.R. Finn Sailing Mystery** series, introduces a government assassin disguised as a boat-bum lazing about the Caribbean Islands. This series is also available in audiobook format.

A LIST of all my books is on the last page; just click on a title or go to my website for more information. If you'd like to know when my next book is released, visit my author's page on Amazon at www.amazon.com/author/clrdougherty and click the "Follow" link or sign up for my mailing list at http://eepurl.com/bKujyv for information on sales and special promotions.

I welcome email correspondence about books, boats and sailing. My address is clrd@clrdougherty.com. I enjoy hearing from people who read my books; I always answer email from readers. Thanks again for your support.

ABOUT THE AUTHOR

Welcome Aboard!

Charles Dougherty is a lifelong sailor; he's lived what he writes. He and his wife have spent over 30 years sailing together.

For 15 years, they lived aboard their boat full-time, cruising the East Coast and the Caribbean islands. They spent most of that time exploring the Eastern Caribbean.

Dougherty is well acquainted with the islands and their people. The characters and locations in his novels reflect his experience.

A storyteller before all else, Dougherty lets his characters speak for themselves. Pick up one of his thrillers and listen to the sound of adventure as you smell the salt air. Enjoy the views of distant horizons and meet some people you won't forget.

Dougherty's sailing fiction books include the **Bluewater Thrillers**, the **Connie Barrera Thrillers**, and the **J.R. Finn Sailing Mysteries**.

Dougherty's first novel was *Deception in Savannah*. While it's not about sailing, one of the main characters is Connie Barrera. He had so much fun with Connie that he built a sailing series around her.

Before writing Connie's series, he wrote the first three Bluewater Thrillers, about two young women running a charter yacht in the islands. In the fourth book, Connie shows up as their charter guest.

She stayed for the fifth Bluewater book. Then Connie demanded her own series.

The J.R. Finn books are his newest sailing series. The first Finn book, though it begins in Puerto Rico, starts with a real-life encounter that Dougherty had in St. Lucia. For more information about that, visit his website.

Dougherty's other fiction works are the *Redemption of Becky Jones*, a psycho-thriller, and *The Lost Tourist Franchise*, a short story about another of the characters from *Deception in Savannah*.

Dougherty has also written two non-fiction books. *Life's a Ditch* is the story of how he and his wife moved aboard their sailboat, Play Actor, and their adventures along the east coast of the U.S. *Dungda de Islan'* relates their experiences while cruising the Caribbean.

Charles Dougherty welcomes email correspondence with readers.

www.clrdougherty.com
clrd@clrdougherty.com

OTHER BOOKS BY C.L.R. DOUGHERTY

Bluewater Thrillers

Bluewater Killer

Bluewater Vengeance

Bluewater Voodoo

Bluewater Ice

Bluewater Betrayal

Bluewater Stalker

Bluewater Bullion

Bluewater Rendezvous

Bluewater Ganja

Bluewater Jailbird

Bluewater Drone

Bluewater Revolution

Bluewater Enigma

Bluewater Quest

Bluewater Target

Bluewater Blackmail

Bluewater Clickbait

Bluewater Payback

Bluewater Survivor

Bluewater Thrillers Boxed Set: Books 1-3

Connie Barrera Thrillers

From Deception to Betrayal - An Introduction to Connie Barrera

Love for Sail - A Connie Barrera Thriller

Sailor's Delight - A Connie Barrera Thriller

A Blast to Sail - A Connie Barrera Thriller

Storm Sail - A Connie Barrera Thriller

Running Under Sail - A Connie Barrera Thriller

Sails Job - A Connie Barrera Thriller

Under Full Sail - A Connie Barrera Thriller

An Easy Sail - A Connie Barrera Thriller

A Torn Sail - A Connie Barrera Thriller

A Righteous Sail - A Connie Barrera Thriller

Sailor Take Warning - A Connie Barrera Thriller

Sailor's Choice - A Connie Barrera Thriller

A Deadly Sail - A Connie Barrera Thriller

J.R. Finn Sailing Mysteries

Assassins and Liars

Avengers and Rogues

Vigilantes and Lovers

Sailors and Sirens

Villains and Vixens

Killers and Keepers

Devils and Divas

Sharks and Prey

Sin and Redemption

Ashes and Dust

Anarchy and Chaos

Deepfakes and Diablas

Call Me Finn Boxed Set: Books 1 - 3

Call Me Finn Boxed Set: Books 4 - 6

Other Fiction

Deception in Savannah

The Redemption of Becky Jones

The Lost Tourist Franchise

Books for Sailors and Dreamers

Life's a Ditch

Dungda de Islan'

Audiobooks

Assassins and Liars

Avengers and Rogues

Vigilantes and Lovers

Sailors and Sirens

Villains and Vixens

Killers and Keepers

Devils and Divas

Sharks and Prey

Sin and Redemption

Ashes and Dust

Anarchy and Chaos

Deepfakes and Diablas

Call Me Finn Boxed Set: Books 1-3

Call Me Finn Boxed Set: Books 4-6

For more information please visit www.clrdougherty.com

Or visit www.amazon.com/author/clrdougherty

PREVIEW OF BLUEWATER VENGEANCE

Read the first four chapters of the next book in the Bluewater Thrillers Series.

Chapter 1 Bluewater Vengeance

"I want what's owed me, bitch," he hissed, his massive head blocking her vision as his lips sought hers.

Dani's mind raced as Nigel Smythe shoved her into the stone wall. A moment's inattention on her part had allowed him to trap her; he had one massive arm on each side of her, and his big belly was squeezing the breath from her lungs. He reeked of alcohol as he leered down at her.

"Stop this before I make you regret it, Nigel."

"Hah! You're the one who'll regret it."

She felt her temper building, even as she fought to control herself.

"You think I'm going to pay you back for what your own foolishness cost you? Forget it, and get off me before I hurt you."

"Oh, I'm scared, all right, missy. Think your rich old daddy can buy your way out of this, do you? It's not money I want now, and you know it. Now give. I'll be rougher if you make me force you."

She felt time slow down as adrenalin flooded her system. The intervals between his words seemed to stretch to seconds as she took a deep breath, centering herself in her slim, wiry body as she focused her eyes on his chest. She was past the point of control now, operating on pure instinct honed by years of bar fights. As her tormentor shifted his weight to pin her against the wall, freeing his hands to paw at her clothing, she slipped to her left slightly, grabbing his shirt, pulling him with her.

Off balance now, he fell toward her as she jerked her right knee up, making solid contact with his groin. He grunted in pain, even through the anesthesia of alcohol. As he gasped for breath, Dani gripped his styled hair with both hands, ducked her head, and smashed her forehead squarely into his face. She felt the satisfying crunch as his nose shattered. He roared with pain and anger, took a step back, and lunged at her. She ducked slightly, stepped under his right arm, and pivoted, putting her left hand on the back of his head and using his momentum to drive him face-first into the edge of the stone wall against which he had pinned her moments before.

Knowing the risk in stopping too soon, especially when your attacker outweighs you by a hundred pounds, she didn't hesitate. As Smythe rolled over, spitting out broken teeth, and raising his hands, she delivered a perfectly executed kick to the point of his chin, breaking his jaw and rendering him unconscious.

"Bastard," she muttered as she caught her breath. "Had it coming for years, I'm sure. Wish your wife could have been here to help." She went through his pockets, looking for the monogrammed linen handkerchief that he always carried. Finding it, she pulled it out and used it to wipe his blood from her face and hands, dropping it to the ground as she turned to walk away.

As Dani made her way past the yachts tied stern-to the dock, she willed herself to calm down, striding smartly to work off the adrenalin high that she always got from a good brawl. Approaching *Kayak Spirit*, she saw that the lights were still on in the main cabin. Phillip and Paul must still be awake. She gathered her thoughts as she climbed aboard.

"It's Dani!" she said, in response to Phillip's soft-spoken challenge, uttered as he felt her weight shift the boat.

"Hi! Come on down. Paul and I just poured a little nightcap. Want something?"

"Sure," she said, climbing down the companionway ladder, her eye on the liter bottle of St. James Reserve on the galley counter. "Neat, with rocks."

"Only way to drink it," Phillip agreed, rummaging for ice in the refrigerator.

"What happened to you?" Paul asked, eyeing her bloodstained T-shirt. "I thought you were going to take a shower."

"Well, I did, but when I came out of the ladies' head, I ran into that jerk from *Ramblin' Gal*. I never really got a chance to talk to him when I resigned from his crew, so I took the opportunity."

"You okay?" Phillip asked, turning to look at her over his shoulder as he put the lid back on the refrigerator.

"You're all bloody," Paul said.

"Yeah," she agreed. "But it's not mine. He had a nosebleed. High blood pressure, I guess. I got him settled down, though."

"Do we need to get the hell out of Dodge, Dani?" Phillip asked, guessing what had happened. He had known Dani since her childhood, and he had taught her to take care of herself when he discovered that she had her father's belligerent temperament.

"Nah, I think it'll be all right. No witnesses. My word against his. That's if his injured pride even lets him go to the cops. He was falling-down drunk. I think he tripped and fell into that retaining wall out near the main entrance. He busted his face up pretty badly. He's probably too concussed to remember what happened, anyway."

Dani went into the forward cabin and closed the door. Rummaging through her duffel bag, she found a fresh T-shirt and put it on. She combed her hair, still damp from her shower, and joined Phillip and Paul in the main saloon. She sat down at the dining table and took a sip of the smooth rum, feeling the tension fall away as she consciously relaxed her shoulders.

"So what's the plan from here?" She glanced from Phillip to Paul, waiting to see who would answer, hoping neither would press her for more information about her encounter with Smythe.

Phillip picked up his drink and took a sip. He set the moisture-beaded glass back in its coaster. "Well, I guess we're done. With *Sea Serpent* sunk on the reef and no sign of Mike Reilly, there's not much left for us to do here, is there?"

"Not that I can think of," Paul said. "Unless you and Dani have other ideas, I'm booked on an early flight back to Miami in the morning. I'll get back in time to have lunch with Mario and the boys. You know they'll want a report."

"I'm sure my father has filled them in by now," Dani said. "How about you, Phillip? What are you going to do now?"

"I just got off the phone with Sandrine; she wants me back in Martinique. I'm missing her, too."

"So, is she the one?" Dani asked, a mischievous smile on her elfin face.

"Well, you know, she just might be. I hadn't given it much thought until your father called and asked for my help. Until this little adventure took me away, Sandrine and I were just kind of having a day-to-day thing. Since I've been chasing around the islands the last couple of weeks, we've both realized it's serious."

"About time you settled down. You don't want to wait too much longer, or you'll end up a crusty old bachelor for sure," she said.

"What are you going to do now, Dani? Back to Paris to see your folks?" Phillip asked.

"No, I don't think so. It's too hard to get away from them, once they get their hooks into me. I'm not sure I want another crew berth, though."

"What, then?" Phillip asked. "Have you thought any more about a yachting-related business?"

"Yes. That was a good suggestion. You know how I love the sea. I'm thinking I'll find something else yacht-related, and I'm like you about the islands. There's nowhere else I'd rather live than down here. I need some time to chill out and think my way through this, though."

"Nothing wrong with that. You've been through a lot in the last couple of weeks. I'm probably going to fly back to Martinique and leave *Kayak Spirit* here for a while, anyway. If you want to boat-sit, you're welcome. She needs a little love from a skilled hand."

Dani's face split into a big grin. "Can I fix her up a bit? Like re-upholster these dismal settees? Put some fresh varnish on the table?"

"Knock yourself out. Treat her like she's yours for as long as you want."

"Deal," Dani said, standing to give Phillip a big hug. "I'm beat. 'Night, guys." She went back up to the forward cabin, and Paul and Phillip finished their drinks and crashed on the settees.

DANI AND PHILLIP waved as Paul got into the taxi the next morning after breakfast.

"Let's go over to Customs and Immigration and get you on the paperwork as the skipper, Dani," Phillip said, as they walked back toward the docks.

With that accomplished, Phillip stopped in a travel agent's

office and booked a flight to Fort-de-France, departing in the early evening. He and Dani spent the rest of the afternoon talking about Dani's ideas for sprucing up *Kayak Spirit*. Before either was ready, it was time for him to catch his own taxi.

Dani cooked a quick pasta dinner for herself, drank a glass of red French table wine from a bottle that she found in the bilge, and stretched out on the starboard settee to think, utterly content.

Chapter 2 Bluewater Vengeance

Liz tore the sheet from her sketchpad and balled it up, throwing it to the floor with her other rejects. Staring through the window of the gallery in frustration, she stood up, rolling her cramped shoulders, gradually working the stiffness from her sore muscles. She could visualize *Sea Serpent* clearly in her mind's eye, but she couldn't get the proportions down on paper. The graceful sheer line, the spoon bow, and the counter stern — she could sketch them individually to her satisfaction, but blending them into the beautiful profile of the old yawl was more of a challenge than she had expected.

She walked out onto the porch and let her gaze wander over the harbor as Suzanne finished wrapping a painting for her lone customer. The gallery was a feast or famine business, depending on whether there was a cruise ship in the harbor up at St. John. When a ship was in port, the tour buses would bring crowds of frantic shoppers to the quaint little shopping center at English Harbour. There were stores offering local rums, "native" crafts, many of which were imported from China these days, and expensive upscale clothing. There was a musty-smelling shop with an eclectic collection of books; some were genuine antiques, but many were by present day, Caribbean-based writers.

The cobwebs and moldy stone walls of the 18th-century building that once was a chandlery for the British Navy made it seem as if the shops existed in some time warp, giving the customers the feeling that they were back in the early 1700s. Then, a splash of dazzling color and light broke the spell; there was Suzanne's Art Gallery. On the days without cruise ships, Suzanne would have one or two customers, usually people who had recently bought one of the condominiums in the marina complex and wanted to decorate with island art.

Suzanne had come to Antigua on holiday after she and Liz had finished their university studies, Liz in finance, with a minor in graphic arts, and Suzanne in art history. Suzanne never went back to Belgium. A holiday romance had blossomed into a marriage to a well-known local artist, and she had found the place where she was meant to be. Liz envied that. Based on her own experience of the past few weeks, life in the islands seemed idyllic. Of course, she hadn't actually tried to live here. She had been on holiday for several weeks, which cast a rosy glow over her experiences, even her most recent adventure, a nearly fatal yachting accident.

She had caught a ride as pick-up crew with a single-handed sailor who was northbound from Guadeloupe, expecting to part company with him in Antigua, where she planned to visit with Suzanne and her husband. The yachtsman had turned out to be an odd character, and she had begun to worry a bit about his strange behavior. He had clearly wanted her to accompany him on his travels beyond Antigua, suggesting an open-ended itinerary that encompassed the entire Caribbean basin. Before their conflicting goals could become a problem, fate had intervened.

She still wasn't sure exactly what had happened, but it appeared that he had fallen asleep on watch with the autopilot steering for the southwestern tip of Antigua. She had sailed through the evening hours, and he had relieved her in the early morning. Exhausted from sailing solo for about 6 hours, she had left him and gone below. She had been sound asleep when *Sea Serpent* had struck the unyielding Cade's Reef.

Thrown violently to the cabin sole by the impact, she had taken a severe blow to the head. She regained her senses as the vessel pitched about, breaking up and filling with warm, tropical seawater as the wave action ground the keel against the coral. Semi-conscious, she made her way through the flooded interior into the cockpit, registering that there was no sign of her host.

As the wreckage settled into the water, she managed to hold on to one of the larger sections. With full consciousness returning, she realized that the water in her immediate vicinity was only a little over waist-deep. She quickly discovered that the current was so swift that she couldn't stand without holding on to the firmly grounded wreckage.

In the soft glow of moonlight, she could make out a silvery strand of beach a few hundred yards away across the surging channel between the reef and the island of Antigua. She knew that the tidal range was only about 18 inches in the islands, so she reasoned that if she could hang on, the water wouldn't get much deeper. She could swim to the beach easily except for the vicious current; it would sweep her out to sea before she could reach the shore. She clung to the wreckage, waiting patiently for slack water. It seemed like an eternity, but eventually the current abated. She swam to the beach, collapsing in the warm sand until the sun woke her up.

"Liz, are you all right?" Suzanne asked, interrupting her recollections.

"Fine, Suze. Just got lost for a moment. Did your customer leave?"

"Yes. I just put some herbal tea on to steep. Let's sit out here on the porch and relax. Looks like you need a break."

When she saw the puzzled look on Liz's face, Suzanne smiled and gestured at the discarded sketches that littered the floor.

SANTIAGO RODRIGUEZ, known as Big Jim to his minions and Iago to his close friends, decided that it was time for an unannounced visit to his operation on Baliceaux. Rodriguez lived on Mustique, a haven for the very wealthy, and Baliceaux was a large island, only a stone's throw away.

Rodriguez and his associates had been using Baliceaux as a transshipment point for drugs and human cargo for several years. The island was uninhabited and privately owned, yet readily accessible by boat. He and his colleagues had donated generously over the years to the 'campaign funds' of key politicians in St. Vincent and the Grenadines to ensure that the island remained undeveloped.

Baliceaux had some historical significance from the early colonial era that made it politically plausible to keep it untouched. The members of the widely dispersed family that technically still owned the island had no interest in it; after 400 years, there were so many heirs that the value of any one person's claim was insignificant, and without the impetus from a developer, no one could be bothered to clear the title to the island. Rodriguez's boss, Juan Camacho, had stumbled upon Baliceaux on one of his sport-fishing excursions and realized its potential.

Rodriguez didn't have any pickups or deliveries scheduled for several days, but he figured that the girl that Rosa was holding captive might have come out of her coma. He wanted to know who she was. Never one to overlook an opportunity, he thought that ransom was a possibility, although he had not shared that with Rosa or that idiot Julio, who had found the girl.

To Big Jim, the girl looked like someone's rich kid; he had a sense about those things. There was nothing specific that he saw. It was more the absence of tattoos, piercing, and needle tracks. Even though she was bedraggled from her time adrift before Julio's crew fished her out of the water, Big Jim sensed that someone cared about this girl, and that she took care of herself.

She might be worth more in ransom than he could get for her from his Arab contact in Caracas.

The crossing from Mustique was short and pleasant, in protected water. He eased his nondescript skiff up to the beach in Landing Bay, a bit surprised that none of his guards had come out to check on the approaching boat. Running the bow into the soft sand, he tossed an anchor up onto the beach to keep the boat from drifting away. He leapt carefully from the bow, landing above the wet sand, and made his way to the shack where his three gunmen lived. Before he stepped up to the door, he could hear the buzzing of flies.

"Hola!" he yelled. "Qué pasa, hijos de putas?"

There was no sound but the buzzing. He shoved the door open and gagged on the stench as he saw the clouds of flies working over the three corpses in their beds. No stranger to such sights, he stepped back, closing the door. He would examine them later to see what he could learn, but right now he wanted to check on the women and their captive. He walked around the side of the shack and followed the trail up the hill, noticing as he passed that the canvas-covered pallets holding his merchandise appeared undisturbed. That was encouraging. His first reaction had been that someone had stolen his stockpile of drugs.

More cautious now, he approached the long, low building where Rosa and her two assistants kept the women they were holding for future sales. Like an old-fashioned, cheap motel, it had a number of rooms used as cells that opened onto a long, shaded porch. He moved quietly along the dirt bordering the porch, noticing that the doors to the cells were all unlocked, including the one that held the girl. She was their only "guest" at the moment.

He stepped up and glanced into the cell where they had kept her. It was empty. Then he saw that the hasp and lock that had secured the door to the girl's cell had been torn out of the wooden doorframe. Reaching to open the door to the room that

Rosa shared with her two helpers, he saw that it was locked from the outside with one of the padlocks that they used on the cells. He frowned at the discovery; this door was normally not locked when Rosa was around.

He had no key. Rosa kept the keys; he had no need for a set. He pulled an old but well-kept Colt .45 semiautomatic pistol from his waistband and blew the lock from the door to Rosa's room. He could have torn it off with his massive hand, but he was frustrated and angry. Pulling the trigger and feeling the kick of the old pistol was satisfying. He pushed the door open and entered the room.

He saw the two assistants first. He would have thought they were dead in their beds, just like the guards, but they were both struggling, wild-eyed, against the cable ties that held their wrists and ankles to the metal bed frames. He looked around for Rosa and saw her about the same time as he noticed the flies on her putrefying carcass. His ears ringing from the gunshot, he couldn't hear their buzzing. He stepped up to the nearest of the two living women and casually ripped the duct tape from her mouth, asking her what had happened. Her mouth and throat were so dry after her long period without water that she was unable to make a sound above a whisper.

"*Agua, por favor, agua,*" she croaked.

Chapter 3 Bluewater Vengeance

Dani's mind was occupied with thoughts of Phillip as she spread the first coat of varnish on the surface of the table in *Kayak Spirit's* saloon. Laying on varnish wasn't careless work; it required a steady hand and just the right speed of application. Too quickly and it didn't spread evenly; too slowly and it would begin to set before it flowed out, making a smooth coat impossible. A veteran of years of crewing on yachts, Dani applied varnish with the same instinctive care that most women used when polishing their nails. It was relaxing and absorbing, but it left her mind free to roam as she methodically laid on a flawless finish.

She was glad that Phillip seemed to have found a soulmate in Sandrine. Some 20 years Dani's senior, he had always been a part of her life; he was the big brother that she never had. A former business partner of her father's, Phillip was in some ways the son that Jean-Pierre Berger had never had, as well. For the most part, though, J.-P. had raised Dani as if she were his son, at least when it came to leisure pursuits.

Her father was an avid yachtsman, not averse to the occasional drunken brawl in a waterfront tavern, and Dani had learned the skills of a deckhand and a street-fighter at his side. He had taken her sailing at every opportunity, and their bond was a strong one. Her mother had no interest in yachting, and her brawling was done on an emotional level, not with her fists. She had been divorced from J.-P. as long as Dani could remember.

While not overly protective of his only child, J.-P. had kept her well away from his business dealings. In that part of his life, Phillip had been his alter ego, his presence in the lucrative markets of the Caribbean and Latin America. Phillip had an awakening a few years ago after a close call involving illicit weapons and corrupt Latin American politicians. No fool, Phillip figuratively backed away from the table, counted his chips, and decided to withdraw from the game. Fortunately for their relationship, J.-P. understood. He had managed to move away from direct dealings with his customers himself. J.-P. operated his various enterprises from a safe distance, and he and Phillip were still close. When Dani had disappeared in the islands a couple of weeks ago, it was natural that J.-P. would turn to Phillip for help in finding her. J.-P. knew that Phillip carefully maintained his contacts in the islands; there was no one better suited for the job.

Dani stood up, wiping her hands on a rag soaked in thinner. She stretched the muscles in her lower back and put the lid on the varnish can, wrapping the brush in the rag to avoid drips. The table had been in better shape than she thought. A light sanding and one full coat of varnish brought the finish up to her satisfaction. She stood, tilting her head from side to side, catching the reflected sunlight from several different angles, checking for flaws. She smiled to herself at the mirror-like finish and took the brush up to the cockpit to clean it. That done, she put away her supplies and went below, reaching down into the refrigerator box for an ice-cold beer.

She sat in the shade of the cockpit awning, relaxing as she pondered what she wanted to do with her life. She knew that she would tire of tinkering with *Kayak Spirit* in a few days; boat maintenance was therapeutic, but she wanted more of a challenge. As she had told Phillip, she had no wish to go back to France; she had fallen under the spell of the islands. Crewing on other peoples' yachts had just been a way to live here, but now that she knew this was her place, she wanted a life of her own. Boats and the islands were her love; the freedom of the open sea evoked a passionate response in her that nothing else had ever equaled.

As she sipped the cold, refreshing beer, she was gazing at a big ketch tied up at the shipyard across the harbor, admiring the classic lines and gleaming brightwork. She could see the fine hand of L. Francis Herreshoff in the graceful sheer line, falling back from the clipper bow to the stern with its wineglass section. A replica of his famous *Bounty* design, she thought, as she noticed the yacht broker's 'for sale' sign hanging on the stern rail. She finished her beer and grabbed her shower bag. A long, cool shower before a tropical fruit salad at the restaurant just up the waterfront had a strong appeal. She cast a last, lingering look at the ketch across the harbor as she stepped off *Kayak Spirit*.

"SHE SAID NOT, J.-P.," Phillip said, the cell phone in his left hand and a café au lait in his right. He was sitting on his veranda, gazing out over the anchorage at Ste. Anne, Martinique. He listened quietly to J.-P. for a few beats.

"I don't think it's just her mother, J.-P. She's looking for the next step, if you want my guess, and it's not in Paris or New York. She has too much energy to work at anything that would require her educational background. She likes action; you know that." He sipped the coffee as J.-P. responded.

"No, I don't want her in our business, either. She might be good at it, but it's not what it used to be. Certainly not worth the personal risk, the way the world is shaping up. Give her some time; she'll figure out what she wants, and she'll tell you when she's ready. She's fine. Quit worrying." He picked up the carafe and refilled his cup.

"Thanks, J.-P. I think so. Sandrine wants to meet you, too. Maybe I'll bring her over when she gets another holiday, unless you want to come out here." He paused, offering a wink to Sandrine.

"You're welcome, J.-P. Good-bye." He disconnected the call.

"Come, Phillip. I am almost being late for the work. For the reality, you will taking me to Paris? Is that it, how you Americans say? It is not sounding okay to the ear, I think."

Phillip shook his head, hiding a smile. He had missed Sandrine and her never-ending quest to master idiomatic expressions in American English. "Not quite, Sandrine. You would say 'For real? You're going to take me to Paris?' You hear the difference?"

"Yes, Phillip. The way I say it, you are buying the tickets. The way you say it, maybe I am buying the tickets. I don't think so, if I am being late for the work."

She giggled at the perplexed look on Phillip's face. "Come, come. I am making the wise crack, Phillip. I hear the difference, for real."

They continued the discussion as Phillip drove her into Marin. He parked his Jeep in the lot at the marina and walked her to the door of the Customs office, receiving a quick hug and a peck on each cheek for his trouble. "I see you this evening, my love," Sandrine said as she slipped through the door. Phillip walked back to the car and drove home, a happy man.

MARIO ESPINOSA WAS HOLDING court at his regular table in one of his favorite Cuban restaurants, this one on Calle Ocho in Miami's Little Havana. Paul Russo had indeed made it back in time to join his cronies for their weekly lunch. In fact, he had his days mixed up and had rushed from the airport to the restaurant yesterday, arriving out of breath to discover that the table was empty. Puzzled, he had called Mario on his cell phone.

"It's only Tuesday, Paul," Mario had said, laughing. "You been down in the islands just a few days, and now you don't even know what day it is. That's boat lag, does that to you. Kinda like jet lag, but not so fast. You sit down and let Gloria bring you a nice *medianoche* and some *pupus fritas*; drink a beer. Go home and get some rest, and meet us there tomorrow, okay?" They ended the call with a laugh, and Paul had taken Mario's advice.

Now that everyone had a good laugh at Paul's expense, they wanted to hear all about his adventure in the islands.

"So, how is Dani?" Mario asked.

"She seemed no worse for wear to me. She stood watches on Phillip's boat with no trouble when we were racing up the islands. Had a little scar on her head, and her hair hasn't grown back over it yet. I knew for sure she was okay when I saw how angry she was that Mike Reilly was lost when his boat hit the reef. She was pissed. She had plans for him, if she'd gotten her hands on him. She's not very big, but I wouldn't want her after me."

All the men except Paul had known Dani and her father for years. They laughed.

"When she was about 13, just a tiny thing, J.-P. brought her over here on a business trip. They spent a couple of days here, and then he was taking her to the Bahamas to do some sailing on a charter boat. While we were eating lunch, right here in this restaurant, she went outside to get one of those free newspapers that has the weekly entertainment guide. Right out there. You see the box?" Mario pointed out the window.

Paul glanced through the window and nodded.

"Well, these two punks backed her up against the newspaper box. One of them was waving a knife around. I got up to go help her, and J.-P. laughed and pulled me back into my chair. By the time I looked back outside, the kid with the knife was out cold. The other one tried to run, but she kicked his feet out from under him and smashed his head into the sidewalk. Then she got her paper and came back inside. Sat down like nothing had happened and started reading. Thirteen, she was. Probably weighed 75 pounds. You think she's something, wait 'til you meet J.-P."

"Sounds like you got to the islands too late for all the fun, Paul," one of the others said. "I talked to Sharktooth the other day about something else we got going, and he told me about how he and Phillip sprung Dani."

"Yeah, I'm sorry I missed that. At least I got to meet Sharktooth. What a name; what a funny character. I'd like to spend more time with him one day. Bet he has some tales to tell. What's his real name, anyway?"

"He keeps that secret," Mario said. "Nobody knows any name but Sharktooth."

"Well, at least I got to know Phillip Davis a little bit. I always heard about him when I was still with the cops. Every so often, when I got mixed up in something with the Feds, his name would come up. He was like a phantom or something. Never could figure out which side he was on, you know?"

"So which side do you think he's on now?" Mario asked.

"The right side, for damn sure," Paul answered. "No question. He's one of the good guys."

Seeing the nods of agreement around the table, Paul continued. "I had a quick trip, and a fine, fast sail up the islands from Martinique to Antigua with Dani and Phillip, but that's about it. Fate took care of that Reilly character. We never laid eyes on *Sea Serpent*. Dani was almost as mad about him wrecking that Concordia yawl of his as she was about what he did to her, I think."

"Yeah, probably so. She and J.-P. do love their boats," Mario said, just as Gloria brought two big platters of *ropas viejas* to the table, effectively ending the conversation as the men began to load their plates.

Chapter 4 Bluewater Vengeance

"All they could tell me was that there were two men," Big Jim said, his hand trembling as he held the encrypted satellite phone to his ear. "One Anglo, probably, but he had camouflage face paint, so they weren't sure. Normal size. The other, he was a big Rasta man, real big. Rosa was about to shoot the one with the face paint when the Rasta man stuck her in the kidney."

"What kind of accent did they have?" The man on the phone asked.

"They don't say not a single word, the women say. Just look at one another and nod when they got the women tied to the beds and Rosa dead."

"Sounds like they done this before, then. Why would they kill the guards and Rosa and leave? You got a shipment sittin' there, right?"

"Yeah. From Julio's last delivery. Full shipment."

"You checked it? You know they didn't take none?"

"All there. Don't even look like they lifted the tarps to look at it."

"And you ain't heard from anybody, Rodriguez? No strange phone calls or emails?"

"Nada, Boss. Nothing."

"You didn't have no women or a *maricón* there? Like maybe on your own account, you ain't tellin' me about?"

"*Ninguno*, Boss. Nobody but the guards and Rosa and her two nurses." Big Jim had beads of sweat on his forehead. If the Boss found out about the girl he got from Julio, it would be rough, maybe fatal.

"This don't add up to me, Rodriguez. You think it's the St. Vincent cops, lookin' for a bigger piece? You think they found out we're runnin' women and didn't pay their cut?"

"I don' see no way that could happen, Boss. We been too careful."

"That woman, Rosa, she was from Cuba, right?"

"Yes. Army medic for many years. Russian trained. She was in Grenada, and Afghanistan, too."

"You think she might have been tight with some of them Russian crooks workin' from Havana?"

"I don' think so, but could be, I guess."

"What about the other two, the nurses?"

"From Venezuela. More likely would be Rosa. Those two, they never been out of the islands. Rosa, she been to Moscow for training, and she was all over with Castro's advisors down here and in Africa."

"Yeah. Something stinks, Rodriguez. You hear about Julio?"

"What about him?"

"Dead. Cops in Grenada think he killed the engineer and then shot himself. Drunk, probably. The cops found him on that piece-a-shit freighter of his. Went out to see why he hadn't cleared in with Customs."

"What about the crew?"

"They don't know nothin'. What do you think? The Customs people in Grenada got *Erzulie Freda* impounded. Cops found some of those microwave ovens in the hold, the ones with the cocaine in the packaging. Julio must have held back a few from his last drop with you. You count that damn stuff when it comes in, Rodriguez?"

"Of course, Boss. I count it all myself. He must get some extra when he take on the cargo. Hide it from us."

"Maybe. Okay, Rodriguez. We'll go on from here, but we gotta be extra careful. I'll send you three more soldiers I can trust. You get rid of the two women. They know too much."

Big Jim noticed the emphasis on "...*I* can trust."

"But who take care of the next shipment of whores, then, Boss?"

"We ain't shippin' no more women or drugs until we figure out what's happenin', you dumb bastard. Now, clean that island up. Get rid of the bodies and the two broads. For all we know, they're part of this. Else, why didn't they get killed with the others?"

"Good question," Big Jim said, trying to keep the relief from his voice. He had been worried about how to explain that the women had died at his hand, trying to convince him that they really didn't know any more than they had already told him. The fish around Baliceaux were eating well.

"You got anything else?" The Boss asked.

"No, Señor, *nada*."

"Okay. Ask around. We gotta find out who hit Baliceaux before we do any more business. Just sit on that shipment for now."

"Okay, Boss, do you..." Big Jim paused, looking at the phone. The Boss had disconnected while Big Jim was still talking, the Cuban bastard. Big Jim put the phone down and pulled out a silk handkerchief. He wiped the sweat from his brow as he wondered whether the new soldiers would have orders for his 'retirement.' He knew he was under suspicion. El Grupo didn't take this sort of thing lightly. He was sure that the man he called Boss was even now answering some hard questions from Caracas. He reasoned that in any case, they wouldn't kill him until they had time to figure out what had happened.

DANI TUNED out the yacht broker's voice as he droned on about all the hand-built custom cabinetry. She would have been happy to explore *Best of Times* on her own, but she knew the broker had to do his job. *Best of Times* was a replica of Herreshoff's famous *Bounty*, just as she thought when she saw the boat yesterday. As the tanned, carefully groomed fool yammered away, she methodically crawled through every space on the vessel, examining everything for traces of poor materials or shoddy workmanship. As she expected with a vessel of this quality, everything she found spoke to her of meticulous care in construction and maintenance. This particular execution of Herreshoff's beautiful design was as flawless as the design itself.

Best of Times was a seaman's dream, custom-built for a life-long cruising sailor from Maine whose health had failed him soon after he and his family brought her to Antigua on her shakedown cruise. They had planned to circumnavigate, but it was not to be. Now his widow was eager to dispose of the boat and put the sad memories behind her. It was eerie to open the lockers and find the couple's clothing and personal belongings neatly stowed, but the broker said that the woman was utterly devastated and wanted nothing to remind her of their broken dream. Everything aboard would transfer to her new owner.

Dani had started her inspection with a trip up the mast, much to the broker's surprise. He had been expounding the benefits of the gourmet galley as they walked down the dock toward the boat.

"Wait until you see the stove, Sweetie," he had said, a smirk on his face. Dani was surprised that he hadn't asked her any qualifying questions to see if she was a serious prospect. She sensed that he was just idle and bored, and that he had decided to amuse himself by showing the boat to her. He certainly wasn't treating her the way he would if he thought that she could make a purchase.

He was already opening lockers in the galley, nattering away about the Wedgwood china, when he looked around and discovered that she had not followed him below decks. When he finally spotted her, she was scrambling up the mast like a monkey going up a coconut tree.

"Wait!" he said. "I'll get a rigger over for a rig survey. You don't have to do that."

"Rigger's not going to buy the boat," Dani grunted over her shoulder, continuing to climb. "I might, but I'll make my own judgments. I'm the one that'll live with 'em."

The broker watched, worry etched on his face, as she scrambled around, free-climbing through the rigging over 70 feet above the deck. He fidgeted nervously for several minutes until she said, "Looks good aloft. Stand clear of that backstay, will you? I'm coming down."

He stepped aside slightly, a puzzled look on his face as he watched her take a handful of rags from her pocket and wrap them around the sloping piece of stainless-steel cable that ran from the masthead to the stern. He watched, open-mouthed, as she swung her feet off the fittings that she was braced on near the masthead. Before he grasped her intentions, she locked her ankles around the backstay and was sliding toward him at a frightful speed. A few meters above the deck, she let her legs swing down and tightened her grip on the handful of rags, braking her descent to land softly beside the stunned broker as he stumbled out of her way. The rags were smoking a bit as she dropped them to the deck.

"Wha-, wha-, what would you like to see next, c- captain?"

"Oh, let's have a look at that china you're so taken with, *Sweetie*," Dani said, with her best poker face.

After spending several hours scrutinizing *Best of Times*, Dani was still impressed with the boat.

"She's asking a million, even," the broker said.

"She might get that. Good boat, in great shape. She'll have to wait a while, though. Too late for this year's season, and besides, the boat's in Antigua."

"So make an offer. What would you give her, for a deal today, delivery here?"

"Same as I'd pay for a deal next week, I expect," Dani said, watching him wince, not offering him any hope. "Look. It's a nice boat. I may make an offer, but I need to think it over."

"I've got someone else interested."

"Good. Maybe they'll like that Wedgwood as much as you do. I'll call you either way when I decide," Dani said, climbing into the cockpit and hopping over the rail, catlike, to land on the dock.

She went back to *Kayak Spirit* and spent the rest of the afternoon pondering her future as she measured the settee cushions. She planned to go shopping the next morning to find some fabric to make covers for them. She had in mind something that would be in character with *Kayak Spirit's* Caribbean origins — bright colors, soft texture. The battered vinyl had probably been in place since the former owner had used the sturdy old boat for smuggling jackiron rum from Grenada to the French islands, many years ago.

END OF PREVIEW of *Bluewater Vengeance*. Read more about it and my other books at www.clrdougherty.com

EXCERPT FROM ASSASSINS AND LIARS

Assassins and Liars is the first book in my new **J.R. Finn Sailing Mystery** series.

Finn is living on a beat-up sailboat in the Caribbean — just another boat bum — or is he? Maybe that's just his cover story.

He's retired from government service. He won't say what he did when he was working, but wherever Finn's sailing trips take him, bad people die.

In *Assassins and Liars*, Finn's leaving Puerto Rico on a mission to deal with some undesirables down island when he meets a woman looking for a crew position. Mary, as she calls herself, is in a hurry to leave Puerto Rico. She tells him she doesn't care where she goes next.

Finn takes her along, thinking she'll provide cover for his mission. Before they even leave, he discovers that there's more to Mary than she's told him.

Read the following excerpt from *Assassins and Liars* and meet a well-matched couple. Or are they? See what you think.

Chapter 1

Her feet were the first things I noticed about her. That may seem strange, but it wasn't as strange as the things that happened later. Still, her feet caught my attention and that led to the rest.

About those feet. They were at eye level. That's why they were the first things I noticed. I was tying the dinghy to a cleat on the dock at the marina, and the feet stepped into my field of view. Tanned, slender, and clean. They looked cared for, but like they worked for a living. No nail polish or toe rings, just nice feet.

Oh, and the soles. She wasn't wearing shoes. Not even flip-flops. The soles of her feet were like mine. Callused, cracked, and salt-cured. Tough as leather. She went barefoot, maybe all the time. Like I said, working feet.

I finished my figure-of-eight knot and let my eyes wander up her legs. Dancer's legs, well-muscled, with smooth skin the color of *café au lait*.

The tattoo of the cobra slithering around the inside of her left thigh was lifelike, startling. It wrapped around her leg, the perspective exaggerated. With its tail hidden behind her thigh, the snake's life-sized head was heart-stopping.

It leapt from her tanned flesh; I felt myself flinch from its strike. Recovering from my shock, I overcame the urge to let my eyes linger and looked up, curious to see her face.

She had even features, no makeup. She didn't need any. Her eyes locked on mine. Gray eyes, almost colorless. They would have been cold and forbidding, except for the creases at the corners. She must smile a lot. Her face gave away nothing. She wasn't smiling now.

"Single-hander?" she asked.

"For now," I said.

"By choice? Or by chance?"

"Does it matter?" I asked.

"It might," she said. "I'd respect your privacy if it's by choice."

"And if it's by chance?" I asked.

"Then I'd offer to buy you a rum punch."

"Reckon it's my lucky day." I climbed up onto the dock.

"Mary," she said, extending her right hand.

I took it, surprised at her grip. She wasn't a slight woman, but she wasn't big enough to have a grip like that, either.

"Finn," I said, matching her grip, careful not to overdo it. I liked the way her hand felt. Solid, with enough calluses to tell me where she got the grip. Like her feet, her hands worked for their keep.

"Irish."

The way she said it made me wonder what it meant to her.

"American," I said.

"Me, too," she said, with a hint of a smile. "I meant your last name."

I nodded. She had a nice smile. "About that rum punch ... "

"Come on, then, Finn." She turned and started walking up the dock.

I skipped a step and fell in beside her, matching her pace as she headed for the tiki bar at the head of the dock. She was about my height, tall for a woman, average for a man. Our strides matched; walking with her was comfortable.

"Finn is your last name, isn't it?"

"People just call me Finn."

She nodded and kept walking.

The bar was an open-air place. When I dragged a stool up for her, it woke the bartender. It was a weekday. The people who owned all the fancy sportfishing boats were in their air-conditioned offices trying to make money to pay for their boats. The real fishermen were out on the water, slaving away in the tropical sun. Things were slow in Puerto Real at best, but during the week, not much moved.

The bartender got up from his chair in the corner and shook his head, blinking, reminding me of an iguana.

"*Buenas tardes,* Finn."

"*Gracias, Julio. Y tu, también,*" I said.

"*Para la senorita?*"

"Rum punch," she said, settling onto the stool and dropping her backpack on the floor.

I sat down next to her. Julio put a glass on the bar in front of her and turned to open the refrigerator. He retrieved a pitcher of rum punch and a bottle of Presidente. After he filled her glass, he pried the top off my beer and returned to his chair in the corner.

"You're a regular," she said. "You live here?"

"For now," I said. "You?"

"Passing through," she said, "looking for a boat."

She picked up her drink and extended it toward me. I clicked my beer bottle against her glass, and she took an honest swallow of the punch.

"Cheers," I said, sipping my beer. "You headed north or south?"

"It depends," she said.

"On?"

"On which way the boat's going. I mostly want out of Puerto Rico. Been here, done it. Time to move on."

She took a sip of her punch, pacing herself after that first slug. I was relieved to see that. I was interested, but not if she was a rummy.

"Where'd you come here from?" I asked.

"Miami. Deckhand on a big Perini Navi."

"Gold-plater," I said. "You cook?"

"I get by."

"Drugs?" I asked.

"You looking for a handout? Or offering to share?"

"Smart-ass," I said.

"Yep." She grinned. "Got a problem with that?"

"What if I said yes?"

"Then I'd thank you for the company and tell you to fuck off."

I laughed. I was enjoying this.

"About the drugs," she said.

I raised my eyebrows.

"I'm clean," she said. "Don't use, never did. You?"

"Same."

She nodded. "But I don't judge people. They make their own choices. Long as they don't mess me up that's okay. Everybody gets to pick their own road to hell."

I liked her. She was clean, articulate, and she was damn good looking. Not in a barfly way, either. And I liked her sense of humor.

This could work for both of us. She wanted a ride. I'd be less noticeable as half of a couple.

"You in a hurry?" I asked.

She frowned and didn't say anything.

"To leave," I said.

"Oh," she said, her face stretching into a smile like a sunrise.

I wondered what she thought I meant at first.

She shrugged. "Sooner would suit me better than later. You got a schedule or something?"

I started to tell her, then thought better of it. She probably wasn't working for them, but why risk it? I was planning to leave this evening; I only came ashore to pick up a few things at the little grocery store across the street.

"I'm itchin' for open water. Sooner's better, for sure."

"Sooner like tomorrow, maybe?"

"That could work. You really don't care where we go?"

"No, I don't. I'm tired of Puerto Rico — too big. Where are you thinking about?"

"We've got a strong northeast wind; looks like it's settled in to blow for a while. A close reach would put us in the Grenadines in four days, maybe farther north if the wind backs a little."

"All the way to the Windwards, huh?" she asked.

"It's either that or beat our brains out hammering into the wind to get to the Virgins. I'd rather spend my time on an easy sail. We could work our way back up the island chain from there if we want to."

"Sounds good," she said.

"You got a passport?" I asked.

She leaned over and picked up her backpack. Unzipping a side pouch, she extracted a dog-eared passport and handed it to me.

I looked at the mugshot; her, no doubt about that. Mary Elizabeth O'Brien. Twenty-four years old. I flipped through it — not many stamps, given the rough shape it was in. I gave it back, and she zipped it away, lowering the backpack to the floor again.

"Want to go sailing for a while?" I asked.

"Sure," she said. "I'm game."

"Should we go get your stuff?"

She gave me a hard look. "There's something we need to talk about, first."

I raised my eyebrows, inviting her to continue.

"I'm a woman," she said, and paused.

I nodded. "I guessed that."

"And you're not."

"Not last time I checked, anyhow."

"There's this thing men and women do. Sex."

I held her gaze and said nothing.

"It could happen," she said, "or not. I'm not narrow-minded, but I'm not easy. If it happens because both of us want it, that's okay. If you think it's how I'm paying my way, get over it."

I nodded. "I'm with you. If it happens, it happens. Or not. We'll just have to see." I was a little surprised that she seemed to take my word for that. Either desperate or naïve, I figured. I was wrong, I was soon to learn. About the naïveté, at least.

"Let's go see this fine vessel of yours," she said, standing up.

She pulled a rumpled bill from her pocket and put it under her half-full glass of punch.

I took a last swig of beer and got up. "Where's your stuff?"

She hefted the backpack and turned. "I travel light," she said, leading the way back to the dinghy dock.

Chapter 2

"Let's go get those groceries," Mary said.

"Now?" I asked. We'd only been aboard *Island Girl* for about ten minutes. In that short time, she stowed her backpack in the empty locker I showed her and went back on deck.

She checked the tension of the shrouds, putting her weight into it, and cast a critical eye over the rest of the rig. Back below deck, she opened lockers and exercised the through-hull fittings, yanking hard on the hoses attached to them. She was no novice; I saw her eyes narrow at a few things that could use attention.

When I thought she was finished, she pulled the scrap of indoor/outdoor carpet up from the cabin sole and lifted the panel that exposed the bilge sump. She stuck her head in the bilge and took a deep breath. Putting the panel and the carpet back in place, she stood up.

"Well?" I asked.

"She'll do," she said, moving on to the galley, opening drawers and lockers one by one.

I was licking my wounded pride; this was my home she was talking about. "She'll do?" I asked, trying to keep the emotion out of my voice.

She looked at me for a long few seconds and said. "Yeah, she'll do. She's no beauty, but she's ready. She'll take us wherever we want to go."

I just nodded, not trusting myself to say anything.

"What do you need from the grocery store?" she asked.

"Peanut butter, a couple of loaves of bread. Some snack food, depending on what they've got."

"That's it?" she asked.

"Yeah, unless you want something."

"You're fond of beans and rice," she said. "Looks like a lifetime supply, and you have plenty of smoked *chorizo* to go with 'em."

"You don't like my diet?" I asked. "What more do you want?"

"I love beans and rice with *chorizo*," she said. "But we need tomatoes and fresh onions. A couple of heads of garlic, too."

"What for?"

"Beans and rice are good for you. Throw in a few extras, and it makes 'em taste like they're worth eating. The *chorizo's* a good start, but the other stuff makes a big difference. You okay with that?"

"Sure. I'm pretty easy when it comes to food; it's just fuel."

"Yeah," she said. "Life's short. Might as well eat fuel that tastes good."

"There's a big grocery store about a ten-minute walk east of town," I said.

"No need," she said. "Not unless you want something else. The little place across the street will have everything we need. Let's go now; I'll cook supper when we get back. We can make an early evening of it if you still want to get out of here in the morning."

"Let's go," I said.

She climbed back up into the cockpit and pulled the dinghy alongside. I untied the painter and held it while she got settled in the little inflatable. I lowered myself into it and started the outboard, heading back to the dinghy dock.

When we got there, she tied the dinghy up and locked it as if she did it every day. That dock was maybe five feet above the water. This is where I came face to feet with her not long ago. I was trying to wriggle by her so I could clamber up and give her a hand. Then she stood up, facing away from me. She was right in front of me, blocking my way.

She put her right hand on the dock, gave a little jump, and vaulted up. I was pretty sure no part of her body touched the dock except the palm of her one hand and the soles of her feet. Damnedest thing I'd ever seen, like a gymnast or something. Next thing I knew, I was standing there in the dinghy admiring those feet again.

I took a deep breath and hoped I could get up there without embarrassing myself. Fortunately, she turned away, so she didn't see me struggling. But I think she guessed. Once I was standing next to her, she looked around at me and smiled.

"You okay?" she asked.

I gave her one of my taciturn nods, and she started walking up the dock. I skipped a step or two and caught up with her, matching her pace again. Damn, I liked walking next to her. "You're pretty fit," I said.

"I work out. You?"

"Well, I swim a lot."

"That's good for you," she said.

By then, we were walking out the marina gate. I've spent a good bit of my forty years in hostile environments. Situational awareness is deeply engrained in me; that's why I'm still walking around. I saw the car idling at the curb on the opposite side of the street and thought it looked out of place. There was a guy behind the wheel and two in the back seat.

With practiced speed, the two passengers jumped out, both on the street side, leaving the door open. One grabbed Mary, and the other took a swing at me. I slipped his punch, hooked his ankle, and gave him a shove on the back of his shoulder. His momentum took him to the ground. The other one held Mary in a bear hug, dragging her toward the car.

I knew the drill; if they got her in the car, it was over, whatever *it* was. I rushed the car. The driver's window was open. He was shifting his eyes from the rearview mirror to the windshield, watching for traffic.

He saw me, but it was too late for him to react. I hit him below his left ear with my right fist, all of my 185 pounds behind it. He flew across the front seat and landed in a pile against the passenger door. I snatched the keys from the ignition and dropped them in my pocket.

I turned, ready to go back and deal with the two who were grappling with Mary. Before I took more than a couple of steps, I watched her go limp in the bear hug. The guy holding her staggered forward, her dead weight throwing him off balance.

The other one was getting back on his feet. He took one step toward Mary and she dug both heels into the pavement and lurched back, legs pumping like mad. She drove the guy holding her back against the wall of the building. He came to a bone-jarring stop against the concrete.

Mary snapped her head back, smashing the back of her skull into his nose with an audible crunch. He let her go, but not before she raised her right foot behind her and raked it down the front of his right leg. She caught her foot on the top edge of his kneecap and put her weight on it. All that happened in the time I took to get to the other man, who was still closing on Mary.

The one whose knee she dislocated started screaming and fell to the sidewalk. Mary squatted and pivoted on her left foot, coming up with her right foot snapping out at head height. Her heel connected with the point of the last man's chin just as I grabbed him from behind. I heard the crack of his jawbone breaking as the force of her strike knocked us both down.

"Good move on the car," she said, as I slithered out from under her unconscious victim.

"I've seen this play before," I said. "As long as they didn't drive away with you, I figured we'd be good."

I got to my feet in time to see her spin and plant another one of her deadly kicks on the side of her first assailant's head. That's when I realized he was screaming non-stop, when she knocked him into oblivion and it got dead quiet.

"About the groceries," I said.

She grinned. "Beans and rice with just *chorizo* can taste pretty good when you're hungry," she said. "I think we should haul ass. Somebody's probably called the cops, after all the racket this crybaby made."

"Walk back to the dinghy fast, but don't run," I said. "Be cool."

"Got it, skipper. It's not my first time, either."

Read more about Finn and Mary at
www.clrdougherty.com

OTHER BOOKS BY C.L.R. DOUGHERTY

Bluewater Thrillers

Bluewater Killer

Bluewater Vengeance

Bluewater Voodoo

Bluewater Ice

Bluewater Betrayal

Bluewater Stalker

Bluewater Bullion

Bluewater Rendezvous

Bluewater Ganja

Bluewater Jailbird

Bluewater Drone

Bluewater Revolution

Bluewater Enigma

Bluewater Quest

Bluewater Target

Bluewater Blackmail

Bluewater Clickbait

Bluewater Payback

Bluewater Survivor

Bluewater Thrillers Boxed Set: Books 1-3

Connie Barrera Thrillers

From Deception to Betrayal - An Introduction to Connie Barrera

Love for Sail - A Connie Barrera Thriller

Sailor's Delight - A Connie Barrera Thriller

A Blast to Sail - A Connie Barrera Thriller

Storm Sail - A Connie Barrera Thriller

Running Under Sail - A Connie Barrera Thriller

Sails Job - A Connie Barrera Thriller

Under Full Sail - A Connie Barrera Thriller

An Easy Sail - A Connie Barrera Thriller

A Torn Sail - A Connie Barrera Thriller

A Righteous Sail - A Connie Barrera Thriller

Sailor Take Warning - A Connie Barrera Thriller

Sailor's Choice - A Connie Barrera Thriller

A Deadly Sail - A Connie Barrera Thriller

J.R. Finn Sailing Mysteries

Assassins and Liars

Avengers and Rogues

Vigilantes and Lovers

Sailors and Sirens

Villains and Vixens

Killers and Keepers

Devils and Divas

Sharks and Prey

Sin and Redemption

Ashes and Dust

Anarchy and Chaos

Deepfakes and Diablas

Call Me Finn Boxed Set: Books 1 - 3

Call Me Finn Boxed Set: Books 4 - 6

Other Fiction

Deception in Savannah

The Redemption of Becky Jones

The Lost Tourist Franchise

Books for Sailors and Dreamers

Life's a Ditch

Dungda de Islan'

Audiobooks

Assassins and Liars

Avengers and Rogues

Vigilantes and Lovers

Sailors and Sirens

Villains and Vixens

Killers and Keepers

Devils and Divas

Sharks and Prey

Sin and Redemption

Ashes and Dust

Anarchy and Chaos

Deepfakes and Diablas

Call Me Finn Boxed Set: Books 1-3

Call Me Finn Boxed Set: Books 4-6

For more information please visit www.clrdougherty.com

Or visit www.amazon.com/author/clrdougherty

Made in United States
Troutdale, OR
09/24/2025

34827169R00169